HUNTED

Fraser Kingsley

For Natalie
X

PROLOGUE

Jake flinched as the door slammed shut, the crash reverberating around his concrete cell. Bloodshot eyes observed him disinterestedly through the viewing hatch before the cover slid shut, and for the first time that day, he was truly alone.

Jake was now a prisoner, fed into the meat grinder of the criminal justice system. In just a few short days, he had been reduced from a thriving member of society to another of its downtrodden, nothing more than a number.

He retreated to the far end of his cell and sat on his haunches, his back chilled against the bare concrete wall and surveyed his drab grey home.

In the corner sat a gleaming metal toilet without a seat and a small metal basin. A barred window high on the flanking wall let in a shard of moonlight but afforded no view of the outside world. His bed, a flimsy metal-framed single cot was securely bolted to the concrete floor. Upon it lay a dirty grey sheet, perhaps white once upon a time and covered with a thin scratchy looking mattress. The pungent aroma of antiseptic and stale sweat bled from the walls.

Above the sink, a square of stainless steel functioned as a mirror. He stood and washed his face then forced himself to look at the man in the reflection.

Fear stared back.

He hardened his stare; fear would get him killed.

He sat on the bed and unwrapped the standard prison issue bundle he had been given and examined the meagre offerings. It consisted of a paper-thin pillow, a tin cup and a breakfast pack of tea and cereal.

He lay down and folded the pillow double, wedging it between his head and the concrete wall.

It would be their bedtime. Claire would be sitting on the end of their bed, reading a story or singing to them.

It was time for their soothing massage. Jake closed his eyes and willed into memory the feel of their warm soft skin as he stroked their delicate backs, gently lulling them to sleep.

When would he next get the chance to enjoy such simple pleasures? Would they still be young enough or would they have transformed into young adults robbed of a father's love for a decade?

This would be the first of many such nights when thoughts of his family would cause him actual physical pain. The tightness clutched at his chest like a vice.

His soul ached, longing to return to them where he belonged.

What will she say?

It would come as a major shock to hear that Dad was not coming home anytime soon.

He now faced a long and lonely period of incarceration. He would need to tap into his mental and physical strength if he were to survive this ordeal and retain any semblance of the person he once was.

His thoughts drifted to the man he had killed. He had taken another man's life, but what choice had he been given?

As his thoughts cascaded between his own family and the man who had died, he indulged the luxury of the tears that came. Tomorrow he would have to face the hardened men who shared his new home. For now, he returned to happier thoughts of his children and wife, clinging desperately to more joyous times.

These were his final thoughts as he collapsed into troubled sleep.

CHAPTER 1

Two Days Earlier

The early morning sunlight piercing through the blinds woke Jake early. Claire slept on huddled under the duvet snoring softly. He leaned across and kissed her forehead gently then slid out of bed.

He dropped to the floor and powered through his routine fifty push-ups to get the blood pumping then strolled to the bathroom and plunged his face into a basin of water. He held it for as long as he could bear, the numbing effect creeping from his face and into the back of his head like ice-cold hands crushing his skull.

He towelled dry and examined himself in the mirror. His skin was smooth albeit with a few crow's feet creeping in at the corners of his eyes. His hair back was cropped close. He flexed. Muscles taut and toned, he was in good shape for his forty-one years.

Heading into the kitchen he flicked the kettle on. Scruffy, his beloved caramel cocker spaniel was snoozing on a blanket by the sofa. She opened one eye and wagged her tail slowly as Jake gently scratched her ears then snuffled down into her blanket. Not quite time to wake up yet.

The sun hung low in the sky illuminating the sparse clouds in fiery shades of purple and pink. Peeking over the trees at the end of the garden, it bathed the kitchen in spring dawn sunlight. Dew glistened on the grass as it wafted gently in the breeze. The garden wind chime rang gently, a soothing backdrop to the early morning dawn chorus as the birds welcomed the new day.

He returned to the bedroom and watched from the doorway as Claire stirred and stretched lazily opening one eye.

"Morning. You made me tea, you angel." She sat up and plumped the pillows, propping them behind her. Her shoulder length chestnut hair framed an elfish face and inquisitive green eyes flashed as she smiled, drawing you into her gaze. "So, what's the plan today?" she asked, cradling her tea.

Jake placed his hand on her knee "Well, I thought I might start the day fooling around with my wife". He tickled his way slowly up her leg. Locking eyes, he raised an eyebrow hopefully. She giggled playfully revealing perfect white teeth with a gap between the front two, something she had been self-conscious about and used to hide as a little girl, but just one of the many things that Jake had fallen in love with.

Leaning in he softly nibbled on her ear and whispered gently. "The kids are still asleep and we can be quiet. Well, at least I can!"

She moaned gently and stroked his face protesting unconvincingly. "They will be up soon though; we don't have time!"

Scruffy lolloped in and jumped onto the bed planting herself between them somewhat spoiling the moment.

"Hey Scruffy, how are you doing girl?" Claire ruffled Scruffy's ears and scratched her on the chin as Scruffy licked them both in turn. She wagged her tail furiously and panted with excitement. Jake discarded his carnal intentions with a sigh, the moment lost.

"Chase, give it back." The slam of a door reverberated around the house accompanied by the stomping of feet across the hallway.

"Mum, Dad, she's stolen my lip gloss again. Make her give it back." Violet appeared at the doorway hands-on-hips. She glared at her parents willing them to intervene. At eleven years old she considered herself practically a grown-up. She was a miniature version of her mother with green eyes and a mane of chestnut hair. Also like her mother, she was quick to anger when the mood suited her.

"I only borrowed it, chill sis, don't overreact." Chase pushed past her older sister into their parent's bedroom taking the opportunity to plant a pointy elbow into her ribs.

"Ow, you bitch. That hurt." Violet shouted her face reddening with anger. She turned away. "You'll need more than lip gloss to make that ugly face pretty," she muttered under her breath.

"Girls, girls, come on now, behave." Claire took charge attempting to diffuse the delicate situation. "Please, you are on your holidays, let's not start the weekend like this."

"How about Dad's pancakes for breakfast?" Jake chimed in changing the conversation. "Chase, apologise to your sister for taking her stuff, and for the elbow dig. I saw what you did. Violet, you too, I don't want to hear language like that."

Chase's face scowled in exasperation at her older sister. "Sorry," she muttered with little conviction.

"Sorry for calling you a bitch," Violet retorted, emphasising the last word and smiling sarcastically.

"Come and sit girls and let's talk about plans for the day," he said planting a kiss on Chase's forehead as she plonked herself down huffing through her nose. He ruffled her hair, and she softened a little, snuggling in for a cuddle.

Violet sat on the end of the bed. Recognising a break in tension, she took the opportunity to offer an olive branch.

"Look, please don't take my makeup without asking. You can borrow it but you need to ask. Deal?" She held out her hand and fixed her sister with a glare, daring her to argue back.

Chase took the hand and shook it solemnly while nodding her agreement. "Deal. Sorry for the elbow in the ribs." She smiled at Violet her face warm with genuine contrition this time. The storm passed as quickly as it had flared.

"That's okay," she said stretching her long gangly limbs out on the bed and yawning widely. "I guess it's good to know you can give it a little. How about after breakfast I do your makeup for you?"

"Really." Chase's face lit up with a smile. "That would be soooo cool." She was two years younger and much more childlike than her older sister. She was pretty in an unconventional manner with brown puppy dog eyes emphasised by thick dark eyebrows.

"Anyway, first things first. Now Dad, how about those pancakes?" Violet enquired. She looked up hopefully, smiling and catching his eye. He winked back at her.

Chase reached out to Scruffy burying her face in the warm fur and scratched behind her floppy ears. "You are too cute Miss Scruffy, I missed you." The dog went to town on her face licking hard prompting sharp squeals of delight.

"So girls, it's Saturday and it's school holidays. What would you like to do?" Claire enquired.

"Well, first it's pancakes," Chase replied. "Then me and Violet are going to do makeup, then some TV for a bit?"

Violet nodded her agreement and chimed in "Then a movie tonight with popcorn and crisps."

"Okay, okay. That all sounds like fun, maybe a bit too much screen time," Claire replied. "We are all going out for a walk with Scruffy before lunch to stretch our legs and get some fresh air."

The girls groaned in unison. Violet rolled her eyes. "Muuum. No. Do we have to?"

Claire sat up raising an eyebrow at Violet. "You begged us to buy you this dog. She needs walking. Besides, it's a lovely day. We are all going out together and that's final. Then you can do what you like after lunch."

The girls both knew better than to push it any further. "Come on Chase, let's go find my makeup." Violet uncoiled herself from the end of the bed and dragged her younger sister back down the hall to their bedrooms.

"I'm onto breakfast then honey," Jake said jumping out of bed. Scruffy followed him downstairs to the kitchen.

"And another tea please mister," she called after him snuggling back under the duvet. "I want ten more minutes in bed."

***

After breakfast they took a long and pleasant walk in the nearby woods. The chirrup of birds serenading each other rang through the trees and Scruffy chased squirrels excitedly as they leaped from branch to branch. The girls ran ahead and climbed to dizzying heights leaving Claire breathless with minor panic.

Jake and Claire strolled hand in hand following behind. They stopped from time to time to enjoy the spring flowers blooming in the undergrowth. As they emerged from the cool woods, the canopy overhead began to thin leading into a wide-open expanse of green parkland.

The early morning chill of spring had gone, and the sun warmed their backs as they strolled. Scruffy bounded about chasing her ball and enthusiastically greeted the other dogs she met.

Jake was raised a streetwise scrapper on a rough estate in the suburbs of North London. He had dreamt of better and of escaping his hard life in the city. That dream became a reality when out at a pub one weekend, he fell madly in love. He was twenty-five. A chance collision into the most beautiful girl with long chestnut hair and cute dimples, spilling her drinks in the process. An unfortunate start to any relationship but in that moment a door was closed on a dark and violent past and a new opened into a new and exciting world. Like Dorothy entering the technicolour world of Oz. There and then they had ditched their respective groups of friends and spent the evening in each other's company. Jake was the sporty type from the city, Claire the bookish musician who lived in the countryside. They had almost nothing in common. Yet something clicked that night and so began a passionate relationship, culminating in marriage some three years later. The happy couple set up home in a country village close to Cambridge and far away from the dark world Jake had previously inhabited and which he had yearned to leave. Violet was born one year later, and Chase soon followed. The Charles family was complete.

"How is Violet doing?" He stopped and turned to Claire. "Have you noticed anything a little off lately? Nothing I can put my finger on, but she feels a little distant. Almost as if she is putting a brave face on something. The rows with Chase are getting worse and she seems, well, just sad."

Claire sighed in exasperation flinging her scarf over her shoulder and fixed him with her stare. Eyebrows raised, hands-on-hips. She reserved this for those relatively frequent times when he needed to be told some hard truths. He braced himself for what was to come.

"You should talk to her. You know, really talk to her. Rather than just watch telly and goof around. The same goes for Chase for that matter."

Jake stopped to face her his face wrinkled in confusion as he bristled at the accusation.

"What do you mean? I spend lots of time with them," he replied. But deep down some buried guilt stirred in him, some kernel of truth she had touched a nerve on. Was she right?

"When did you last spend one on one time and really listen," she continued. "To ask what's troubling her, either of them for that matter?" Claire waited silently tapping the elegant toe of her cowboy boot as she waited for his response.

He looked away and gazed at the girls affectionately as they played together on the swings. "I guess that's a fair criticism. Perhaps I could spend more time with them. But you know what I am dealing with, trying to keep the business going. I guess I left the girl chats to you. I don't think I am emotionally equipped to deal with pre-teen girl's problems."

"It's nothing like that you moron," she guffawed snorting through her nose. "But she does have worries about school." She punched him affectionately on the shoulder. "You may not have noticed but since she has gone up to secondary, she has had some issues. Some of the girls in her class are verbal bullies. Right bitches from what she has told me."

"Really. Why didn't you say something?" he said taking her hand. "That I can help with. Been there myself."

Claire took his hands in hers, brough furrowed with curiosity. "Really. You bullied? I can't imagine such a thing."

"It was a long time ago. Anyway, I'll talk to her," he replied.

You're a good dad Jake Charles, but sometimes you just need to be more present with your children. This is a big deal to her."

***

"Hey Violet. How are you sweetie?" Jake put his arm around her neck, pulling her in for a hug.

"Dad!" she complained, pushing him away. "Not in public please. Don't you think I'm getting a bit old for that?" She glared at him, eyebrows raised, one hand on her hip. He hid a smile behind a cough as he reflected on the startling similarities with her mother. Right down to the disapproving expression.

"Sorry sweetie. I forgot. To me, you are always my little girl. I'll try and remember though." They settled into a pace together walking on in awkward silence.

"I was talking to your mum. She tells me you are having some issues at school. Want to tell me about it?"

Violet sighed, her head dropping visibly. "What do you want to know?" she said forlornly. "That I have no friends in my class, that some of the girls are right bitches to me."

Turning to face his daughter Jake lifted her chin gently. "Bitches how? Tell me, maybe I can help you."

"I doubt it dad." she groaned. "What would you know about it?"

"Believe it or not I was also young once. I had problems when I was at school. Some of the boys used to beat me up. It was horrible. I got it every day for a while."

"Really. She stopped and looked at him with renewed interest. "I never knew that. Why didn't you tell me?"

"I guess it never came up. But every day after school two boys used to beat me and steal my lunch money. I was about the age you are now."

"And, what happened," she pressed, enthralled for a change in what her father had to say.

I battered them both unconscious and nearly got expelled.

He looked away from her, his pulse spiking as he recalled the distant memory.

"I stopped them." He turned back to meet her gaze. "I don't want to go into the details, but I refused to be a victim. Then they stopped harassing me. After that everything was fine."

"She eyed him quizzically. Did you fight them Dad?" Her face creased with a widening smile. "You did, didn't you." She tugged on his arm excitedly. "Did you win?"

He stifled a smile and pinched her cheek. "Maybe. The point is you don't always have to fight to beat bullies. You just need be prepared to stand up to them. It's the one thing they hate. Let's spend some time tomorrow morning. I'll teach you a few tricks I know. Conflict resolution, that kind of thing. Then lunch afterwards for reward. Anywhere you like, your choice."

She flung her arms around his neck, hugging him tight. "That would be brilliant. Thanks Dad. You are the best." For one glorious moment her self-imposed rules of fatherly affection were discarded.

"Love you too sweetie." He picked her up and swung her in circles, her face beaming and her mane of hair flowed out behind her. She squealed in delight. Despite the grown-up clothes and makeup, she was still his baby girl at heart. Hopefully for a little while longer at least.

***

"Bye girls." He kissed them both in turn on the forehead and ruffled their hair. Engrossed in their show they mumbled their goodbyes and carried on watching.

"I'm off now honey," he shouted to Claire. She bounded through from the kitchen, covered in flour, her hair in a messy bun.

"Bye sweetie. What time are you home?"

"I'm out for a few drinks later with Natan after training so it could be late. Don't wait up!"

Claire's face dropped and her body stiffened. "Out drinking again? Is that a good idea given our financial situation?

I thought you were worried about the business."

Everything about her had changed. The light and airy tone replaced by something darker simmering beneath the surface. She stared at the floor unwilling to look him in the eye.

Please, not again. Not now.

Jake puffed out hard recognising the familiar opening act of a well-rehearsed play.

"Look at me honey." He moved in close placing his hands on her shoulders and lifted her chin tenderly forcing her to meet his gaze. "I am worried about the business. But I can't fix our problems by sitting at home fretting. Besides, I need time away to blow off steam with the guys. You know that."

"So it's fine for you to waste money on a night out with your mates while we struggle to pay the bills. Is that it?"

She sighed turning away from him, her anger building with barely concealed resentment.

Jake steadied his emotions burying his own anger. He chose his words carefully. "It's only money. I can always make more."

He leant in and kissed her on the forehead. "I don't want to do this now. I'm late. Let's talk tomorrow."

No reaction. She continued to look at the floor. He left closing the door behind him and slung his kit bag in the boot. He headed off to class, his mood grim. All the while remaining oblivious to the dark corner into which he was about to stumble.

CHAPTER 2

"Guard up Jake, come on!"

The vicious blow landed on his left temple dazing him. The instructor, a giant bear of a Welshman named Evan circled Jake and his sparring partner watching carefully and barking instruction. Further remorseless blows came raining in and Jake parried as best he could, but he was taking a pummelling from Mike, his tank of an opponent.

"You're static Jake, attack. You need to move and fight back."

Jake snapped out a palm heel strike to the face, catching Mike's attention. He followed up with a brutal kick to the groin extracting a satisfying grunt. He lunged forward clubbing his opponent's head knocking him backwards, then locked onto the arm and crunched his forearm into the jaw. A final knee to the groin and the fight was over. His partner collapsed onto one knee coughing.

"Good Jake. Well-done boy." Evan clapped him on the shoulder eyes beaming beneath his shaggy eyebrows. "Shaky start but impressive when you got going"

"Mike, you started well," he continued, turning to Jake's opponent. "But you let him overwhelm you. Next time push your advantage. Get a drink guys. Three-minute recovery then onto the bags. Who's next?"

Jake touched gloves with Mike and nodded his appreciation. They had been sparring partners for around three years now. Mike joined the class soon after Jake and had risen fast. He was a natural-born brawler, squat, strong and vicious in attack.

He exited the ring still blowing heavily from the clash and drank greedily from his bottle, desperate to slate his raging thirst.

The class was run from an old boxing gym by Evan, shaggy-haired and bearded like a frontiersman from a bygone age. He was once a minor celebrity in the boxing world but one too many bloody defeats and a frank discussion with his doctor had put paid to his fighting career before he made it to the top. Now he earned his income teaching boxing and more recently Krav Maga, an aggressive fighting style developed in the 1930s by persecuted Jews desperate to defend themselves from the rage-filled fascists rampaging across Bratislava and Czechoslovakia.

The gym was functional rather than aesthetic, a cavernous space decked in varnished wood. The walls were adorned with photos of Evan's glory days alongside posters promoting upcoming bouts from his stable of fighters. Two men clashed in the ring spurred on by Evan. Others skipped or crunched blows onto heavy leather punch bags strung throughout the gym. The smell of sweat and testosterone was pervasive.

Jake sucked in oxygen exhausted, hands on head. He was a capable fighter by the class standards, regularly defeating his sparring opponents and even giving Evan a bloody nose on one memorable occasion. He trained hard and looked after himself, but he also liked a few drinks. These days he felt the effect, particularly during heavy sparring sessions. Still, the high-intensity combat and the buzz of victory kept him coming back. As the session closed, he was drenched with sweat and close to vomiting.

***

The scorching water sliced into Jake cleansing him of the sweat and grime of training. He turned the temperature to freezing, blowing hard through the spray as the icy water speared into his skin like a thousand needles until he was tingling all over. His muscles were taut from the workout, loose and strong. That quasi painful feeling he so enjoyed. He dressed and packed his kit away then headed to his car.

"Quick pint at The Crown Jake?" Mike shouted across the car park.

He checked his watch then turned to Mike, squinting into the sun hanging low in the sky. "Sounds good, I've time for a quick one," he replied.

He pushed the door aside and surveyed the bar. It was a traditional old-style English tavern with peeling paint and oak panelling and the ceiling was stained yellow from decades of smoking. Pictures of grand looking monarchs and British statesman hung on the walls, while Union Jacks were proudly on display behind the bar. Raucous youngsters drinking at the bar eyed Jake suspiciously as he entered, while a few old boys sat quietly in booths contemplating times past or playing cards with a mate.

Two men sat in the corner by the fruit machine caught Jake's eye. The younger was in his mid-twenties and even while sitting Jake could see he was tall and wiry with gym-honed muscle. He commanded presence, regally regarding all around as if he owned all that he saw. His companion was a scrawny weasel-faced man who was wearing an ill-fitting tracksuit and worn trainers. As he brayed sycophantically at his companion's jokes, he revealed a mouthful of stained, tombstone teeth.

Without warning, the bigger man with some predator instinct of being watched turned to look directly at Jake directly. For an instant their eyes locked.

Danger.

Jake's lizard brain registered it. He quickly looked away conscious not to stare. The incident, while trivial, left him unsettled.

He found Mike sitting on a corner table already set up with a pint for each of them.

He wore thick wire-rimmed glasses atop a beaky nose

lending him a bookish air. He had a disarming habit of staring intently while speaking, his unblinking eyes magnified through the thick lenses.

Jake took a seat looking around the bar. "Why do you come here Mike, what a shithole," he laughed.

He settled back in his chair, clinking his glass against Mike's and took a long pull of his beer. "Good class today mate. You fought well."

"It was tough for sure," he replied, scanning the bar area. "You beat me fair and square though. I thought I had you, but you came back strong. Not bad for an old blo..."

He was interrupted by a commotion next to the fruit machine in the corner. The two men Jake spotted earlier were arguing with another group of four. Jake could not hear but the taller man was acting aggressively while the others tried to calm him. It seemed they knew each other.

Jake watched carefully as he sipped his drink recognising the warning signs of an imminent attack; clenching of fists repeatedly and looking from side to side.

It's gonna kick off.

Sure enough, the big guy exploded into action launching a vicious uppercut to the jaw of the man in front of him, rocking him to his toes. The poor sap went down cold. Turning to the man on his left, he crunched a headbutt into the face, his entire upper body delivering the blow from his waist. Blood exploded from the man's nose as he was knocked back over a chair and onto the floor. His two mates froze in fear, their faces drained white with shock.

The bar fell silent.

Other patrons watched from the corner of their eyes, too frightened to be caught staring. The tall man grabbed his scrawny companion and strode confidently towards the exit.

"Be seeing you," he said over his shoulder to his victims.

Jake looked on shocked at the brazen violence in a public place. The man sauntered past, cocksure and fearless. He stared down intently at Jake, almost daring a challenge. For the second time that evening he looked away, recognising trouble when he saw it. The men left, kicking the bar door open and slamming it behind them.

"Jesus, that was intense," he said to Mike, who sat calmly drinking his beer.

"Call an ambulance!" he shouted to the barman before heading to attend to the injured men.

Jake placed a bar towel behind the head of the unconscious man who was beginning to blink his eyes and come around slowly, dazed and shaken. The other man held a towel against his face to stem the bleeding from his busted nose.

"Are you alright mate?" Jake enquired guiding the man into a seat. "What was all that about?"

"Minor disagreement among friends, nothing serious," he replied. Blood streamed down his face staining his shirt.

"We should call the police," Jake continued. "That man should be locked up. He's an animal."

"No. No police, it's okay. I know him," the man replied quickly his eyes darting around shiftily. "He's a friend, well, more of an acquaintance. It's not worth getting the police involved. Trust me, they won't do nothing over an argument between us. Appreciate your help but it's not your problem pal."

Jake stepped away shaking his head, confused. "Okay. Your business, not mine. I think you both need medical attention though."

Paramedics arrived shortly and after assessing the injuries took the two men outside for further attention.

"Don't you think it's a bit weird?" Jake asked as he returned to Mike at their table. "The bar staff didn't call the police. Those guys did not want them involved. All a bit odd if you ask me."

Mike smiled knowingly. "First time in this boozer I guess? It's like this every weekend mate, and the cops are spread thin these days. When did you last see any officers on the street? My car was broken into six months ago and my laptop was nicked. The police didn't even show up."

"I guess so. Sign of the times," agreed Jake.

"Sad really," Mike replied. "The thugs are taking over round here. See the way he looked at you? Nasty piece of work."

Jake nodded. "Scary guy. Showed no fear. He's trouble to be avoided at all costs."

"Amen to that," replied Mike. "That's why we train. So we don't become victim to these scumbags." The two men clinked their glasses and drained them.

"One for the road?" Jake asked looking at his watch. "I've got twenty minutes. Let's have another quick one then I can be on my way."

Jake returned with more drinks, and they continued to muse over the incident, analysing it from each participant's perspective.

"They allowed him to get in close," said Jake. "As soon as he was in striking range they should have been prepared. Ready to defend and run if possible."

"Easier said than done," replied Mike. "They were backed up to the fruit machine with chairs blocking them. Nowhere to go and they looked scared."

"He wouldn't have got me in the corner like that, that's for sure." Jake checked his watch again and downed the last of his beer. "It's been interesting to say the least, but I need to get going. I'm off to another bar and thank fuck it's nicer than this dump."

"Listen to your lordship," Mike replied grinning. "Take care mate. Have a good one." He punched Jake playfully on the arm.

Jake left his car and walked the ten-minute journey. The incident had left him unnerved and cautious. He scanned anyone who approached carefully, scrutinising and assessing their demeanour, watching their hands.

The fight had reminded him how quickly a seemingly innocuous situation could explode into extreme violence.

CHAPTER 3

Jake approached Nouveau, an upmarket bar close to the centre of Cambridge where the young and chic came to play. It compared to the Crown as Harrods does to the pound store.

He nodded to the doormen who returned the greeting, stepping to one side and politely opening the door for him. The head doorman smiled as he passed, a towering hulk bulging from his suit like a magician had made him from balloons at a child's party.

Rhythmic bass rumbled from the sound system, throbbing through Jake's head and chest. The bar was all steel and soft blue neon lending the bar staff an alien, ethereal glow. Polished black marble floor tiles sparkled silver and blue in the dim light.

Jake liked to come here from time to time as a pleasing reminder of the single life he had enjoyed before he committed to Claire. Although still early, it was busy with people chatting and laughing on bench tables dotted throughout, their faces illuminated by candles.

He edged past a group of young women congregating by the bar while a group of well-groomed men hovered at the fringes trying to work up the courage to initiate conversation.

He smiled to himself. He sometimes missed the social dance but that was all behind him now.

He scanned the bar for his friend and spotted him at a table towards the back corner lounging on a sofa hugging the far wall. Natan stood nodding his greeting and his face cracked into a wide grin as he pulled his friend in for a deep hug.

"Look at you." Jake said smiling. "You look great. How are you keeping?"

Natan was long and lean in body and face and was dressed sharp in jeans and a sleek black tee hugging his toned frame.

"I am good man," he replied slapping his friend on the shoulder.

"What you after, I'll get some drinks," Jake said heading to the bar.

Natan waved his glass as Jake headed to the bar returning quickly with their drinks and sat down. "So, life is treating you well?" he asked.

Natan nodded nursing his drink. "Can't complain. Work is pretty busy."

Jake remained silent fidgeting in his chair his eyes darting around the bar unable to focus. The argument with Claire was weighing on him.

Work is fucked for me.

Natan sat forward eying his friend thoughtfully. "You do not seem yourself. Is everything okay?"

Jake bristled at the question rubbing his head as his ego fired tiny flashes of anger. He chewed his lip nervously. "I'll be fine," he replied tersely.

Natan sat back in his chair reflecting on his friend's demeanour and took on a cooler tone. "Now I might be inclined to take offence." He paused looking hard at his friend. "How long have we known each other?"

Jake recalled the skinny kid who arrived on his building site fifteen years before having fled his homeland desperate for work and seeking a more tolerant society.

"Longer than I care to say out loud," he relented smiling.

"You gave me start here all those years ago when I was forced to leave Poland. And later with Karen. Well, you probably saved my life..." He tailed off gazing into the distance. His eyes were shining, and he brought his hand to his mouth.

The dark days of Natan's wife's death were a topic rarely dwelt on. Jake remembered those long nights in hospital comforting his friend as he sobbed uncontrollably into Jake's arms as the final days approached.

Natan regained his composure and shuffled forward in his chair placing his hand on Jake's arm while locking eyes intently. "What I am trying to say is you have always been there for me. So don't fob me off with some bullshit. Tell me what's wrong."

Jake sat back heavily in his chair puffing out his cheeks and laughed nervously.

"Okay, you got me. Bottom line is I'm going through a dry spell at work. I got stiffed on a final payment from a client. Claire is worried about money and giving me shit about it. We had a row before I came out and not for the first time. It's not been a great few weeks I have to say." He ground his teeth slowly, a nervous trait he had been unable to control since childhood.

Natan sat back in consideration. "Sharing is caring my friend. Please don't hide from me?"

Jake relented nodding. "You are right. I'm sorry, male pride is a fucker."

"Pride before the fall," he warned theatrically wagging his finger. "Besides. Maybe I have something for you," he said pointing at Jake with a smile. "I have a client who wants an extension built. Nothing major but it's probably six months work and must be completed this summer. It's a nice little job for a lovely couple. I can't take it on right now, too much else on my plate. Why don't you come with me next week to see them? I can make the intros and you can take it from there."

This could be the answer. Money coming in. Work for my guys. Claire happy.

Jake had not really noticed the constant low-level tension twisting and ravaging his body and mind, it was just always there recently. He felt it flow from him like someone had opened a tap to relieve it. His face relaxed and he stopped chewing at his lip.

"Really? That sounds perfect." He reached across the table and pulled Natan in for a hug. "Thanks, buddy I appreciate your help."

***

The evening progressed and they were joined by Anton, a friend of Natan's. Anton was mid-twenties and a typical surfer type, all tousled blonde hair and face bronzed from days working outside. The drinks flowed and conversation moved onto lighter topics.

While Natan and Anton headed to the bar for drinks he sat back on the sofa nodding along to the rhythmic music as he surveyed the bar casually.

As he scanned the bar people watching, the trilling of laughter from a nearby table caught his attention.

He turned to see two women deeply engrossed in animated conversation.

They were both in their late twenties or perhaps early thirties and striking. The taller of them had long blond hair framing a soft oval face and dusky almond eyes. She wore a silver dress slashed at the thigh revealing long tanned legs tucked into elegant heels. Her friend had high angular cheekbones and milky white skin, almost translucent. A stark contrast to her deep scarlet lipstick.

Once upon a time, he thought, with a wry smile.

Then he saw them.

His face dropped and his heart began thumping in his chest like a bass drum. Next to the women was a table with two men on it. He recognised them instantly. It was the big guy from the pub fight earlier and his scrawny companion. He tried to shake off the feeling of sudden unease and turned away.

From nowhere bedlam flared up behind him, and he glanced over his shoulder to see the dark-haired girl stand and throw her drink over the tall guy. In an instant his expression changed from leering nonchalance into something much harder and more aggressive.

"Who the fuck you think you are?" he shouted in his thick Eastern European accent. He towered over her, spittle spraying from his mouth twisted into the snarl of a hyena. She refused to back down meeting his gaze defiantly.

The man began to clench and unclench his fists like Jake had witnessed in the pub earlier.

The jovial atmosphere and low murmur of conversation was gone. Like the fun had been sucked out of the room leaving an altogether darker mood as people looked on startled at the disturbance.

He's going to attack her. Do something.

His heart raced and his palms began to sweat, nerves getting hold of him. But he forced himself to move quickly across the bar and positioned himself between them.

"Come on now guys, lets everyone remain calm. Relax and take a deep breath," Jake said raising his palms. Was his voice wavering?

Instantly the man's attention and aggression shifted towards Jake. "Who the fuck might you be? We know each other?" He stared coldly at Jake with dead eyes.

"I'm nobody mate. Only a concerned bystander. I just want to make sure there is no trouble."

"We are not how you say, mates," he snarled back, his face twisted with anger as he moved closer towering over Jake. "If don't want trouble, suggest you fuck off." He rocked back and forward on the balls of his feet, staring intently and puffing out his massive chest.

This guy is a psycho. Don't let him get close.

He kept his eyes forward but noticed the man's companion had also stood up, his hand clenched around a bottle tensed and ready to strike. Chilled adrenaline bathed Jake, the chill running down his spine as the fear clawed at his guts.

What have I done? This can't be happening again.

He was aware of sucking in oxygen as his mind flooded with visions of a violent past. lying battered on a pub floor twenty years before. The world closed in, tunnel vision blurring the outside world to all but the imminent threat. The urge to run was pervasive and overwhelming but he fought to control his fear, breathing slow and calm preparing himself for the fight.

As the three men stood off, Anton and Natan sped over from the bar to join Jake.

"Everything cool?" asked Natan eyeing the two men suspiciously.

"Everything's cool," replied Jake. "Just a misunderstanding that's all."

Thank fuck.

The relief of reinforcements arriving crackled through him like electricity, filling him from within with a surge in power. His hands tingled and the hairs on the back of his neck raised as he waited, ready to kick off.

They all stood their ground. Jake kept his eyes on the chest of the man directly in front while continuing to monitor the other out of his peripheral vision.

By now the doormen had noticed the disorder and were approaching fast. With the numbers shifted against them, Jake sensed the change in the body language of the big guy as he deflated like a popped balloon. He looked at Anton and Natan then sideways to his accomplice and gave a slight, almost imperceptible shake of the head.

The snarl disappeared in a flash, painted over with a forced smile as he backed away. "Your friend is correct. Just a misunderstanding. Now we are leaving."

The two men put their bottles down and pushed past. His eyes never left Jake as he barged through, fixing him with that dead-eyed emotionless stare.

And then they were gone. Jake exhaled blowing away the tension and turned towards the girl. Her hands were shaking, and tears formed as her initial bravado melted away.

"Well, that was exciting," he laughed, trying to lift the dark mood. "Who was that guy?"

She picked up her glass and took a long pull of wine. "I don't know him," she sobbed. "But thank you for your help."

Her turned to her friend and they hugged, comforting each other warmly.

"Let's have a drink," Anton interjected heading to the bar.

"I'm Jake," he said extending his hand. "Pleased to meet you."

She took his hand returning the greeting. "Thanks again. I'm Jasmine and this is Alice. That guy was an arsehole. Him and his scumbag mate have been eyeing us up since they got here and making crude comments. I snapped and lost it. I threw my drink at him. Stupid I know. Well let's just say he did not take kindly to that." She laughed nervously.

"Well, at least you stood up for yourself," Jake replied with conviction. "This is Natan and the guy at the bar is Anton. You can relax and enjoy your evening now they have gone."

They sat down and conversation came easily. Jake replayed the story of the incident he had witnessed earlier to their astonishment. As the evening progressed, the drinks flowed, and everyone relaxed, soon able to laugh off the earlier incident. Jasmin and Alice were easy company, smart and fun to talk to.

Natan and Jasmin had gravitated towards each other. The tell-tale signs were there. They sat close, laughing at jokes together and touching each other's hair. Alice and Anton were also getting along, drinking shots and talking about heading to a nightclub.

These guys are hitting it off, he thought with a wry smile.

Thoughts of Claire snuggled up in bed, warm and inviting tugged at his heart and ignited his desire to be home with her. He stood up.

"That's enough for me. It's been a pleasure, but I am heading home."

Jasmine stood and pulled Jake in for a warm hug. "Thanks again for your help. I'm glad you guys were here, our knights in shining armour."

Jake returned the hug and said his goodbyes to the others before heading out of the bar.

As he exited the cool night air washed over him. The biting cold of winter had long given way to the pleasant chill of a May spring evening. The sky was cloudless, and the stars peppered the sky like a billion dancing fireflies.

He pondered taking a taxi as he surveyed the street.

He took off up the street heading for home. He failed to notice the car parked in the side street opposite the bar. The occupants saw him though. They had been waiting.

CHAPTER 4

"How long we sit here?" Narc protested shifting in his seat and scratching his neck.

Yuri Vasin glared at his accomplice with disdain. "Mudak," he swore under his breath in his native Russian. "We have been here two hours only, what is problem? Sit tight and we have fun when those bitches come out. Have smoke and relax," he said passing the joint.

Narc took it gratefully and dragged deeply. "Why we must stay in this fucking town? I want to go back to London."

Yuri's hands clenched tight around the steering wheel, knuckles white. "We go when I say," he hissed through clenched teeth.

"Can we put heating on? It is cold." Narc rubbed his hands blowing into them.

Yuri stared again at his so-called friend and imagined the pleasure he would glean from driving an elbow sharply into his temple.

His name was Narcissus but he was known as Narc due to his unrelenting drug addiction. He was of Russian origin like Yuri but grew up in some shithole province that made him worse than a Georgian in Yuri's eyes.

Narc scratched continuously at his pale sweating face. His teeth were crooked and stacked chaotically in his mouth like a pile of rotten wood. Squinty ferret eyes darted nervously in sunken sockets always searching so he never seemed to look directly at you.

Yuri closed his eyes and rubbed his temples slowly in a futile effort to rid himself of the tension. Narc was a parasite and always induced tension.

***

"I need you in Cambridge," Vlad had instructed that morning. "You must collect from the Jacob brothers. They owe us. Take Narc."

The red heat fired in his brain fuelling him with defiance.

"No. I will not do it," he had replied shaking his head firmly. "I go nowhere with that fucking junky moron. He is liabili..."

"Just do what you are told moy brat," his brother had scolded cutting him off.

He turned to him lifting his chin until they were eye to eye. Yuri shrank under Vlad's dark and malevolent gaze. He placed his hands on Yuri's shoulders adopting a softer tone.

"I need you to do this for me brother. We can spare no one else. Deliver this task and we can give you more prominent responsibilities." He clapped him on the shoulder and grinned. The corners of his mouth turned up in an approximation of a smile, but the eyes remained dead.

Yuri nodded meekly as the familiar feeling of self-loathing consumed him. "Of course, brother. I can do this," he replied softly dropping his eyes to the floor once again complying with his brother's instructions.

***

So here he was. He clenched his teeth and gripped the steering wheel hard, fighting the urge to reach over and choke the life from that thin week body. Now he would have to explain to Vlad that the Jacobs had failed to pay and he was forced to beat them.

The dread mounted slowly rising from his toes. His feet felt like lead weights dragging him down as he imagined delivering the news and bearing his brother's silent disappointment at his failure to deliver such a simple task.

"What is this?" Yuri's attention sharpened as the door of the bar opened. He sat up straight "Look, it is pizda who got in our way earlier?"

Narc squinted through the windscreen. "Sure boss that is him, but we wait for those two bitches for our fun, no?"

Yuri's hands tightened on the steering wheel and he ground his teeth as his lust for revenge and pure red anger burned through him like fire.

"We get our kicks different way tonight," he hissed through clenched teeth. Get ready."

Yuri watched his target moved off down the main road. When he was a discreet distance away he gunned the engine and pulled out of the layby following slowly.

The anticipation built from within as he pictured himself face to face with his victim, savouring the terror in his eyes when he had him cornered. He could almost smell the fear

Yuri turned right stalking his target with caution and maintaining the distance between them.

"He is turning into alley. We get him now."

He opened the glove box and handed a cosh to Narc. "Take it."

Narc fingered it nervously. It was about eight inches in length with a handle of stitched black leather expanding into a bulbous end containing a heavy metal ball. Narc tested it, thumping it into his hand rhythmically. The dull smack echoed around the car.

"I drop you at end of alleyway. You wait there and cut him off. I drive to other end and we trap him in middle. Be ready in case he runs."

Narc took deep breaths psyching himself up for the fight.

Yuri glanced at him. His eyes were wide with fear and for a split-second Yuri felt the sharp stab of indecision.

He cast the thought focussing on the task at hand. He dropped Narc at the alley entrance before speeding around the crescent to the other end.

A single streetlamp away up the road provided the only illumination leaving the alley dark and isolated. He cut the engine and pulled a bag from his pocket. He took a coin and snorted a generous portion into both nostrils before rubbing more on his gums. The coke hit instantly, bitter on the back of his throat and numbing his mouth and nose. His heartbeat surged and his vision focussed with heightened clarity, like the world before him had switched in a flash from black and white to high-definition colour.

He grabbed the bat from under the seat and stepped out of the car swinging it, feeling its weight and heft. Fuelled by the drugs and seething in anger from the earlier humiliation, his fury raged as he sucked in deep breaths fuelling his lungs with oxygen. Any passing innocent bystander would have described a raging monster snarling through clenched teeth, spittle flecks flying from his mouth. Eyes bloodshot.

He concealed the bat behind him he stepped into the alleyway. His target was directly in front only ten yards away jogging towards him.

He moved into the light and their eyes met.

Yuri savoured the sweet moment of recognition. That split second of terror as his target registered the danger. He drew the bat from behind his back and rapped the ground slowly. He felt the familiar surge of power and dominance expand in his chest as his victim froze in place momentarily, eyes wide and paralysed by fear.

In a flash as if some switch had flicked inside, his victim turned and ran sprinting fast back into the alley.

They had him trapped.

***

Jake left the main road heading into a side street. After a few hundred yards he turned into a dimly lit alleyway. His pace quickened as the claustrophobic space closed in. He registered the sound of car tyres screeching, the noise sharpening his senses. He turned to scan behind. It was empty but some something did not feel right. The hairs on the back of his neck prickled and his heart started beating faster. Like a gazelle on the plains dimly aware of some hidden predator stalking from the reeds he was on edge, nervous. He could not see anything, but some acute sense had fired alerting him that a threat was close.

The end of the alley was around thirty yards ahead now. He heard a car approaching in front of him. He glanced behind again. This time a man was stood there, dimly lit and distant.

This is bad.

His heart was hammering now. Primal fear coursed through him. He felt chilled to the core, like his veins had been pumped full of refrigerant. Twenty yards from the end he broke into a jog, desperate to be in an open space and free from confinement of the alleyway. Only ten yards to go.

A man stepped into the alleyway directly in front stopping him in his tracks. Illuminated from the streetlamp above Jake recognised him instantly as the thug from the bar. He produced a bat from behind his back knocking it with purpose on the concrete floor. The sound echoed menacingly from the alley walls like a ticking clock counting down the seconds to Jake's imminent death. His bowels turned to jelly and he froze, paralyzed with fear. He was trapped.

Run Now.

His flight response triggered and he turned and sprinted. The other man was around thirty yards away silhouetted against the dim light at the far end of the alley. He accelerated fast as cortisol coursed through him shunting blood to his major muscles and fuelling him with raw energy and power.

The man was armed with a small club in his right hand.

Don't stop. Get past him.

He now faced the prospect of fighting two armed attackers in a confined space. He was in a fight for his life and if he did not prevail, he would die in this alley tonight.

He closed in and lifted his arms in front of his face. All his attention was focussed forward with no time to consider the man behind him. The man stood his ground and raised the cosh to strike.

Jake smashed into him at full pace landing a forearm blow directly to the jaw. The man's head snapped back hitting a concrete fence post with a sickening crack. Gravity took over and he collapsed like a dropped sack of potatoes.

The impact threw Jake off balance, and he went down losing precious seconds. He quickly regained his feet but the other attacker was upon him with the bat raised high above his head roaring with anger. Hatred flashed across his face and spittle oozed through clenched teeth as he snarled like a rabid animal.

Jake charged and crashed into him striking for the face with his elbow. The bat thrashed down towards his head, but Jake ducked in close and it glanced off his back. He held on tight to his attacker's arm and struck out repeatedly at his eyes and throat with his free hand landing crunching blows. He clamped onto the neck and drove his knee sharply into his groin eliciting a howl of pain.

The man collapsed wrapping his long arms around Jake and they tumbled to the floor. The wind was driven from Jake as he found himself pinned beneath the weight of his attacker. Struggling to breathe he lashed out smashing fists and elbows into his attacker's face. He clamped on tight to the back of the neck and pulled him in tight. He took a bite from his ear provoking a sharp scream.

He sensed movement of the man's right arm. Then he heard it. The unmistakable click of a flick knife.

Is this the end?

He waited for the sharp bite of steel sinking into his ribs. He was seconds from death and fought franticly to draw in oxygen as his strength weakened. He saw the silver flash of the blade in the moonlight inches from his face and grabbed hold of the knife arm with both hands as the blade pressed down towards his throat.

His eyes locked onto his attackers. Black and lifeless like a mannequin. There was no compassion. Only pure fury and anger. The end was close for Jake and he had little fight left. Visions of his children flashed though his mind.

Summoning the last of his strength he screamed and bucked his body crunching his knee into his opponent's groin. The strike connected driving the wind from his assailant. Jake managed to twist the knife away from his throat and towards his attacker. They rolled and Jake forced all his weight down driving the blade away from him. He felt a sudden rush of hot wet on his hands and face. With an animalistic roar he sat up and pulled his hand back to strike the finishing blows and end the fight.

The man lay flopping limply beneath him, his hands

clawing weakly at the blade. It was buried to the hilt in his throat. His legs thrashed, kicking spasmodically as he coughed gouts of blood flowing down his chin black as oil in the moonlight.

The eyes were fixed on Jake. All the anger and hatred had gone, replaced by the fear of certain death and the final journey to the next world. Jake surged with mixed emotions as he watched the man die, feeling the power flush through his body lighting up every nerve and filling him with energy and vitality. Millions of years of evolution celebrating victory over a slain enemy. For how long he sat there he did not know. He gasped in oxygen and his skin prickled with intensity as his lungs filled and his heart pumped the blood round his body bathing him in warmth.

Jake stood and surveyed the carnage. Blood pooled around the dead body staring lifelessly into the night sky. The second attacker was regaining consciousness and Jake turned and stomped his boot forcefully into the groin. He ran from the alley returning to the safety of the main road near the bar.

As the reality of the situation began to sink in his stomach churned and he turned and vomited into the gutter. His mind and body were overwhelmed by mixed emotions and feelings. His imminent death, utter exhaustion from the fight, the exquisite ecstasy of victory, the death of a man by his hand.

He was shaking uncontrollably as he tried to pull out his phone and it clattered to the pavement. He retrieved it and sat on the curb fighting to control his breathing and called for help.

They arrived less than five minutes later. A police car pulled up next to him and two officers got out circling him warily while keeping their hands on their batons.

They approached Jake cautiously who put his hands on his head. "Are you hurt Sir? "the younger officer asked. "Did you make the call to the emergency services?" He was of a calm bearing with a stocky frame and kindly eyes.

"Yes, it was me. Two men attacked me in the alleyway back there," he replied thumbing over his shoulder. "I think one of them is dead."

The second older officer eyed Jake suspiciously and made off towards the alleyway to assess the situation while the younger one remained with Jake.

"It's all going to be okay," he said one hand out towards Jake. "I'm PC Jackson. Let's start with your name please Sir. You are safe now but please keep your hands where I can see them." Despite his size and presence Jackson possessed an easy demeanour that calmed Jake down.

"My n.. n.. name is Jake Charles," he stuttered through ragged breaths. His hands were still shaking and his legs felt heavy, like he was dragging concrete boots as the effects of the adrenaline rush began to leave his body

"Okay, that's good. Can you tell me what happened?" Jackson noted Jake's responses as he spoke.

Jake replayed the incident to Jackson who listened intently and recorded his comments. "So, the man got stabbed with his own knife?" he asked raising an eyebrow. "Did you try to stop the bleeding?"

Alarm bells tingled quietly in the back of Jake's mind.

Be careful what you say.

"There was nothing I could do," he replied. "He died in seconds and I was scared the other man would come after me again. They were both armed. I think they were trying to kill me."

Jackson regarded him thoughtfully. "Did you kill the man Sir?"

The question stung Jake like a scorpion to the base of his

spine sending a jolt of nerve through his body.

Did I kill him?

"No, of course not," he replied angrily. "I told you already, he attacked me and pulled a knife." Yet he recalled the animalistic thrill he had felt as he had roared in victory atop his enemy and the energy that had flowed through his body like fire in his veins.

Stop. Don't do this to yourself. It was him or you.

He checked himself rapidly.

More police cars and an ambulance had now arrived lighting the surrounding streets with the flash of blue lights. The area had been taped off to keep the public at bay. The commotion brought people into the streets keen to see the excitement. Natan and Jasmine were standing outside Nouveau watching the events unfold, shock and confusion written across their faces.

Jackson beckoned one of the ambulance team. "Please can you check this gentleman for injury?"

"Of course, this way please Sir." The paramedic approached, a young lady with a soothing tone and friendly demeanour gestured towards the waiting ambulance.

Jake managed to catch Natan's eye and mouthed at him, "Phone Claire."

Natan nodded his understanding as his friend was led to the ambulance, bloody and beaten.

The paramedic directed Jake to sit on a trolley. "I'm Christine Spencer and here to help you. Are you hurt?"

Spencer was short and slight dressed in paramedic greens and black boots. Her blonde hair was pulled tight into a ponytail revealing an oval face with soft features and a wide mouth. The ambulance smelt faintly of antiseptic.

"I don't think so," Jake replied. "The blood is not mine mostly."

"Let me take a look." Spencer sat Jake down and removed his t-shirt then wiped the blood away with a surgical cloth before examining his torso thoroughly. "You have some bad scratches and bruises, but you seem okay. I can't see any puncture wounds." She busied herself cleaning him with iodine and applying plasters. He flinched at the sting of the brown liquid.

"Any blows to the head, any pain?" she asked, shining a torch in his eyes.

"No. I feel fine," he replied which was far from true as he turned over the events of the evening and what might have been.

Spencer nodded. "You are going to be fine. As I said, a few minor scratches. You are a lucky man. Most people involved in a knife incident come away with horrific wounds. Or worse."

His thoughts turned to his family. He could be the dead man heading for a slab in the morgue. He pictured the girls waking to their mother's howl of anguish as the police arrived to deliver the news of their father's death. He was desperate to get home to see and hug them, to tell them everything would be alright.

Once Spencer was finished, she led him from the ambulance. Jackson was waiting. He approached Jake with a grave look on his face placing a firm grip on his shoulder.

"We need to take you in to make a statement. Jake Charles, I am arresting you on suspicion of murder. You do not have to say anything, but it may harm your defence if you do not mention when questioned something which you later rely on in court. Do you understand the caution?"

Murder. Surely not. No this cannot be happening. The gravity of the situation folded in around Jake enveloping and overwhelming him. His stomach churned and he wretched on his empty stomach.

"Surely you cannot be charging me. I haven't done anything wrong," he replied aghast at the turn of events. He had defended his life and now covered in another man's blood was being arrested for murder.

"Of course, we need to make that determination Sir," he replied. "That will all come in due course, but we need to take you in for questioning. Please hold out your hands."

Say nothing more.

He snapped to his senses. He held out his arms as instructed, and Jackson cuffed his wrists and guided him into the back of the waiting police van.

CHAPTER 5

What's happening to me. Am I in real trouble this time? The thought returned repeatedly pecking away at the back of his mind like a hungry bird.

His heart yearned for Claire. It was gone midnight and he was desperate to speak with her. She would expect him home by now or at least a message to say he was staying out late. Hopefully Natan would have contacted her and would be there to lend support.

His thoughts flipped between his family and the man who had died.

Did I kill him?

Was there a pang of guilt gnawing at his insides?

The van slid past the wide green expanse of Parker's Piece. Late night stragglers mingled on the moonlit parkland, living their lives while Jake's slowly crushed in on him.

They pulled into the rear car park of a dull grey concrete building housing the police station. Only the blue sign out front marked it as different from any other office building on this side of town.

Jackson frogmarched Jake to a metal door and placed his security card next to the magnetic lock. It opened with a soft click. He was led through a long corridor, silent but for their footsteps and the flickering of harsh fluorescent strip lamps. At the end of the corridor double doors opened inwards to the custody suite. The Sergeant looked up from his paperwork as Jake was led into the room.

"Haven't we had a busy night Sir?" he commented looking Jake up and down. "I am Sergeant Ainsley."

Ainsley sat ramrod straight in his chair crisp in a pristine white shirt. His sleeves were rolled up revealing sinewy tanned forearms and strong hands with stubby fingers. He peered at Jake with hard grey eyes.

"So, what are we in for?" he turned to the policeman escorting Jake. "Are you the arresting officer Jackson?"

"Yes Sir, I am." Jackson pulled out his pocketbook and consulted his notes from the arrest. "I attended the scene following a report of an attack. I arrived to find this man, who identified himself as Jake Charles covered in blood. He claims to have been attacked by two men in an alleyway. He says one of the men pulled a knife and during the ensuing struggle the man sustained a fatal wound."

"And has Mr Charles been cautioned?" Ainsley replied.

"He has Sir." Flipping the page on his notes he continued, "Mr Charles was cautioned at the scene and placed under arrest for murder at 11:53 pm."

Murder. There it was again. Such a stark and unflinching word. Coarse. Unambiguous. It had no double meaning

Ainsley turned to Jake. "Is there anything you wish to say at this time?"

Jake shook his head firmly. "Not until I have spoken with a solicitor. Please can you arrange one?" he replied.

Ainsley nodded his agreement. "Of course. Are you on any medication? Any health concerns that we need to know about?" He made notes as Jake spoke.

"No, nothing like that," he replied softly, staring into the middle distance.

"Any further questions you wish to ask me?" he asked looking up at Jake?

"Can I phone my wife? I would like to let her know what has happened."

He shifted nervously on his feet as the dread ball formed in the pit of his stomach and expanded through his torso.

What will I say to her?

"All in good time Sir. First, we need to take your clothes as evidence." He turned to Jackson and gestured to the corridor behind the desk. Jake was escorted to a cell while Ainsley followed carrying a large polythene bag. The blood-soaked t-shirt was placed inside by Jackson who had retained it at the scene. Next, they went over his entire body with a metal detector wand searching he assumed for concealed weapons.

"Please take off your clothes and place them in this bag," Ainsley instructed.

Jake stripped as he was told, depositing his jeans into the bag. He stood in front of them, naked and shivering in the cool of the cell.

"No one likes this but I'm afraid it is required. Please bend over and pull your cheeks apart."

For fucks sake. Is this really necessary?

He completed the humiliating procedure. Seemingly satisfied he was not carrying anything illicit, Ainsley handed him a cellophane bag containing fresh underwear.

"Can I shower?" he asked as he dressed.

Ainsley nodded. "Soon, but we need to finish processing you."

Ainsley gestured to another officer who had entered the

room. "Forensics will complete the examination, then you can clean yourself up. Please sit."

The contents of his fingernails were scraped into an evidence bag. Dried blood was picked from his torso with tweezers and placed into another bag.

"Open your mouth please."

Jake complied and a sample was taken from the inside of his cheek. Finally, it seemed it was all over. Ainsley handed him some clothes, grey jogging bottoms, t-shirt, and a hoodie along with a towel and a bar of soap.

"The showers are down the hall. Jackson will escort you and wait outside. I have called for a solicitor. Someone will be here first thing in the morning. Once you are cleaned up, we can get you something to eat if you are hungry."

Fear and adrenaline had fuelled the emotional rollercoaster of Jake's evening and he had not thought of food once. Now, the gnawing chasm of emptiness in the pit of his stomach was calling out for food.

"What can I get, pizza?"

Ainsley nodded. "We can manage that. I'll arrange it while you shower."

Jake nodded his thanks then Jackson led him down the corridor to the shower block. As the door closed behind him, for the first time since this nightmare had started, he was alone. He undressed and stepped into the shower cubicle. The powerful jet enveloped him, washing away the grime and blood.

Am I going to prison? Surely not. He had not stabbed anyone or even touched the knife. It was an accident, and the facts would emerge in time.

The shower cleansed his body and mind leaving him primed and ready to face the music. He dressed and opened the door to find Ainsley waiting with pizza.

"Would you like to make your phone call before you eat?"

The pit of dread returned. He nodded and was escorted to a small stark room, bare and oppressive with no windows. The only furniture was a metal table with a black phone handset and a flimsy silver chair. He closed the door, sat and picked up the handset. He hesitated, staring blankly at the phone.

What the fuck am I going to say?

He sighed heavily and slumped forward in the chair. Head in his hands. Elbows on the table.

Finally, with shaking hands he dialled the number. It barely rang before she picked up.

"Jake, is that you? Thank God. Where are you? Are you okay?" The anxiety in Claire's tone was unmistakable. She had been crying. He could picture her sat in the living room, eyes red and face taut with worry. "What happened?"

"Hi baby, it's good to hear your voice." He kept his voice low and tone soothing. He had his own demons to deal with, but he needed Claire calm and strong for the children.

"I'm fine. I'm not hurt, just a few scrapes. I've been involved in an incident. I won't go into the details, but I was attacked by two men. One of them pulled a knife."

Claire gasped. "Jake, that's awful. You could have been killed."

He sat upright staring vacantly at the wall and took a deep breath. "There is bad news." He paused, unsure how to continue. "The guy with the knife. He died. There was nothing I could do."

Silence.

He closed his eyes and let out a long sigh.

"It gets worse. They have arrested me for murder. It was clear self-defence, but the police seem to think there is a case for me to answer. I'm waiting to find out if I'm going to be charged."

He flinched at the sound of Claire's broken sobbing.

"My God Jake. Arrested for murder. This can't be happening."

Nausea overwhelmed him as he prepared to deliver what came next. "There is something else you need to know. Something about my past. Way back before we met."

This is going to change everything. He swallowed nervously, yet unable to remove the lump in his throat.

"I've been in trouble with the police before. As a kid." He paused, staring at the phone willing her to respond.

"What do you mean?" she finally replied quietly. "Surely nothing serious?"

"I have a conviction for fighting when I was younger. And for carrying a knife. You know I came from a tough neighbourhood. It was a jungle. I did what I had to do to survive."

A chasm of silence had opened. An empty void he felt compelled to fill with his words. "Speak to me baby, please."

Finally, she responded. Her tone was low and quiet, cold. "You lied to me. Why didn't you tell me?"

"No Claire. I never lied to you," he begged. "I just didn't think it was important. That was the old me. When we met, I changed overnight. I am a totally different person now. I never wanted to dredge up old feelings and problems from my previous life. I guess I just did not want you to think of me that way."

"You should have told me Jake," she said icily. "I always imagined we had no secrets from each other." She spoke quietly, eerily calm now. The wracking sobs gone.

I can't lose her now.

"Please baby. You have to trust me," he pleaded.

He felt she had drifted away. Distant irrelevant of the physical separation. Like some of the mooring lines tethering them together had been snipped.

He pressed his forehead onto the table and fought back the tears that threatened. His voice wavered.

"I know baby. I should have and I'm sorry. But please, now is not the time for division between us. I need you. I'm in deep trouble and I can't do this on my own."

"What shall I tell the kids?" she replied.

He yearned with all his heart to be with her. To have this conversation face to face. To comfort and hold each other and breathe in her scent. With a sudden jolt of fear, he wondered how long it might be before that materialised. Would it be the same as before? Something had changed. It was like they had been side by side but now they stared at each other across a gaping crevasse that had cracked open between them.

"Tell them the truth but without the detail. I was attacked by some bad men but I'm okay. One of the men tried to hurt me. I defended myself but unfortunately the man was severely injured and died. The police want to ask some questions about what happened and I'm talking to them now. That is all they need to know at this point. We can work out the rest later."

The idea of his children thinking him a killer, even in self-defence sickened him. He felt hollow. Like all he knew about himself had been ripped away.

"I can't believe this has happened," she continued. "It's a lot to process Jake. I need some time to think. The kids are sleeping, I'll leave them and explain in the morning."

He took a deep breath, "I have to go now. Take care of the girls. They will need to see you are not afraid. I love you."

Time stretched eternally as he waited for her response.

"I love you too. Take care." The words were there but

without feeling. Tears slid down his cheek. He knew there and then. Things would never quite be the same between them. He had made a terrible mistake not confiding in her.

He hung up the phone and sat back heavily in the chair suddenly exhausted. He opened the door and gestured to Ainsley that he was finished. Another officer led Jake to his cell where he slumped on the bed and lay processing the unbelievable series of events.

A day that had started so normally. Enjoying time with his girls, a family walk, kissing them all goodbye. Now that day came crashing to a close.

Flashes of the evening tumbled in his mind alongside fears of an unknown future. He fell into an anxious, sweaty sleep filled with dark dreams of violence and incarceration.

CHAPTER 6

The early morning light streaming through the barred window woke Jake from a fitful sleep. He lay on the bed, his mind torturing him with what-ifs.

What if I had fallen on the knife? What if I get charged? What if I spend the next twenty years behind bars? How will Claire and the girls cope?

Anxiety clawed from within like some alien in his chest trying to burst free as the adrenaline surged. He tossed and turned in bed wracked with fear.

Stay in control.

His mind could be his worst enemy, but it could save him if he were strong.

He went through his morning fitness routine. Burpees and press ups until he were doubled over panting and sweating profusely. It had the desired effect. The anxiety evaporated, replaced with steely determination to face whatever the day threw at him. The viewing hatch slid open, and a new officer Jake had not seen before nodded a greeting. Keys jangled in the lock and the door swung open.

"Good morning Mr Charles. How are we this morning? I'm officer Stephens" He smiled warmly. He was young and keen and friendly.

I'm in prison for a murder I did not commit.

I'm fine thank you," he replied quietly staring at the floor.

Stephens laid a tray on the floor next to Jake.

"Tea and toast. It's not much but it will keep you going. Also, your solicitor has arrived. She is waiting to speak with you. I'll be back in five minutes and will take you to her."

Jake murmured his thanks. Hunger growled in his stomach, and he demolished breakfast in two minutes flat. He nursed the tea until Stephens returned and unlocked the cell.

"Please follow me Mr Charles." They followed the corridor and stopped in front of a slate grey door at the far end. "Wait in here please." He opened the door and led Jake inside. The room was windowless and sparsely furnished with a metal table and four chairs. Fluorescent strip lamps made the yellow walls shine slick like butter. Cameras faced into the centre of the room and a large mirror dominated the far wall.

Who is watching, he wondered as he peered up close.

The door swung open, and Stephens entered with a confident young woman in her early thirties. She was smartly dressed in a blue business trouser suit over a white blouse. Dark hair. Oval face. He guessed of Asian ancestry.

Jake stood as she extended her hand to greet him smiling warmly. She radiated warmth and competence putting him at ease instantly.

"Hello Mr Charles, I'm Sarah Millbank. Please call me Sarah. I will be representing you. Can we talk?"

Jake gestured to the seat across the table. "Of course. Please call me Jake."

Stephens closed the door leaving them alone. Millbank took a seat opposite and laid out a legal pad and pencil squarely in front of her. She adjusted both carefully, so the edges were perfectly square to the edge of the table.

"To business Jake. I have been briefed by the desk sergeant. Please can you tell me what happened?"

Millbank made notes as he relayed his account of the previous evening's events.

"I was attacked by two men in an alleyway. They had followed me from a bar where we had a previous altercation." He shifted nervously in his seat. "One of them pulled a knife and took a serious wound to his neck in the struggle. He died quickly. There was nothing I could do."

Does she believe me? He scrutinised her expression, but her face was impassive giving nothing away.

Millbank nodded making further notes. "Understood. That's the short version. Now I want you to take me through it from beginning to end. A full and detailed account. I can only defend you properly if you are completely honest with me."

Jake laughed nervously. "Defend me? I have not done anything wrong," he said incredulously. "I was attacked and acted purely in self-defence?"

She took a deep breath and laid down her pencil then looked him directly in the eye.

"Make no mistake. This was a serious incident in which a man died. Self-defence in the eyes of the law is effectively an admission that you were involved. You have been arrested for murder and according to the desk sergeant there is a second witness who claims you attacked them following an argument in the pub." She watched him closely waiting for his response.

"That's a lie. They attacked me," he replied calmly.

"Understood. Then it's your word against his for now. Please continue."

Jake replayed the evening's events in detail as Millbank interjected with questions probing his account. Once satisfied, she stood and paced the room.

"There is another matter to discuss. The desk sergeant informs me you have a criminal record for violence in the past.

This may have implications for your case."

It was twenty years ago," he said quietly. "I was a stupid kid." He drummed his finger nervously on the table. "

"Maybe. But as far as the police are concerned you have a record for violence including a charge for carrying a knife," she continued consulting her notes. "They are not your friends Jake. They will use dirty tactics to trip you up and find a way to charge you. They may claim you acted with excessive force in defending yourself. You need to understand the worst-case scenario."

Do I really want to know? He wondered.

"And what is the worst-case scenario?" he asked. His voice wavered.

She took another deep breath. "If the police believe this was a fight which got out of hand, you will be charged and appear before a magistrate Monday morning. If the court decides there is a case to answer you will likely be bailed to appear later."

She paused looking away as if preparing to give bad news to a child. "However, given there is a surviving witness and with your past criminal record...."

She hesitated before continuing. "The prosecution may argue that witness intimidation is a possibility and ask for you to be remanded in custody."

Jake swallowed. His throat dry and head pounding as the statement sunk in. The stark yellow walls seemed to close in around him. Beads of sweat appeared on his forehead and his heart throbbed as panic reared.

This can't be happening.

"They tried to kill me. What was I supposed to do?"

Millbank took on a soothing tone. "I know this is a lot to take in but please remain calm. I am preparing you for the worst but let's hope for the best. I can get you through this, but you need to stay focused. Let's get some tea and then tell me everything from the beginning again. I want your recollection crystal clear before you give a statement."

Jake closed his eyes and took deep slow breaths.

Don't lose it. Stay in control. She knows what she is doing.

Millbank opened the door and requested refreshments. They settled into a lengthy questioning session as Jake recounted his evening once more. At last, it seemed Millbank was satisfied they had covered every angle. She stood and paced the room while laying out their case.

"We will not dispute you were involved in the incident. That would be folly. You will claim you acted in self-defence when two armed assailants targeted you in an alleyway. In defending yourself one of them unfortunately died. On your side we have supporting witnesses who will corroborate what happened in both bars earlier in the evening."

Millbank consulted her notes. "Against you will be the second assailant. He claims you instigated the incident in the bar and followed them into the alleyway to attack. I don't know the credibility of this witness, but I will investigate that. The police want your statement and are ready to interview. The best strategy is to relay the events of the evening honestly. Exactly as you have to me. Do you agree?" she asked standing directly in front of him with her palms on the table as she looked him directly in the eye.

Jake nodded meeting her gaze. "Of course, you have my full trust."

"You. Did. Not. Direct. The. Fatal. Blow. Or. Touch. The. Knife." She enunciated the words emphasising each with a bang on the table then paused to let the statement sink in. She placed a hand on his shoulder. The first friendly human contact since arriving at the station. She took on a softer tone and continued. "I want you one hundred per cent clear on that point. If the police believe you picked up or directed the weapon intentionally, they will charge you with murder. Do you understand?" she stared hard, daring him to disagree.

"I do," he replied firmly.

"Are you ready?"

"I'm ready," Jake replied standing.

"Good. A few ground rules. If you are unsure of any questions, ask for clarification. They will try to get you to admit something that can be used in court. If I challenge their question or answer on your behalf do not interrupt or contradict me. If you are unsure about anything confer with me before you answer. Clear?"

"Clear," he replied taking a deep breath. "Let's get this done."

CHAPTER 7

"So, how have you been Sam? It's been a couple of weeks since we last spoke." Counsellor Michael Anderson peered at DCI Samantha Raynes over horn-rimmed spectacles perched on a long-beaked nose lending him the appearance of a learned old bird. A mop of unruly grey nested on his head. Same for his eyebrows. He displayed an expression of intense concern which Raynes imagined was an effort to lull his patients into a soporific feeling of ease and comfort.

It never worked.

"Well, I haven't had a drink now for over a month," she replied quietly forcing a smile. She dropped her gaze to her foot which bounced uncontrollably as if attached to a stranger's leg.

Maybe just one glass tonight to celebrate, she thought as the gnawing craving for alcohol consumed her like a vampire's bloodlust. Her face reddened and her lips tightened as the hot flash of shame washed over her for permitting the notion. Memories of the last time filled her mind. Waking naked in her flat surrounded by bottles and empty wrappers of coke and soaked with her own urine. She forced the image from her mind and painted the smile on her face again.

"Well, that's wonderful news. Good for you." He watched her carefully with watery blue eyes at which he dabbed constantly with a tissue causing Raynes to blink involuntarily herself. "And are you still following the twelve-step programme and attending the meetings?" He laid his hands flat on the table in front of him smiling and tilting his head to one side like a dog listening to his owner.

"I am not sure the meetings are for me," she replied softly meeting his gaze.

"And why is that?" he replied, cocking an eyebrow.

She stared at his fingers drumming slowly and recalled the circle of loathing at the last meeting. Those poor tortured victims revealing their innermost secrets and fears. Yet she reserved the most vicious loathing for herself.

"My job makes it... Problematic," she replied monotonously. The truth was her stomach twisted into knots as she recalled spewing her shameful story to a room of strangers.

"I understand," he replied nodding thoughtfully. "And how are you feeling. Any depressive or suicidal thoughts?"

Raynes flinched and looked away shaking her head. "Nothing like that no," she lied.

In truth every night was a battle.

A handful of pills and a bottle of vodka and it could all be over. This was a mantra she repeated on a nightly basis. But the job kept her going, the one positive force in her life.

"And what about... 'Him'. Are you still experiencing the dreams and the visions?"

The question she knew was coming still stabbed like a knife to the heart. She chewed her lip as a solitary tear slid down her cheek. The protective armour she constructed around herself each day fell away as she recalled the horrific image seared into her brain as a little girl. She felt it now as she did then, the utter helplessness as she witnessed her mother laying dying at 'his' feet. She started sobbing quietly.

Anderson pushed a box of tissues across the desk between them, Raynes took one gratefully wiping her eyes. He morphed into business mode, connecting the tips of his fingers in front of his face.

"You have used alcohol and other substances in the past to mask these thoughts and feelings. To drown them if you like. Now you are sober, it's to be expected they will come to the fore more often. Are you keeping a journal as I suggested? It is important to explore your innermost feelings both good and bad. It will help with your recovery."

She pictured herself at her desk each evening. Night after night she toiled over her treasured journal, filling page after page with echoes of her tragic past and desires for a new future. Fuelled with endless cups of coffee she wrote into the small hours. It was the one thing that could quell the infinite craving for alcoholic oblivion.

"I am," she sniffed, finally smiling through her tears. "It helps. Really it does."

He smiled exhaling deeply with satisfaction at the breakthrough. "That's great Sam. It's not an easy path you are on. The trauma from your past is manifesting in your present. But you are doing well. And you must learn to forgive yourself."

Raynes emerged from her shell slowly as she always did in her sessions with Anderson. He chipped away delicately at the tough exterior, coaxing information and encouraging openness. Gradually he found a way through, peeling back the layers built up over decades.

***

"And when you are ready, please open your eyes."

Raynes blinked slowly orienting herself back to the room. She was slumped deep in her chair. Her breathing was slow and measured. Her hands and feet tingled. Momentary calm and peace washed through her as Anderson concluded their meditation session.

I'm afraid that's all we have time for today," he said glancing at his watch.

Back to the real world. The sadness poured back in as sure as if someone were filling her being up with jugs of pure misery. As it rose, it displaced the fleeting calm until all had spilled from her body. Gone as if it had never been there.

Brick by brick she began to reconstruct the mental wall Anderson had so meticulously dismantled. He was the only one to ever meet this version of Raynes. The vulnerable child and addict.

"Until next time Sam. Be kind to yourself." He smiled and stood from the leather chair. He uncoiled his lanky frame and smoothed his tweed blazer in place. They shook hands as she dabbed at her eyes, wiping away the tears the wider world could never see.

***

Light traffic rumbled above, crossing the bridge that spanned the river. Raynes cut a solitary figure alone on the park bench gazing at the water. Sunlight peeked through the trees on the far bank glittering on the ripples as a light breeze ruffled the river. Boaters passed from time to time, nodding their greetings as they punted up the river enjoying the springtime air. They would notice a sad but striking look woman. Difficult to place in age but likely twenty years from either college or a bus pass. Her face was thin and angular, the gaunt face of an addict with the broken capillaries of alcohol abuse expertly covered by makeup. A trick she had learned from her mother.

A pair of swans sailed by, majestic and proud with a trio of cygnets following close in their wake. A strong bonded family unit. Both pen and cob hissed at passers-by who came too close, fiercely protective of their young. Raynes watched those young cygnets wrapped in the warmth of their parent's love and envied them for a life she never had.

***

Her earliest memories were lying in bed at night drawing the sheets tight under her chin. She buried her head under the pillow desperate to drown out the shouting and screams from the bedroom next door.

But she never could.

For as long as she could recall her mother had worn cuts and bruises. They came and went, sometimes fading to reveal a pretty face on a shy and timid lady who doted on her only daughter. She did her best to cover them. An expert with makeup and sunglasses, yet nothing could hide the haunting fear in her mother's eyes. That never went away.

Raynes was five when she first received his attention. She remembered like it was yesterday. Her crime was to take a biscuit from the tin without his permission. For that transgression he had come at her belt in hand, snarling and vicious while her tiny sparrow-like mother desperately tried to stop him. Of course, she never could. He was far too strong, but it diverted his attention away from her daughter.

Then one day it seemed her mother could take it no more. Finally plucking up the courage she fought back. He stood silhouetted in the doorway, belt hanging loosely in his hand. She charged, screaming and spitting as she clattered the hammer into his head. He was knocked to the ground, blood seeping from a deep wound in his temple.

It was not enough.

He regained consciousness within seconds. Nine-year-old Samantha looked on as he rose, drawing his massive frame to its full height. Like a cat toying with a wounded bird, he stalked towards her as she struck out feebly again and again with the hammer. He knocked it away as if it were made of paper. Then he closed those massive hands around her throat and slowly squeezed the life from her body.

Numb and unable to watch or help Sam had opened her bedroom window and jumped, hoping to kill herself. She closed her eyes as she fell waiting for the welcoming oblivion.

She landed in the bushes below unhurt and tumbled to the grass lawn. She ran blindly, desperate to get as far away as she could. She was half-naked, and her feet were bleeding. Rescue came from a passing driver who took her straight to the police station.

Recollection blurred from there, but the truth was coaxed from her gently. The police visited the house to find her mother dead and her father missing. It took some time, but they caught up with him eventually. Sam could recall later clutching her teddy as she sobbed the full horrific story out.

He did not last long. The prison hierarchy was cruel to such men.

When the police came to Raynes as a young teenager and informed her he had been killed in prison she recalled feeling no emotion. His throat had been slashed from ear to ear. Her only regret that she could not have been there to see it.

All alone now in the world and deeply scarred.

She was adopted by a kindly couple who did their best to heal the damage and cast out her demons. As time went on, with counselling and sheer force of will she was able to focus and do well at school. A passion was ignited inside to do some good in the world and bring justice to evil. Eventually, she passed the exams to join the police and a career was born. Raynes had risen fast in the male-dominated environment. The trauma of her past equipped her with a mental toughness that stood her out from the crowd, and few of her fellow male officers could match.

Privately the hurt was always there lingering in the back of her mind. Sometimes all-consuming. She self-medicated to make it all go away, hiding it well from her colleagues who never guessed at her troubles. There was barely a copper in the force who did not drown their sorrows after work. Raynes blended well into this environment, viewed as a solid member of the gang who enjoyed a tipple. So, she was able to hide her rampant alcoholism in plain sight, barely raising an eyebrow from her superiors who were more than willing to overlook the odd transgression from a talented officer who always delivered results. High profile cases flowed her way and somehow, she managed to balance the demands of the job with her problems.

***

She blinked away the tears banishing the memories of her past. The sunshine had given way to grey clouds which rolled ominously across the sky. The warmth of the day had gone. She drew her coat tight, shivering in the wind as it tugged at her clothes.

The swans had long since passed by, leaving the river empty and Raynes alone. She checked her watch and took a deep breath, steeling herself.

Game face on Sam, time to face the world.

CHAPTER 8

Raynes drove past the public entrance to the station and turned down an adjacent side street. She followed the road round to the right and approached the rear car park entrance stopping to be identified. Security had become a major factor in recent years following the increased threat from domestic terrorism. She opened her window to be greeted by a cheery male officer.

"Morning Ma'am. How are we doing this morning?" He touched his cap greeting her with the respect her rank afforded.

"Morning," she replied forcing a weak smile mimicking friendly warmth. The raw emotion stirred by the counselling session had exposed her soft underbelly. Her nature was to hide her true self (or obliterate it with alcohol). Opening up so candidly left her feeling like a frightened puppy cowering in front of a snarling rottweiler. Now she must strap on her armour again.

The officer sat waiting patiently for Raynes to present her security pass. He knew who she was, and they had been through this charade countless times. Yet he took the time to examine her pass paying due diligence. They both knew not to do so would cost him his job. He gave the car a few moments of attention peering carefully through the windows.

"Thank you, Ma'am, you may proceed." The barrier raised and Raynes advanced coming to rest in front of three raised metal bollards. The reinforced steel barrier closed behind boxing her in. While there was no one in obvious sight from where she was sitting, Raynes knew she could be surrounded by highly trained firearms officers at a moment's notice should she demonstrate any security threat.

So very British, she mused. Polite and understated so bad actors with nefarious intentions were tilted off guard. Yet behind the scenes lay a swift and lethal response ready to strike.

Raynes turned to a monitor while her face and retinal pattern were scanned. After a few seconds her name and rank flashed on the screen and the three bollards receded silently into the ground. She drove down the ramp into the underground car park and pulled into her allotted space. She took a few moments to check her makeup in the mirror. Her eyes were bright and her skin looked fresh giving her a clean and healthy glow untainted by the ravages of alcohol for a change.

She exited the car and headed for the lift. She held her security pass against a magnetic reader stirring the motors into motion. A dull whirr rumbled from deep inside the lift shaft. The doors opened and she selected the top button for the main station concourse. She strode out confidently nodding at the desk sergeant as he looked up.

"Ma'am," he greeted as she swept through another security door to the main area of the building. A long corridor led to glass double doors which emerged onto an open plan office space buzzing with activity. Officers and clerical staff huddled round desks holding muted conversations. Telephones rang and printers spat out reams of paper filling the room with a cacophony of background noise like an orchestra tuning before the curtain for the show raised. Junior officers offered a courteous nod as she passed, heading across the open space towards her office in the far corner.

"Raynes." A gruff voice barked out from behind her stopping her mid stride.

Crawford. Please, not now.

She spun on her heel to find Superintendent John Crawford standing at the door to his office arms folded tightly across his chest. His blunt impassive features showed no hint of emotion. He was a relic of a bygone age, deliberately obtuse to the political correctness he perceived to be infecting his force. He was bull necked and stocky, standing a shade over six feet tall and built like a rugby forward. He used his bulk and presence to intimidate junior employees and criminals, treating both with equal disdain. Dark hooded eyes stared intently, searching for the next victim of one of his legendary verbal assaults.

"Morning Sir. How can I help?" she enquired forcing a smile.

"That case I put you on. The dead Russian and the vigilante. The file is on your desk. I want you to report directly back to me. Understood?"

"Of course, Sir" she replied to his back as he turned away not bothering to wait for a response. Crawford had never been one for small talk.

Raynes headed into her office and slumped heavily into the black leather swivel chair, a luxury item she had treated herself to when promoted to Detective Chief Inspector. She eyed the file on her desk thumbing it cautiously like a suspected letter bomb. She picked it up and skimmed the pages. A dead Russian with known links to organised crime killed by a knife wound to the neck in alleged self-defence by one Jake Charles.

Vigilantes and Russian gangsters. A scalding hot potato. She reflected on the political implications of such a case. The public loved a have-a-go hero. Senior management not so much.

The file showed Charles was known to the police from some time ago. Most likely a drug deal gone wrong was her first guess. She tossed the file back on her desk and stared absently out of the window before checking her watch. 10.30 am. Still forty-five minutes until the interview with the suspect. Time enough for a quick visit to evidence.

She left her office opting to take the stairs instead of the lift. These were less frequently used, and she wished to avoid inevitable exchange of small talk and irrelevant pleasantries. She descended two floors swiftly turning back on herself after the bottom step and followed the corridor to the security door that accessed the evidence treasure trove.

Detective Sergeant Thompson was leaning casually against the wall staring intently at his phone. He looked up startled by her sudden appearance. He snapped the phone shut and placed it in his jacket pocket.

What is he up to now?

He shifted nervously on his feet. Anxious. Furtive. Unable to look her in the eye. Was he down here hiding? Carrying out some private activity away from prying eyes? Maybe she was imagining it, overreacting to an entirely innocent situation. Maybe he was texting a girlfriend, or boyfriend for that matter.

She had never warmed to Thompson since the day he had been appointed as her DS. This was not the first time she had surprised him unexpectedly. There was something she did not trust about him but could never quite put her finger on.

Thompson was young and bookish. Mid-thirties. Crumpled black suit and shoes. Creased white shirt. Blue tie loosened at the neck. Thick glasses. More like an accountant than a detective. He always managed to look like he had slept in his clothes. Raynes took pride in her appearance and took an automatic dislike to anyone who did not adhere to the same standards.

"Morning Ma'am." Was she imagining it or was there a patronising tone lingering beneath the surface?

"Thompson," she acknowledged. She was about to ask

what he was doing down here, but he got in first.

"The interrogation starts soon Ma'am. I have a couple of things to do first. I'll see you in the interview room." He nodded as he headed towards the stairs.

She let him go saying nothing. She stood in thought for a moment then turned and pressed her security pass against the scanner. A soft click from the door and she was clear to enter. The evidence department was a well ordered and tidy place. The exact opposite to the chaos of the upstairs office where paperwork and files were stacked high and strewn across desks.

She pulled on surgical gloves and approached the sergeant in charge. She asked for the evidence related to the Vasin case and flashed her security pass. He disappeared for a moment and returned to place a carboard box on the countertop between them. She opened it and checked the contents. Clothing stained in blood was sealed in plastic bags. The centre piece was the flick knife also in an evidence bag. She picked it up, examining it closely. The blade was still open. It was heavily stained with blood.

"You can sit over there," the sergeant said waving towards a line of desks alongside the far wall. "Sign here please." He pushed the evidence logbook towards her.

"No that's fine. I just needed a quick look. I'm done now." She examined the log carefully. She paused with her pen, poised and ready to sign. The last entry was for Detective Inspector Jones from narcotics dated the previous day at 2.17 pm.

"Was DS Thompson in here a short while ago?" she asked.

"Yes Ma'am. You just missed him. He was also looking at the Vasin case evidence."

"He does not appear to have signed the book," she stated pointing to the previous signature.

The sergeant turned the book to face him, looking mildly

perplexed. "Oh, it must have slipped his mind. He did seem to be in a hurry all of a sudden. I think an urgent message came through on his phone. I'll call and remind him to come and do it."

Raynes paused a moment in thought. "Don't worry. I'm meeting him right now, I'll remind him for you."

The sergeant smiled nodding his appreciation. She signed the book and headed back upstairs to the interview room mulling a multitude of thoughts. Not least of which was the odd behaviour of DS Thompson.

CHAPTER 9

"We are ready." Millbank instructed the officer stationed outside the interview room.

He nodded his understanding. "Follow me please. I will inform the DCI."

He led them back down the corridor and into another interview room much the same as the one they had just left. Windowless walls were painted drab green like two-day old pea soup. A metal table was against the wall. Four flimsy plastic chairs provided the comfort. A microphone hooked up to a recording device sat on the table. Cameras in the corners focussed inward, multiplying the claustrophobic and intimidating atmosphere. Jake took a seat facing the door and Millbank sat next to him.

"Can I get you anything, tea, coffee?" the officer enquired.

"Tea would be nice, thanks," Jake replied. Millbank requested the same.

His leg bounced nervously. This was not the first time he had been in a police interview, but was by far his most serious encounter. The door opened and they were joined by two officers. A young man and an older woman.

"Good morning Mr Charles. I'm Detective Chief Inspector Samantha Raynes and this is Detective Sergeant Bill Thompson." She extended her hand smiling thinly. She was a rather severe looking woman. No humour in her eyes. All business. She wore heavy makeup and was dressed in a tailored grey trouser suit. Expensive looking. A woman in command. No nonsense. Probably needed to be to succeed in the police. Thompson shuffled in behind Raynes. Meek and unimpressive. Like he would be more at home stacking shelves in a homeware store. He was slight in stature and seemed to shrink in Raynes shadow. He stood behind her shifting nervously from foot to foot. Raynes took a seat and began.

"We need to get to the bottom of last night's incident." She started the audio equipment recording.

Jake glanced across at Millbank who nodded her encouragement. He returned his focus to Raynes. "Okay. Where would you like to start?"

"I need to remind that you are under caution. Anything you say will be recorded and can be used in court. Do you understand?"

"I do." Jake nodded his agreement.

"I want you to use this opportunity to give us your account of last night's events," she continued. "Please start at the beginning. Where you met your friends. The incident in the bar. What happened on your way home. Please be as detailed as you can."

She pulled a thick folder from her bag and placed it on the table in front of her. It was an inch thick and had Jake Charles scrawled across the front in bold sharpie. She eyed him closely with just a hint of a smile.

Stay calm. Standard intimidation tactic, he schooled himself.

He sat up straight and tall looking Raynes directly in the eye and began. "I went to my fitness class in the afternoon. Then a friend and I went for a drink at The Crown straight after."

Raynes made notes on a pad in front of her laying her pencil down each time she spoke.

"What type of class do you take?" she interjected.

"It's a combat class. It's called Krav Maga," he replied confidently. "Mostly for fitness and self-defence."

"You have some fight training?" she asked raising an eyebrow. How long have you been doing that?"

Can they use this against me? The first kernel of doubt began to form in Jake's gut. Almost imperceptible at first, but it was there.

"Around five years," he replied. His voice was strong. No wavering.

"So it would be fair to say you have some fighting experience, and you know how to defend yourself?" Raynes continued staring straight at him, emotionless.

He hesitated. His right leg bounced as he watched it from the corner of his eye unable to make it stop.

"Yes. I would say that's fair."

"What happened in The Crown?" Thompson spoke for the first time leaning forward.

"That was the first time I saw them," Jake replied. "There was an altercation with another group. The man I… the man who died last night knocked out two men."

"Were you involved in this incident?" Thompson continued.

"No. It was all over in a flash. The two men left straight afterwards. He stared at me as he left but that was it."

"Did anyone call the police?" Thompson asked.

"I don't believe so. An ambulance was called for the injured men. It did seem strange though. No one seemed to want the police alerted. We figured it was up to those involved to make the decision."

"Fair enough," Raynes acquiesced. "What happened next?"

Jake replayed the incident in Nouveau as Raynes listened intently and continued to take detailed notes.

"After the incident I stayed for maybe another hour. My two friends were still there when I left. They seemed to be getting along well. Anton and one of the girls Alice decided to go clubbing. I am not sure what Natan and Jasmine had planned.

"You had been drinking for approximately four hours? You must have had a few?" Raynes enquired.

Careful. His hackles raised sensing danger in the question. He snapped his eyes back to Raynes who was staring intently. Thompson sat forward in his chair, his hands clasped in front of him.

"I had a few drinks. We all did. I was not drunk if that's what you are implying. I left the bar at around 10:30 and decided to walk home since it was a nice evening.

"Were you aware of anyone following you?" Thompson asked.

"Not at first no. Only when I turned into the alleyway." He hesitated, staring into the middle distance. "That's when they came for me," he said softly returning his gaze to Thompson.

"Did you recognise them?" he asked.

His heart started pounding as the memory came flooding back. He took a deep breath. "He was right in front of me. Well-lit from a streetlamp. I recognised him instantly as the tall man from the bar. He was armed with a bat. It was clear I was in danger and under attack. I turned and ran as fast as I could."

He continued through the events in the alleyway, his voice wavering with emotion as he recalled the crucial final moments.

"We fell to the ground. He was on top of me. I was aware

of his arm moving to his pocket and I heard a click. It was unmistakable. A flick knife being deployed. I thought he was going to kill me."

"Unmistakable you say. I guess you know knives then?" Raynes enquired flicking lazily through the file in front of her. She returned her gaze to him. Stone faced. No hint of emotion.

That was twenty fucking years ago. Jake felt the first chilly tendrils of fear as cold sweat began to slide down his back. Like someone had dropped an ice cube under his shirt collar.

"I've seen enough movies. It's a distinctive enough sound," he replied hesitantly watching for her reaction. None came.

"The knife flashed in front of my face. I lashed out to block it." Sweat began to form on his brow and drip down his cheek.

"It was in his jugular. He bled out in front of me. I knew there was nothing I could do for him. He died in moments. The other attacker was starting to come around, so I ran. Out of the alley and back towards the bar. I called the police and ambulance from my mobile. And... well you know the rest."

He was careful to omit the flash of thrill he had felt in the moment of victory. He slumped at the table exhausted.

Raynes looked at Thompson and nodded. "Is there anything else you would like to add to your statement at this stage? Else I will pause the interview and we can take a break?"

"That's everything I can recall. Please can we break?" he replied softly.

Raynes checked her watch. "We will resume in thirty minutes. Interview with Jake Charles is paused at 11:20 am Sunday 24th May."

She opened the door and addressed the officer standing outside curtly. "Please can you organise some drinks for Mr Charles and his solicitor?" She marched off with Thompson in her wake without waiting for reply.

Jake turned to Millbank breathing heavily. They don't believe me, do they? What happens now?"

Millbank tapped her pencil thoughtfully on her legal pad. "Don't worry. It's standard practice to try and rattle you. You did well. Clear and concise. A lot will now depend on the other witness statements."

***

The door opened and Raynes and Thompson took their seats at the table. "Ready to continue?" she asked staring directly at him.

Jake pulled himself upright again. He was twisting up inside, even as he desperately tried to appear outwardly calm and confident. "Of course. Let's continue and get this over with."

Raynes started the recording again and checked her watch. "Interview with Jake Charles resumed at 11:53 am Sunday 24th May. Mr Charles, I will remind you that you are still under caution. Please can you take me through the incident in the alleyway again?"

Jake once again explained how events unfolded. Raynes opened the file next to her. She pulled out a single sheet of paper and laid it squarely on the table in front of her. She paused, revelling in the long silence that endured.

As it dragged on, Jake felt almost compelled to fill it. To say something, anything.

Mercifully she eventually continued. "We have a witness statement that contradicts your version of events. He claims you followed them into the alleyway and attacked. He says you slammed his head into the wall before stabbing Yuri Vasin in the neck. That he managed to fight you off and you ran away. What would you say to that?" She raised an eyebrow quizzically as she waited for his response.

Stay calm. Don't rise to it.

He forced himself to breathe slowly. Fighting the red-hot anger that threatened to boil to the surface, like a volcanic eruption rumbling from within ready to explode.

"That's a lie. And quite ridiculous. Why would I do that? Surely you don't believe him?"

Raynes considered his question. She sat back in her seat and sighed. "It's no more or less plausible than your story. It's your word against his."

Raynes and Thompson shared a glance before she opened a new line of questioning.

"This isn't the first time you have had a brush with the police, is it?" She turned to the file and retrieved another page, placing it in front of Jake for him to read. "You have been involved in violent incidents before haven't you."

She paused, staring at him. The cordial tone at the start of the interview had long disappeared as she took on a more combative approach. "In fact, quite a few incidents. Arrested for suspected GBH, ABH and affray on several occasions. Doubtless others that have not come to the attention of the police."

She placed a manicured finger on the document in front of him. "You have a conviction for ABH and possession of an offensive weapon. A flick knife no less. I think you have been lucky to stay out of prison."

"So far." She let the statement hang in the air between them.

Jake stared at his bouncing leg willing it to stop but it would not. His past was coming back to invade the present. Cold sweat soaked the back of his shirt as he felt the situation spiralling out of his control.

"That was twenty years ago. I was a kid and grew up in a rough neighbourhood. I got in a few fights. Playground stuff. It's not the same."

"There was also an incident in a pub some years later when you were twenty-five," she continued flicking through the file without looking up. "Numerous statements given, but you were not charged. What happened there?"

She stopped and once again returned her gaze to him, staring intently with cool blue eyes that seemed knowing. As if she had all the answers before she asked the questions. He wanted to look away but forced himself to meet her eye to eye. He shifted nervously in his seat in a vain attempt to force his bouncing leg to quieten. Thompson sat forward. Head to one side listening intently.

"Again, stupid kid's stuff," Jake continued. "I was in the pub with some mates when a gang from another town came in and started throwing their weight around. There was a fight. The police dropped it. Look, I put all that behind me long ago. I got in a couple of tangles as a kid. Who doesn't growing up on an estate? People are ruthless in that environment. If you are marked as weak you become a victim. So you learn to stand your ground. That does not make me a violent criminal who would attack two men and kill one of them. Does it?"

"I don't know. Does it?" Raynes shot back. "I have two conflicting accounts for the incident. One of which makes you guilty of murder. Now I have to decide how to proceed. It seems there is sufficient evidence to have you charged. Then it's up to the prosecution service. They will decide if there is enough evidence to warrant a court case."

Finally, it became too much. The raging caldron of fury in his chest exploded out of him like a dragon breathing fire. He stood up flinging his chair back and slammed the table with both hands. "Charged? You can't be serious? I was defending my life."

Millbank put a hand on his arm, alarm flashing across her

73

face. "Sit down Jake, you need to remain calm." She spoke coolly watching as Raynes and Thompson stole a glance at each other.

Thompson eyed him with regained interest. "It seems you have a temper Mr Charles. Did you lose that temper in the alleyway last night? I suggest you listen to your legal counsel. Calm down and please sit."

Stop you prick. Don't make their case for them. He checked himself rapidly and took a deep breath. He sat as instructed making no further comment.

Raynes broke the silence. "We will finish the interview here." She checked her watch. "DCI Raynes terminating the interview with Jake Charles at 12:10 pm."

Raynes and Thompson stood and left the room. Jake's legs felt hollow as he stood. Like someone had removed the bones. The gravity of the situation closed in enveloping him as he was led from the interview room back to his cell to stew alone.

CHAPTER 10

The hours dragged agonizingly slowly affording Jake an unwelcome glimpse of time behind bars. The rattle of keys jarred him back to the present and the door swung open. Raynes marched in accompanied by a uniformed officer.

"Hello Mr Charles." Her manner was frosty and forthright. Jake took a deep breath and stood up. "Please follow me."

She turned on her heel striding off down the hall. Jake followed, nudged along by the other officer. They followed the corridor to the custody suite where the sergeant and Millbank were waiting. He looked to Millbank for guidance. She gave nothing away.

Raynes took control. "Jake Charles. You are charged with the murder of Yuri Vasin. Due to your past criminal record and inherent risk of witness intimidation, you will be remanded in custody until your hearing before a magistrate which is scheduled for tomorrow morning. The charges are laid out on this sheet.

Charged with murder. This cannot be happening.

Charged with murder. It played over and over again in his mind. Jumping back like a stuck record. His stomach heaved. He nearly threw up. Millbank placed a hand on his shoulder. He stumbled reaching to the wall to steady himself as his head swam like he was drunk. After the formalities were complete, he was led back to his cell struggling to process the turn of events.

Millbank stepped up and took charge. Jake was in no

condition for rational thought. She spent the next few hours guiding him through his defence in preparation for the hearing.

She left after a shared lunch of burger and chips purchased from a local takeaway bar. He spent the rest of a lonely Sunday afternoon in his cell with nothing to do. He had been given some books but was unable to concentrate long enough to read a single sentence. He was bored senseless. His mind wandered to the potential horrors of remand while waiting for trial.

How is this possible?

He boiled inside, seething in anger at the injustice. How could society imprison an upstanding member of the community with a wife and children to support? He had been attacked by thugs, one of who was walking free while he rotted in jail. Evening crept around slowly. Another pizza for dinner. The night dragged longer still. He tossed and turned struggling to find relief in broken sleep.

***

He woke early the next morning. Still dark. A chink of moonlight shining through the barred window cast gloomy shadows around the cell. Crushing reality pressed down on him from the moment he opened his eyes. Like an elephant's foot applying steady pressure to his chest.

Distant dreams of his wife and children were swept away. Scattered like leaves in the wind. He tried to cling to sleep but it was gone. He rose from bed, filled the sink and plunged his face in. His skin constricted, like a force trying to crush his brain. He embraced the pain. Like self-flagellation to cleanse him of his transgressions.

After completing his morning exercise routine and stretches, he sat back on the bed sweating and panting hard. An officer brought tea and toast which he devoured hungrily before taking a shower.

Millbank had arranged for his clothes to be delivered. He dressed in his best suit and shoes. It had been more than a year since he wore them. He searched the pockets and pulled out a folded order of service. His breath caught as he opened it to see the beaming face of his father transporting him back to that bittersweet day.

I love you dad.

He folded it and placed it back in the pocket taking some comfort from its presence. Was it a good omen?

The police van droned through light Monday morning traffic. Jake watched the world go by, envious of those free to go about their business. Something he had taken for granted only two days previously. They arrived at the courthouse near the Grafton shopping centre in Cambridge city centre. He must have past it a thousand times but had never really noticed the sandstone building sandwiched between shops and flats. Yet it was just a short five-minute walk from the location of the offence for which he was now to be judged.

Claire.

There she was outside the court speaking with Millbank. His heart bolted.

How will she react?

Their recent conversation came flooding back. Would she remain distant? Frosty even? He could not bear it. As the van pulled to a halt, he rushed to her and embraced her smothering his face with her hair. He inhaled deeply. She smelled of shampoo and soap. Tears pricked his eyes as they held each other. The first intimate human contact he had experienced since the incident.

"It's going to be okay," she told him taking his face in her hands. Her sparkling green eyes fixed on his. "The battle is ahead now. What's past is past. You need to be strong to come through this for your children, for me, for yourself."

Relief washed through him quenching his fear and doubt like water on smouldering coals. They locked eyes. He drew strength from the resolve and depth of character that lay within. He touched his forehead to hers. They stood like that a full minute, oblivious to the passing world.

Millbank guided them inside with Jake flanked by two police officers. They were led through a foyer bustling with lawyers and their clients huddling in corners. They passed through a long corridor and were directed to an empty room to wait.

The minutes on the clock dragged by. Claire sat with him holding his hand. There seemed little to say. Would this be their last time together for a while?

The door finally swung open, and Millbank entered flanked by the two policemen. "It's time Jake. You're up next."

He stood and embraced Claire then followed Millbank back down the corridor through a doorway into the courtroom. It was larger than Jake expected. Wood panelling throughout lent the room a grand, imposing air. Three magistrates sat at the front watching Jake carefully. Two men flanked a woman who occupied the middle seat. She was in charge. The prosecuting lawyer occupied a table on the far side of the court while a dozen people were present in the observation area behind him. The background murmur hushed as Jake took his place. Raynes was sat at the back. She nodded curtly to him. Most of the people in the room were unfamiliar to him. Journalists he presumed.

One man caught his attention. Well dressed in a charcoal suit with a black shirt and tie. Jet black hair slightly greying at the temples was swept back to the collar. Maybe Jake's age, early forties. He sat impassive. His face emotionless like carved from stone. He did not acknowledge Jake or offer any greeting leaving him feeling cold and unsettled.

Instinctively he knew two things. First, this man was related to the person who had died. Secondly, he was dangerous.

For the first time a new and frightening thought occupied Jake's mind. Perhaps prison and separation from his family were not the worst possible consequences of that terrible night. He forced his attention back to the front of the room as the magistrates began conferring in hushed tones. The woman in the middle took charge. She was a portly, middle-aged lady with a kindly smiling face which put Jake somewhat at ease.

She addressed him directly. "Please stand and state your name and address for the court."

His chest tightened as he stood. As if his lungs were being squeezed like a balloon. He struggled to draw in oxygen. Millbank gave his hand a reassuring squeeze.

"It's okay," she whispered.

He took a deep breath and began. He kept his face solemn and his answers crisp as Millbank had coached him.

"Good morning madam, my name is Jake Charles, 42 Adams Street."

"Mr Charles, you have been charged with murder. How do you plead?"

The court fell silent.

"Not guilty madam." Loud and clear. Spoken with conviction.

She nodded and consulted her notes before turning to address the prosecution.

"I see you have made an application for Mr Charles to be remanded in custody. Please elaborate?"

The prosecution lawyer stood and cleared his throat. He removed his glasses and paused theatrically. His voice was high pitched and enunciated. No doubt from decades of expensive education "Madam. There is a material witness to this incident who was also involved in the altercation with Mr Charles. The witness is fearful of retaliation and intimidation from the accused. Additionally, Mr Charles has a history of violence including a criminal record for weapons offences."

Millbank stood to interrupt. "Madam, if I may interject. My client is a family man of good standing in the community. He has a wife and two children who depend on him. The criminal record of which my learned friend speaks is from twenty-five years ago. Nothing but childhood scraps and bad decisions made as a youth. My client has long since moved on. The so-called 'witness' to this crime attacked my client with a weapon." The word witness was spoken with as much sarcasm as she could muster.

The magistrate listened intently and conferred with her colleagues for what felt like an eternity. Jake strained to listen in but could hear nothing.

Why is this taking so long?

She turned back to face the room. "Thank you both for your submissions. The court decides there is a case to answer Mr Charles. A preliminary date for the committal hearing shall be set for two weeks from today. It is also the position of this court, given your previous record and the potential for witness intimidation, the prosecution has argued successfully you should be held on remand for the duration of the trial. Please take Mr Charles down."

No. It can't be.

His stomach felt full and heavy. As if someone had filled it with cold soup. He swallowed desperately trying not to wretch. The words reverberated around the courtroom. Jake barely able to process what he was hearing. He turned to Claire. Her eyes filled with tears and longing. She held out her hand and they brushed fingertips as he was bustled towards the door by his police escort.

Millbank caught his arm as he passed. "Try not to worry Jake. I'll appeal this decision. I'll come and see you and we can discuss the next steps."

The police swept Jake back down the corridor. His head throbbed as he struggled to comprehend the worst of his nightmare visions playing out in real-time. He pictured Claire back in the courtroom breaking down and sobbing uncontrollably as she contemplated their fate. They led him down steep steps into the underworld of the court. At the end of a long corridor was a small holding cell. They pushed him inside and locked the door behind him. Then they were gone.

He was alone.

The cell was tiny. A barren windowless room with nothing but a bed and toilet. Jake took deep breaths to calm his racing mind.

"I'm going to prison." He spoke the words aloud listening to them echo around the bare cell. When all was quiet, he questioned his sanity. Had he said those words at all? Was this actually happening? But it was all too real. Was it possible to believe that just two days ago he was going about his normal business? Happy and content. Now imprisoned. Accused of taking another man's life.

His thoughts turned dark as he considered the terrible possibilities that lay in his family's future. His mind skipped from one awful scenario to the next.

What will prison be like? Frightening images of violence and gang rape tormented him. The man at court who had frightened him so badly. Would he take retribution while Jake was not there to protect his family? Tears pricked his eyes as he thought of his two girls and when he would next get to see them.

A knock on the door interrupted his thoughts. It swung

open and Millbank entered angst written across her face.

"I'm sorry Jake. I will do everything in my power to have this decision reconsidered."

He placed a hand on her shoulder looking her straight in the eye. "It's not your fault. Please just do whatever you can to get me out. What happens now?"

She composed herself and recovered her business-like manner.

"Transport will be arranged, and you will be taken to prison later today. I will also begin investigations into the principal witness against you."

She touched his hand tenderly. "I have to go now Jake. I'll come and see you soon to begin planning your defence." Their eyes met as the door swung open. Jake could see strength there. A certain defiance that steeled him for the battle ahead. He felt there and then she would never give up on him.

He spent the afternoon making notes about the incident. Every scrap of detail he could recall. Determination fuelled him to find something, anything that could support his defence.

Deep in thought the time passed quickly though it was several hours before he was called on again. The door swung open, and the courthouse guard stood waiting.

"Time to go. Your transport is here." He beckoned Jake from the cell and took him by the arm cuffing him securely. He led him down a hallway and out into the rear car park. A dusty prison transport van was idling and belching black clouds of diesel fumes into the air. Bars lined the dirty windows. A grizzled prison guard dressed in a khaki uniform hauled his bulky frame down the steps. His belt strained from the massive gut spilling over.

"On you get son. Welcome aboard," he growled looking Jake up and down.

Jake climbed the steps and greeted the surly driver who ignored him. The van roof was low causing him to stoop. There was one other prisoner on board. Jake glanced and nodded keeping his expression respectful and neutral. He took a seat towards the back and was cuffed in his seat by the fat and stinking guard.

A few minutes later the gears crunched, and the van pulled away.

Fear and dread flooded Jake as for the first time in his life he was on his way to prison.

CHAPTER 11

Jake pulled his cap low and glanced left, right. Police lined the walkway either side of the road. The crowd streamed down the middle. Like an army of ants marching on through. He was with two others, a close unit operating together within the wider crowd. There were others among them. He recognised faces dotted throughout the throng. Silent nods were exchanged as they walked on.

The crowd began to thin as other fans bled off towards their destinations. At the same time, Jake's group began to coalesce. Drawn together in common purpose. They were away from the ground now. The police presence had long disappeared as the residential streets gave way to industrial units.

He stuffed his hands deep in his pockets. His palms were sweating despite the chill. His breath crystalised in front of him as he breathed in and out. Long and slow as he worked to harness his fight or flight response. His heart rate began to pick up, pulsing deep in his chest as they approached their destination. It was all prearranged. Time, location, numbers. The sky was crystal blue.

No words were exchanged. They marched on, footsteps drumming against the tarmac. Jake silently appraised the gang. They were around twenty strong, a decent turnout. Mostly hard men that he knew well. A few new faces he didn't. Youngsters keen to make a name for themselves. They looked tough enough. No hangers on today.

They spread out across the road in an arrowhead

formation. Jake was in the second row behind the tip of the spear. Not quite in charge but close to the top of this particular food chain.

They left civilisation and followed a stony dirt track hugging the railway line. His heckles prickled as they passed through the choke point. Perfect spot for an ambush. Hemmed in all sides, the railway line to the right, high fence to the left Nowhere to escape. He turned to check their rear for attack. All clear. No strangers following on behind. No heads popping out from behind a bush. He caught Sampson's eye as he turned to check for the same threat. They nodded silently to each other. He focussed forward again as they strode on.

The stony path turned a corner and emerged onto waste ground. A concrete jungle broken up by weeds and time. Perhaps once a car park for the surrounding buildings that now lay derelict and empty. Windows smashed by bored kids with nothing to do but pass the time.

There they were. Jake appraised them in an instant as they closed in. Similar in numbers and strength. Some faces he recognised from past skirmishes. Some he did not.

Excellent. He smiled to himself as he scanned from face to face, seeking the strong and the week. Instant determination on who were the lions and who were the lambs.

"Come on then, let's have it you fucking cunts." The rallying charge went up from the opposition leader as he swaggered, arms out in the monkey dance gesturing them forward. Jake focussed his attention that way. That was his target. Take out the strong first. They picked up the pace and with a roar Jake darted forward leading into the fray.

***

"Did you see his nose. It exploded blood everywhere." You made a right mess of that kid's face Jake."

Jake sat quietly as the throng around him whooped and shouted, congratulating each other on a campaign fought and won. Downing pints in celebration. He was the focus of much of the attention and it was eating him up inside.

"You are the man Jake." Sampson clapped him on the shoulder and raised his glass. "To Jake, my fearless lieutenant."

Jake forced a weak smile and finished his pint, the fizzy liquid joining the churning turmoil in his belly. The crowd around the table nodded their platitudes of respect. They all looked the same to Jake. Eyes shining. Grinning and chattering like Jackals. Drunk on the power of victory. Strong as a group but weak of character and individuality. He knew he was just the same and it was burning him up.

"You're a true warrior son." Sampson shouted. "Born three hundred years ago and they would have made you a knight of the realm. Someone get that man another pint." He turned and glared hard at one of his juniors. He was around forty and tall, well over 6 feet. He wore a hip length heavy black leather jacket and black jeans. Strong heavy boots. Good for crushing bone and cartilage. His face was cruel. Small eyes set close together that sought out weakness to exploit. His hair was immaculately styled. Straight from the salon. He was tanned, also from a salon. He projected importance and command. His lackey did what he was told and headed to the bar.

The platitudes continued. One by one he was congratulated on a job well done. He was taken through every crunching blow he landed. Every nose he busted. And it made him sick to the pit of his stomach.

Something had changed. Something fundamental inside him. He thought back to the young boy. He could have been no more than sixteen or seventeen. Jake had destroyed him. Knocked him to the ground with a clubbing punch that stunned him. He lay prone. Immobile with Jake towering over him. Shaking like the frightened animal he was. Cowering. His hands out begging for mercy. And Jake had stamped on his face anyway.

His head swam as he remembered. His stomach roiled and twisted. He stood up and staggered. Dizzy. He painted on a forced smile and dashed to the toilets to cheers and hollers from his so-called friends. Thankfully it was empty. He only just made it. He headed to one of the cubicles and slammed the door behind him then vomited the contents of his stomach into the toilet basin. The barely digested half time hot dog mixed with yellow bile stared back at him. He wiped his mouth with a tissue and flushed the chain. He staggered to the sink and doused his face in cold water. He raised his head and stared at the reflection, hating what he saw.

"What are you doing with your life Jake Charles," he asked the stranger staring back at him. This life had to come to an end. He was no longer feeling the buzz. He had spent his youth following Arsenal, graduating into the big leagues of their top hooligans and he couldn't stand it anymore. Once upon a time the Saturday buzz was all he lived for. The early meet in the pub. The days spent boozing. The anticipation of combat. The elation in victory, standing over a defeated foe. Recently it had started to wane. Now it was gone forever.

He felt empty. Guilt consumed him at the damage he had inflicted on that young boy. A boy who had sought out the camaraderie and approval of supposedly stronger men. And Jake had put him down and stomped him unconscious. This was someone's son, someone's brother. He could have killed him. He pictured the boy in a hospital bed as machines breathed for him. A sad lady sobbed into the sheets next to him holding his limp hand in her own. What was it all for? The cackling approval of violent thugs he detested. It had to stop. Here. Now. Today.

He left the toilet and headed back to grab his jacket. It was time to move on. He figured some lame excuse about his mother being ill would suffice for now. Then he would work out a longer-term explanation to extract himself from the group. He mulled over in his mind what he would say to escape without raising suspicion.

His mind wandered as he moved swiftly through the bar. Suddenly she appeared directly in his path. She was facing the bar away from him as he nudged through the throng. A curtain of auburn hair cascaded down her back. She turned abruptly with a bottle in her hand, moving with purpose and speed but was not looking where she was heading. Her body and movement preceded her perception of the man approaching behind her. He carried on his own trajectory, slow to react. Physics did the rest. The collision was swift and perhaps preordained?

The bottle in her hand arrived first slamming into his torso as she whipped her head around and briefly caught his eye. Then she arrived, her head slamming into his chin as the bottle clattered to the ground smashing into a thousand pieces. The obligatory cheer went up. The British salute to a dropped drink. Her head bounced hard off his chin, and she blinked twice. Stunned. She wobbled and raised a manicured hand to her brow where she had slammed into him. She staggered and he caught her by both arms and steadied her. She raised her head and looked into his eyes. Time stopped.

The background noise disappeared and all that was left in the world was him and her and that moment in time. Deep pools of liquid green stared back at him. Like swimming in the ocean. She smiled. Then she laughed. Her face lit up at the absurdity of it. He could not help himself. He felt warmth rising through his body. Like sunshine from within. His feet felt lighter, like he was floating. He smiled back and laughed with her. She dropped her gaze and tucked a lock of hair behind her ear then raised her head again. Drew him back into her gaze. His mind was blank. He went to speak but nothing came out. What was happening to him?

Say something. Anything.

"I... I think I owe you a drink," he finally blurted. "I'm Jake."

"Claire." She replied smiling. "Nice to meet you Jake."

CHAPTER 12

The bus rumbled on through the flat, featureless landscape of East Anglia. Wide-open fields punctuated by an occasional farmhouse was all Jake had seen for the past hour.

The dread built slowly. Filling him up from his toes till his legs felt heavy. Leaden.

He watched his fellow prisoner from the corner of his eye, assessing his demeanour. He showed no nerves, seemed comfortable almost. He was whistling a tune. Like a man easy in his skin. He looked at Jake and nodded. "How ye doin'. The name's Zaph." He spoke with the lilting drawl of the Southern Irish.

Zaph was whippet lean with angular features. A barbed wire tattoo crept up from beneath his collar winding around his neck.

"Jake." He introduced himself returning the nod.

"First time Jake?" he enquired raising an eyebrow. "Ye have somethin' of the green about ye."

Be careful.

He dipped his toe in cautiously. "Yeah. First time," he responded coolly.

"Well, it's nice to make yer acquaintance my man. He cracked a wide smile and winked then turned away again.

His first prisoner interaction. Not so bad. He breathed

deep to calm himself and draw on the tiny sliver of relief.

In the middle distance a red brick structure began to emerge against the backdrop of the slate grey sky. Metal fencing topped with razor wire surrounded the perimeter. Inside was a second smaller fence containing a black tarmac yard. As they drew nearer, Jake could see groups of men walking the yard in circles or working out. Four long buildings snaked away from a central compound like a palm with outstretched fingers.

His belly roiled like it was filled with writhing eels as the building and the men in the yard imposed their presence on him. This was to be his home for the foreseeable future where he would have to cohabitate with guards and prisoners alike.

A large double gate rumbled open as the bus approached. The guard tipped his baseball cap to the driver. They swapped small talk as the driver handed over the paperwork. The bus pulled slowly into the yard and the guard came on board. He wore a khaki uniform stretched tight across a barrelled chest. He was short and squat with a thin, mean face and wet rubbery lips like a fish.

"Good morning gentlemen. Welcome. You will address me as Sir. I will take you through to reception from where you will be transitioned into the prison. Let's go."

Jake stood and shuffled forward following Zaph off the bus descending the steps to the tarmac. The piercing gaze of the circling inmates burned into him.

"New crew, welcome." The cry from one of the inmates set the rest off whooping and clapping. Jake watched Zaph saunter off the bus real casual. Like a man without a care in the world.

"Let's move it gentlemen," urged the guard hustling them along. Jake stood tall. Head high. Expression neutral. Eyes straight ahead. A picture of fabricated confidence. Yet his mouth was dry as desert sand.

Can they see my fear?

His first test. The inmates watched to see how he reacted. Sizing him up as a victim to exploit or fellow con to be afforded respect. Zaph shouted greetings to acquaintances. Almost like he was pleased to be back.

Jake shuffled on. Heavily tattooed and muscled men lifted weights, the heavy metal plates ringing as they thudded rhythmically into the blacktop. The atmosphere crackled with barely contained disorder. Like static electricity. Like a powder keg ready to ignite in an instant to chaos and violence.

His eye was drawn to a man sitting on a bench conferring with other inmates. He was bare-chested and corded with wiry lean strength. Scars streaked across his face and torso and his right arm was sleeved with tattoos. He watched closely as they passed.

He is the main man.

Jake knew it in an instant. The other men in his vicinity acted deferentially marking him out as a powerful force. He squirmed uncomfortably under the scrutiny, his heart thumping violently. He strolled on casually playing the role. Calm. Controlled. Expression neutral. Conscious not to stare anyone down but not to turn away either. The man whispered to one of his companions who nodded as he stared at Jake. Tall and lanky with jet black hair slicked back. His biceps and forearms were roped with veins. Jake could feel the hostile stare boring into the back of his head as he passed.

They followed the guard through the yard to the sound of the shouting inmates. A steel door opened, and the guard gestured them through. The racket of the yard subsided as the prisoners' excitement waned.

"Line up toes on the yellow line," the guard barked at

them.

Jake complied. He faced a desk behind which sat a bored-looking guard. He scanned them with disinterest and spoke in a dull, monotonous tone.

So began the dehumanising and mind-numbing process of prison induction. Jake was hustled from one place to the next. One by one, all links to the outside world were severed.

First stop was a sparse and uncomfortable holding cell. Nothing but grey concrete walls and floor with a bench running down the middle. The cloying smell of damp seeped from the concrete. They sat in silence

He was taken to a small private room for the humiliation of a strip search. He removed his clothes and stood in the middle of the room naked while a burly guard pulled on rubber gloves and examined him roughly. That unpleasant experience over, he was issued prison clothes and taken to see the medical officer for a rudimentary examination.

His photo was taken, and he was issued paperwork detailing his prison number and charges. A breakfast pack was dispensed for the next morning. A few biscuits, coffee, milk, cereal. Next, he was led into a drab windowless room with a table and a couple of cheap metal chairs.

"Wait here," the officer instructed closing the door behind him.

He sat and closed his eyes. Slowed his breathing. Unclenched his jaw. Relaxed his balled fists. He opened the water he had been given and gulped half down desperate to slake the dryness of his parched throat.

Stay relaxed.

The initial terror had waned.

Another officer entered eying Jake with contempt. He was short and slight. Tight buzz cut hair. He had the look of ex-military about him.

"I'm Officer Michaels. I'm in charge of the wing." He seemed pleased with his lofty station in life. "I see this is your first visit to the prison. I suggest you make yourself aware of the rule book you have been issued with. I tolerate no disruption on my wing so toe the line and we will get on just fine." He delivered his speech enthusiastically. Not for the first time Jake figured.

"You have been sent here on remand. You get different treatment from the convicted inmates. You will not have to work if you do not want to. You will be given a personal cell. Other than that, you eat, shower and associate with the other prisoners as normal. Any questions?" he barked.

Thank fuck for that. The last thing he wanted was to bunk with some psychopath.

Jake shook his head gratefully. "No. All crystal thank you."

"Good. One of my officers will escort you to your cell. Doors open 7:30 am sharp. You are expected to have had breakfast and be ready for the day."

Michaels stood and opened the door and handed Jake over to yet another grim-looking officer with a paunch hanging over his uniform trousers. He smiled revealing tombstone teeth yellowed by decades of coffee and cigarettes.

Jake followed him down a long corridor. Security cameras were everywhere recording everything. They approached a barred door leading into the main prison wing. It buzzed and the officer pushed it open. Jake followed. The smell was the first thing that assaulted his senses. Sweat and fear. The prisoners were locked up for the night leaving the wing eerily empty. Muffled shouted conversations and catcalls from the cells reverberated around the wing.

A grey metal walkway skirted the edge of the rectangular building. Gunmetal cell doors were spaced around the permitter wall every two meters or so. A long metal staircase ran up the centre of the building linking three identical levels. Jakes was the middle tier. Guard rails and roped nets protected the edge of the walkway.

The guard stopped in front of one of the cells.

"Open 42," he shouted.

The door buzzed and the guard pushed it open leading Jake inside. A chink of moonlight streamed through the small, barred window providing a sliver of natural illumination. A single fluorescent tube on the ceiling lit up yellow-painted concrete walls marked with the scribing of previous occupants.

Home-sweet-home.

All gleaming metal. All bolted to the floor. A single cot bed topped with a thin mattress and a scratchy green blanket. A toilet with no seat next to a basin. The reek of decades of sweat and cigarette smoke.

He threw his paperwork onto the table and sat down on the bed. The guard turned on his heel and slammed the door behind him.

Sleep arrived slowly that first night alone in his cell. Nothing but time to contemplate his situation. He spent an uncomfortable, sweaty night suffering the insomniac's torture. Dreams and reality distorted with nightmares and visions. Finally, blessed sleep consumed him and rescued him from the confines of his cell.

CHAPTER 13

Jake stirred from broken sleep as the first light of dawn cast grey shadows around the cell. It was eerily quiet. Almost silent but for the gentle drum of rain on the window.

He turned to reach for the warmth of Claire, but his arm found nothing but cold empty space.

Where am I?

He rubbed his eyes and sat up. Reality bit as the weekend's memories flashed through his mind. He yearned to scream out at the injustice.

Get hold of yourself.

He sat on the bed. Eyes closed, breathing deeply. Fighting to calm his troubled mind.

It was still early. Before 5 am he estimated. The grey was slowly giving way to tinges of yellow as the first rays of dawn crept slowly across the ceiling.

He dropped to the floor and worked through a punishing exercise regime. The effort left him sweating hard. Muscles Aching. Tight. He finished with stretches, washed up then devoured breakfast.

The prison was cranking to life. Jake could hear the guards pacing outside his cell, boots drumming against the metal walkway. Inmates were shouting out to companions in nearby cells. Guards were barking instructions.

"Cells open."

The magnetic lock clicked, and the door swung inwards. He stepped onto the walkway alongside reams of men lining up. Dozens of pairs of eyes sought him out. Who is the new guy?

At the guard's instruction they filed along the gangway tramping down the stairs to ground level, the stomp of feet rattled the metal grating like an advancing army. Jake shadowed the crowd walking with purpose. Head high. Face neutral. Determined to appear strong and controlled.

His morning activity was induction. The first of many spirit-crushing meetings, lectures and interviews scheduled for the day. He followed signs to classroom D finding it at the end of a short corridor. The door was ajar. It looked much like any classroom with chairs lined up facing a projector screen at the front. A bored-looking prison officer sat drumming his fingers on the desk impatiently. He looked up as Jake approached and gestured to one of the chairs. Zaph had already taken his seat and they exchanged nodded greetings.

The officer stood and hitched his trousers over his ample gut. He had the bulbous nose of a heavy drinker lined with burst capillaries. The rancid stink of stale booze clung to him. Probably had a livener for breakfast. Rheumy eyes swept from Jake to Zaph and back again.

Without introduction he launched into his presentation unenthusiastically, as bored as those on the receiving end. It was a simple slide deck revealing riveting information about topics such as laundry facilities, canteen and gym timetables, how to access the library, educational or work opportunities and visiting rules. He droned on monotonously for more than an hour. Jake struggled to focus and stay awake. It concluded with a video on prison safety, focussing on bullying and the importance of reporting mistreatment to the guards.

Utter Bullshit, Jake told himself. Snitching to the guards was not an option under any circumstances. Rule one in the prisoner's handbook if you wanted to stay alive.

After the lecture Jake was hustled to meetings with further representatives of the prison bureaucracy. The entire process was laced with monotony and delivered by staff who like himself clearly wanted to be somewhere else. He met with the drug team who enquired on addiction issues. He was examined and given a clean bill of health by the medical staff. Then finally the chaplaincy. A pious but guilty-looking Scotsman was keen to discuss Jake's salvation through Jesus.

And just like that he was processed and inducted into prison.

All day he had remained separated from the bulk of the inmates. Now he was directed to the yard for association time.

Be confident. Calm. collected. You can do this, he schooled himself.

The sun was high in the sky. The heat scorched the back of his neck as he left the relative cool of the prison emerging onto the blacktop yard. Weights clattered noisily as heavily inked men worked out, muscles glistening in the sun.

As Jake ambled the yard, he spotted Zaph sitting with some other prisoners smoking and chatting. Jake nodded. Zaph returned the greeting with a smile and ambled across slowly.

"Mind if I join ye for a stroll?" he enquired.

"How's it going," Jake replied coolly. Relief flooded him to find a friendly face. They circled the yard together. Others did the same sticking to their tight-knit groups.

"So how was your first night? Plenty to think about and process I imagine?"

"Fine," he lied. "Slept like a baby."

Zaph turned to him and raised an eyebrow saying

nothing.

"It was a long night, but I've had worse," he replied. He knew he was caught in the lie. "When my kids were in hospital. Or the day we lost one of them on the beach. A night in prison is a cakewalk compared to that."

Zaph stopped and looked at him directly. There was an openness in his face. Wide smiling eyes faintly creased at the corners.

"No kids of my own but I can imagine. Ye can be straight with me Jake. I want you to know that." He placed a hand on Jake's shoulder.

They walked on in silence, circling the compound till they returned to the main seating area.

There he is.

His body stiffened and hands clenched as he noticed the scarred and tattooed man he had seen the day before. He was sitting with his entourage talking quietly. Seeing everything. Keen and observant. From time-to-time other prisoners would approach and conduct some clandestine business or other. It was clear the guards in the towers were turning a blind eye.

As they passed, Jake could tell from his peripheral vision that they were being watched.

"Friend of yours?" he enquired of Zaph.

He shook his head slowly. "More of an acquaintance ye could say. The main man is Taylor. As ye can tell he runs the show in here dealin' drugs and other contraband. Kind of the go-to guy when you want somethin'. No one can touch him or his guys. A few have tried but he buried em all. Word is he is an ex-soldier. Some kind of special forces badass. I know one thing. He is a serious guy not to be fucked with. He only keeps the toughest in his circle and is real selective about who he recruits. And don't think I didn't notice him eyeballin' you. Done anything to upset anyone?"

The man I killed. Does he know him. He shivered involuntarily as he considered this possibility.

"Nothing I can think of," he replied. "Jesus. Only been here one night and I've already made enemies."

Zaph stopped and turned to him. "Yer reputation somewhat precedes ye. News travels fast in here and Taylor knows what ye did outside. It makes you an unknown quantity. Maybe he just wants ye to know he is top dog. Stay out his way and ye'll be grand."

Fine by me.

"How about you then? What did you do to land yourself in here?"

Zaph laughed heartily. "Nothing so dramatic as ye my man. Spot of bank fraud tis all. I've been dabblin' since I learned to fake me ma's handwriting to play hooky from school. This time I got twelve months. Not so bad."

The bell rang signalling the end of association time. Jake followed the other prisoners back inside.

The rest of the day passed without incident. He sat with Zaph at dinner. Lumpy mashed potato and a stew of unidentifiable meat and vegetables. After dinner he returned to his cell to be alone. His solicitor was due the next morning so he spent the time preparing his notes searching for any useful snippet of information that could help his case.

As the guards completed their rounds he lay back on his bed clinging to memories of happier times with Claire and the girls. Exhaustion finally overtook him, and he drifted into an uneasy sleep.

CHAPTER 14

Lunch was a limp sandwich with a rizla thin slice of ham in between two slices of stale bread. And an apple. Hardly the Dorchester but he wolfed it down nonetheless.

After lunch he returned to his cell to read and work out, then headed to the showers to clean up. His fellow inmates were mostly in their cells or in the games room playing cards. Waiting for the call for dinner. The prison landing was unusually deserted.

As he drew close the drum of water splashing on the tiles told him he was not alone. Steam drifted from the door like fog creeping across the moors. Visibility was poor.

His hackles raised instantly when he heard enraged voices. The hairs on the back of his neck and arm pricked up and tingled. An argument was taking place. He knew better than to get involved in other people's business and began to retreat quietly.

He stopped in his tracks when he heard Zaph's pleading voice.

"No, please don't. Why are you doing this to me?"

You have to help him.

He waited and listened intently, chewing his lip as indecision clawed at his insides. Zaph was his friend, his only friend in this place. He could not leave him at the mercy of some prison thug's beating.

Or worse.

He crept forward slowly using the steam for cover. Two men towered over the prone figure of Zaph who was lying on the floor of the shower naked and bloody. One had his knee pressed firmly into Zaph's neck. Ringing slaps reverberated round the shower block as he struck him repeatedly across the face. The other watched, pinning Zaph's arm to the floor with his foot. One final slap cracked his head against the tile floor and the pleading stopped. Blood pooled around him swirling dark crimson against the white tiles as it washed into the drain.

"Stop, leave him alone." The words escaped his mouth before he had a chance to think.

No No No. What are you doing Jake?

The man who had been beating Zaph turned slowly to look, malice burning in his eyes. He was stocky like a wrestler. Head shaved to the bone and shining like a bowling bowl in the steam.

He stood and moved stiffly stopping close to Jake's right side. The second man turned his long gangly frame away from Zaph and approached from the other side. He towered over Jake his long arms swinging by his side like an orangutan.

Oh shit.

Icy fear descended his spine leaving his fingers and toes tingling and twitching. He stood ready to defend against an attack.

The wrestler spoke first staring him down. "Well well. What do we have here then? Who the fuck are you to get involved in our business?"

Jake took a half step back trying to maintain some distance.

"Look, I don't want trouble. I just heard my friend cry out. We'll go."

The wrestler wagged a fat finger at Jake shaking his head slowly. "Newbe ain't you? You should know better than to interfere in other people's affairs. Now it's your problem too."

Jake came alive. The familiar feeling of adrenaline bathing his body ready for fight or flight. Evolution at work. His pulse increased and his focus sharpened. He watched for signs of movement with his peripheral vision.

The wrestler lumbered in swinging wildly with his right fist. Jake stepped forward and blocked then pivoted scything his right elbow across his attacker's temple. Lights switched out instantly. The body crumpled to the floor like the bones had been removed.

Orangutan was slower to react and lunged at Jake roaring in anger. One to one he was no match. Jake stomped his foot hard to the knee with a sickening crack that reverberated around the shower. The ape collapsed to the tiles clutching his leg, screaming in agony. It was all over in ten seconds.

Exhilaration. The heady brew of adrenaline and dopamine released by the brain for the fight bathed him, pouring into every fibre of his body leaving him tingling all over. His heart pounded as he sucked in oxygen.

Zaph was coming to life. He sat up blinking and surveyed the mayhem around him. He looked up at Jake eyes wide with surprise. He sat up stunned.

"Jake, what are you doing here?" He shook his head. There was fear in his eyes. "No. No ye don't understand."

"Come on Zaph. It's okay now. Let's get out of here," he replied holding out his hand.

"You don't know what ye've done." The anguish in Zaph's voice gave him pause for concern. "These are T..." but he was cut short.

"Taylor's men." The voice came from behind. Deep and

guttural. Ominous in the gloom.

He spun around peering into the swirling steam but couldn't make anyone out. The shower faucets were turned off slowly. The sound of running water dyed away as an eerie silence descended. Gradually the steam cleared, and a figure began to form like a statue. Cold and observing.

Instinct told Jake he was in terrible trouble. He froze. Rooted to the spot with dread.

Taylor stepped from the shadows closing in on Jake. Up close he was formidable, standing six feet tall, eye to eye with Jake. His face was scarred and battle-hardened. Piercing blue eyes bore through Jake as the two men stood facing each other.

"Why are you interfering in my business?"

"Hey Taylor. Yer man didn't know what he was doing. He's only looking out for a mate…" Zaph was pulling his clothes back on, blood dripping from his squashed nose.

"Quiet." Taylor snapped his head to face Zaph, stopping him in his tracks. "This has nothing to do with you anymore. It's between me and him." He returned eye to eye with Jake circling him slowly like a jackal circling a wounded animal.

You are no match for him.

Fear descended fast sweeping away the exhilaration of earlier victory. He gulped back bile as his stomach flipped threatening to vomit. This man was different. He could feel it.

"Look Taylor. I don't want trouble," he pleaded. "I saw my friend. He needed help. That's all."

"It's too late for that. You attacked my men and now you must pay." The calm in his voice left Jake cold.

Taylor turned his attention to his men. The wrestler was coming around. A livid purple bruise formed across his temple. He hauled himself to his feet snarling at Jake. Ready to attack once more. Taylor held out his hand. "Enough. Leave us Bones. I will deal with you later. And get him to the infirmary." He waved his hand dismissively at the injured man who clutched his knee, snivelling. Bones hauled his companion to his feet and dragged him off. He turned once more to Jake with a look of pure hatred and anger.

"You too Zaph. Leave now," Taylor continued. "We need to talk."

"Please don't hurt him," he begged. "He's green. He didn't know they were with ye." Zaph clasped his hands in front of Taylors face.

Taylor stared silently, daring him to carry on. Zaph knew better. He gathered his things and scrambled away from the shower block.

You have to fight. Don't back down.

Every instinct told him to run away. The door was right behind him. He could retreat to the safety of his cell in an instant. He swallowed. His throat was tight as if being squeezed by some unseen giant. His pulse raced so fast he could feel the throbbing in his temple.

"It seems you know how to fight. Fancy your chances? Let's go for it here and now. Just for fun?" Taylor's eyes lit up in anticipation.

Jake stayed silent and backed up a pace, out of striking range.

Taylor advanced slowly circling Jake. The two men continued to face each other down. He stepped forward and flashed out a left jab. Jake reacted fast. He slipped inside and launched a palm heel strike at Taylor's nose.

It never even came close.

Taylor darted to one side and jabbed his fingers sharply into Jake's throat. He clawed at his neck in desperation, unable to breathe. Taylor finished him with a strike to the solar plexus driving the remaining wind from him.

The world went dark.

He collapsed writhing on the floor in agony. Excruciating pain exploded in his chest as he desperately battled to draw in air. Taylor dropped to one knee and looked upon Jake like a child toying with an ant.

As his senses slowly returned, Taylor's face loomed close. Jake came close to defecating as all pervasive fear wracked his body.

"Breath now. Suck it in. You will be okay." Slowly he lifted a finger to Jake's forehead and pinned him to the cold tiles with controlled force, like a butterfly on a lepidopterist's matt.

"You think I fight like those other morons? Think again. No one interferes in my business. You now owe me and someday soon I will come to collect."

Taylor stood uncoiling his body gracefully. He moved off silently leaving Jake prone and cowering on the floor, shivering in abject terror for what his immediate future might bring.

CHAPTER 15

The most basic tasks weighed Claire down like an anchor chain round her neck. Dragging herself out of bed to rousing the children. Making breakfast. All of the day-to-day tasks normally taken in her stride seemed like mini battles against life itself. She did her best to shield the girls from her worries, but they were perceptive. Violet eyed her mother cautiously over the breakfast table as Claire absently stirred her tea.

"Are you okay mum?" she prodded nervously.

"I'm fine sweetheart," she replied robot-like. Preprogramed. Her eyes never left her teacup.

"I'm worried about you," Violet said placing her hand on her mothers. This simple gesture forced Claire back to the moment. Their eyes met.

Lines had appeared in Claire's face almost overnight. Her mouth was drawn tight, and her usual easy smile had all but disappeared. She was dressed as normal and her hair was brushed. Like some cursory effort at her appearance had been made, but something had changed. It was as if some supreme being with life's remote control had adjusted the settings. Turned down the colour and the brightness a notch or two on Claire. Her eyes told the whole story. Once shining beacons of joy and laughter were now dull and lifeless, projecting her fear and worry for all to see.

Violet wrapped her arms around her mother's neck. Claire pulled her in close, inhaling the lemon scent of freshly washed hair. For that one moment, she drew strength from the love of her daughter before the crushing fear and worry returned. Overwhelming and pervasive. With herculean effort she shifted it temporarily to one side to make way for a sliver of normality and a simple conversation.

"It will all be okay angel," she lied to herself as much as to the children. "I'm just worried about dad is all. Go and brush your teeth. You too Chase. We leave for school in five minutes."

"Why is dad in prison mum?" Chase asked twirling her hair nervously around her fingers. Unable to look her mum in the eye she kept her gaze on her breakfast. "Did he do something bad?"

Did he?

The question snapped yet another twig from the tree in Claire's core.

The tree had grown stronger and broader with new branches appearing as she lived her life. Branches had sprouted for school, her friends, her passion for music and dance.

Later had come the strongest branches of all. Those for family, her husband, her children. But now the branch for Jake felt somehow heavier than before. It weighed her down, lopsided. She no longer felt centred.

She mustered her strength and recited her prepared response monotonously. "No darling. Daddy did not do anything wrong." She pulled Chase onto her lap. "He was attacked by some men. He managed to escape but unfortunately one of the men was hurt very badly in the struggle. So badly in fact that he died. The police need to talk to daddy about it and they are keeping him safe until they do."

The words sounded hollow as she spoke them. Muted and unconvincing. But her instinct told her not to worry the children.

Chase lifted her gaze as did Claire and they locked eyes. "I can't wait for him to come home," she nodded sagely. "My heart tells me he will be fine mummy. Try not to worry."

Claire looked upon her youngest daughter in amazement. Such strength from one so young. The three of them stood silently drawing into a tight embrace. Claire revelled in the energy and vitality of her children and for one moment a kernel of hope nestled. Like the first blossom of spring blooming on her tree. Tears slipped silently from her eyes.

She kissed each of them on the forehead. "Teeth now." She managed to form a weak smile for the first time that day as the girls skipped off to the bathroom.

***

"Bye Chase. Have a nice day at school." Claire kissed her younger daughter hugging her tight and forced a smile as she ran off through the school gates to greet her friends excitedly.

She turned to leave, desperate to blend in anonymously. She kept her eyes low, avoiding the snatched glances of the other parents.

Do they all know?

School gate gossip was always rife. On more than one occasion Claire had joined in, revelling in some titbit of scandal or other. But today was different. Today she just wanted to escape, to finish her errands and be home. Away from the stares and stolen whispers behind the hands of the other parents.

With horror it dawned she was approaching. Helen. She was the mother of one of the girls in Chase's class. Not someone in her close circle, but a person she had shared tea and cake with at children's parties over the years.

She walked with purpose, closing fast as she stared straight at Claire. There was no escape. She stopped right in front of her. Fear slipped down Claire's spine expanding into her chest and stomach at the sheer dread of friendly conversation.

"Claire my dear. How are you?" She planted her hands on ample hips. Her thin, wet lips drew tight into a smile of false sympathy. "I have been so worried about you. My Arthur was at the football yesterday and he said his friend Danny saw your Jake being taken away by the police on Saturday night. Is everything okay?"

She drummed her fingers together expectantly as she cocked her head to one side like a spaniel waiting for instructions from its owner. She raised her eyebrows in anticipation.

Claire stepped back a pace, excruciatingly uncomfortable at this intrusion into her personal space and private thoughts. The question floated unanswered in the continuing silence. She opened her mouth to speak but nothing came, the words caught in her throat.

Everything is a long way from okay.

Helen filled the conversational gap. "Well, is there anything I can do to help? You must tell me." She nodded theatrically. "After all, a problem shared is a problem halved. Would you like to go for a nice cup of tea and tell me all about it?"

So I can provide you with gossip for your coffee morning? Why don't you mind your own fucking business?

Claire forced a smile as her nerves shot tiny bolts of fear around her body. Her instinct was to get home where she would feel safe and could avoid conversation. With titanic effort she forced a response.

"That's very kind Helen but I have some things I need to take care of today. I appreciate your concern, but I don't want to talk about it right now."

"Oh that's a shame my dear," she said her brow knitting into faux concern. "Well, if you need anything please do let me know." She took Claire's hand patting it gently as if consoling a small child who had lost a favourite toy.

Her hands were rough and dry against Claire's. She recoiled and pulled her hand away sharply at the intrusive touch. The forced sympathy was still painted on Helen's face but now clouded with the tinge of disappointment. Claire nodded and thanked her quietly. She dropped her gaze once more to the floor and pulled herself away from the awkward encounter.

***

She browsed the aisles of the village shop absent-minded and unable to focus her attention on any task for a sustained period. Her thoughts always returned to Jake. Her husband had killed a man and maybe she would lose him to prison for a generation.

She paid for her shopping and began the short walk home. Each step like lifting a leaded boot.

Then she saw it.

It was parked in a side street facing her. A sleek silver sports model. It was alien against the Range Rovers and people carriers typical of the village. From a distance, she could just make out two men sat inside. Were they staring as she passed? She felt a jolt of fear like a cold knife to the stomach. This was her home. Where she lived and her children walked to school. Now was she being watched. Followed even?

Something snapped inside.

Her initial fear was overshadowed as anger took hold inside her.

How dare they come to my hometown.

Her cheeks flushed and she gritted her teeth as the hot red fire coursed through her entire body exploding into her brain. She dropped her shopping and walked with purpose towards the car, staring intently.

The engine gunned and the car took off fast, tyres screeching as the car spun off into the distance. She did not get a good look at the occupants; it had all happened so fast. Their reaction made it clear though. She was being followed.

She ran home leaving her shopping where she dropped it. Anger and frustration boiled over. Tears coursed down her face. She fumbled the keys in the lock and finally, mercifully she managed to get the door open. She retreated from the outside world to the relative safety of her home. Inside she sat with her back to the door sobbing uncontrollably. She could barely focus or hold a single coherent thought for a second. Her mind a seething cauldron of burning worries.

How would she manage the bills? How would she cope as a single parent? How would Jake survive in prison? What would the neighbours say What does she tell the school? What would be reported in the papers? Who was the man he killed? Who were these people following her? Would they seek retribution? Who was her husband really?

This crushing thought kept returning. Her prime worry under which all other worries were subcategories.

Did she know her husband?

It was like she had married two men. The Jake she knew and loved and bore two children with. And this other man. A man with a violent and dark past he had concealed from her. A man who was now labelled a killer. Could she still trust him?

Her heart thumped as panic began to set in, racing uncontrollably. She ripped her shirt away staring at the throb in her breast as if expecting to see some alien claw itself out of her. The dread rising from the pit of her stomach washed through her like refrigerant as her chest tightened. She felt like she was inhaling through a balloon. Each breath harder than the last with less oxygen available. She could not breathe. Could not get the air she needed.

Internally she was screaming, wailing like a banshee. Nothing would have given her greater release than to give it a voice, but she swallowed it. Pulled herself back to the moment. She closed her eyes fighting to regain control of her breathing. She forced herself to count.

Breath in two three four, out two three four.

Slowly the panic began to subside. The ragged gasps gave way to controlled breathing. The rising dread dissipated but left a cold, empty feeling inside. She stood and walked to the kitchen, staring at the bottle of whisky on the side. She poured herself a hefty slug and tipped it back in one, savouring the burning sensation in her throat and stomach, anticipating the sweet release that would come. She poured another but caught herself just in time. As she stared into the glass, she stopped and hurled it across the kitchen smashing it against the far wall.

She could not serve her children, her husband or herself by numbing her mind with alcohol. She emptied the bottle down the sink and did the same with a half-empty bottle of wine that she had started the night before. It was time for a change.

Did she have the right to judge him so harshly for his actions as a youth, years before they had even met? Surely every man deserved a second chance. He had never exhibited any characteristics of his violent past since she had met him. He was gentle and kind. At least until now. Was it unfair to question his actions so critically? He had explained what had happened. This was no random act of violence. He was defending his life. Humankind's most basic survival tool. And he was still alive. Still breathing oxygen that his heart pumped around his body. Still able to think and experience joy, happiness, loneliness, and fear. And what was the alternative had he not fought so hard? He would be lying dead on a cold gurney in a morgue. No longer a father or a husband. Just a slab of dead meat.

A seed of gratitude took hold inside of her. A warming feeling of love and joy that he was still alive given the awful alternative.

Flashes of their past lives together took over her thoughts as she sat at the kitchen table staring into space. She remembered the day of their wedding. Remembered walking down the aisle with nerves buzzing like bees in her stomach, only to be washed away by the happiness welling within as she approached her husband to be as he stood waiting for her. They held hands and smiled nervously at each other as they began the next stage of their journey together. They recited vows and pledged themselves to each other through good times and bad.

The good and the bad. I must stand by him

The day of Violet's birth. Thrashing on the bed with inescapable agony burning her centre as she pushed. The waves of pressure overwhelming her until she thought she might die of the pain. Jake was there by her side, holding her hand, encouraging her, urging her. Tears in his eyes as their baby girl was born into the world so small pink and helpless, announcing her entrance bawling and screaming. The midwife placed her on Claire's breast. The desperate pain of childbirth gone, a distant memory replaced by pure love, joy and contentment. Like sunshine lighting her from within. This tiny being. Someone for them to love and nurture, to teach and help grow and learn.

This was her family. Jake may have done bad things in the past, but that was long ago. This was now and she had to fight for him.

She banished the fears from her mind and rose from the table with a newfound strength within. These fuckers would never harm her babies. Jake would come through his ordeal and screw anyone who whispered behind her back, or stole glances at her in the shops, or outside the school gates. None of that mattered. Her only concern was Jake and her children. Their family unit would be as one again. She would stand by her husband and see him through this dark time. And any person who came between her and her children was going to suffer.

CHAPTER 16

Zaph appeared at Jake's door the next day, shuffling from foot to foot, his face etched with grave concern.

"So sorry my man. I never wanted this for ye." He paced the cell wringing his hands, unable to look Jake in the eye. "But I appreciate yer standing up for me mind."

"Don't sweat it." He played it cool, concealing the true fear that lay within. "I couldn't leave you like that."

"I'll speak to him. See if I can squash this," he replied. "Ye didn't know, but I'm in his crew. Not on the enforcement side but I have certain skills and contacts that he makes use of. I stepped out of line and took a beating. It's the way of things in here. I didn't want ye to get dragged into it."

Taylor won't let this go. I'm fucked.

"It's not your fault. I should have thought before I acted," he replied. "Don't worry, let's just see how it plays out."

***

Jake spent the next few days in a state of constant high anxiety. Anyone who approached was suspect. He scanned hands for weapons. His skin crawled and heart pounded in fear of retribution. Every sound was a perceived attack. A trainer that squeaked on the floor behind him and he would spin in terror of finding a shank buried in his ribs.

You're on your own.

Zaph couldn't help him. He sat alone in his cell doing his

best to stay relaxed, yet he was anything but. He churned with inner turmoil, fear, and adrenaline as he waited for the attack in his room.

How easily the system had turned him. He had been a prisoner for just a few short days. In that time, he had been in a fight and now trembled in a state of constant readiness for reprisal attacks, prepared to battle for his very survival. Prison would expose the hidden warrior that lurks in every man.

He played many scenarios over and over in his head. Who would come to him? Would Taylor send his men or come himself? What had he meant by 'come to collect?' Would they just beat him badly and that would be it? Should he just take it?

No. The first rule of prison is to fight back. Or to at least try. That was how you earned respect. He had no chance against Taylor himself. The man possessed speed and power Jake had never witnessed before. Abilities that could kill a man a thousand ways in seconds. But still he resolved to fight no matter what. Whoever came, he would hear them out. Then if called for he would go hard at the vulnerable areas. Eyes, throat, balls. Disable quickly and move on. He gave himself no chance of winning, but he wasn't going down without a fight.

They came two days later as he lay on his bed reading.

He heard the approach from the gangway to the left. Footsteps slow and purposeful. He readied himself, easing off his bunk so he could not be taken lying down. They appeared at the open doorway. The taller one wrapped mockingly on the door and smiled sadistically.

"Knock knock. Time for a chat?" He was lean and gangly with dark hair slicked back. His eyes were set close and sunken in hollowed sockets. It was the man Jake had seen on the yard with Taylor, his right-hand man. He was closely followed by another guy. Shorter than Jake but thicker set and built like a tank. His head was shaved to the bone, and he fixed him with maniacal eyes. Jake trembled in fear. He tensed. Ready for action.

Play it cool.

"What can I do for you?" He kept his arms loose by his side projecting confidence even as his guts turned to jelly.

"I'm Slick. This here is Arno." The taller one did all the talking. "Do you know who we work for?" he continued, closing the door behind him. He moved to Jake's right-hand side while Arno stood to his left. He was cornered.

"You are Taylor's men. Look I don't want trouble." He put his hands out in a gesture of compliance. Slick moved his face in close revealing a mouthful of brown rotten teeth. His breath stank of stale cigarette smoke.

"Relax. We are not here to hurt you. For now anyway." He paused letting the words sink in. "But you stepped on Taylor's toes," he continued. "Now he wants to talk."

"Talk about what?"

Slick stepped back giving Jake some breathing space. "That's between you and Taylor. Just here to deliver the message." He smirked and gave a theatrical bow. "Sir. You are cordially invited to dinner."

Arno stepped directly in front of Jake and fixed him with a cold dark stare. He spoke for the first time. His voice was low and gravelly. "Be there tonight. Or we come back. And then no so friendly."

Jake nodded his acquiescence. "I'll be there."

They left slamming the cell door behind them.

He rushed to the toilet, crouched on one knee and vomited. Dry heaving against an empty stomach. He moved to the sink and splashed his face with cold water looking at the man in the reflection. There was fear in those eyes gazing back at him.

Can they all see it?

Time ticked agonizingly towards the call for dinner. Jake paced the cell haunted by dread.

What does he want with me?

This was the last place he wanted to be. When the time came, he filed down with the other prisoners and joined the line.

"Evening my man, how's it going?" Zaph sidled up to him.

"Well. I'm still alive, "Jake replied. "They came to see me. He wants to talk."

"I heard." Zaph glanced across at Taylor's table. He was sitting flanked by Slick and Arno and was watching them both intently. "When the guards call the end of dinner stay behind. The room will clear. He'll will be waiting for ye." Zaph turned to face him. "Listen, I wanted to say thank ye. For what ye did for me like. If I can ever repay the favour I will."

"Is this going to turn nasty?" Jake asked, nodding his head towards Taylor.

"I doubt it in here. He only wants to talk. Who knows after that?"

"Thanks," he replied, bumping fists with Zaph. He collected his food and took a table at the edge of the room. Facing in so no one was behind him. Taylor's crew scrutinised him carefully. He scanned the room. Outside of Taylor's circle no one paid him any attention. This was between him and Taylor. News had not yet circled the prison grapevine. A testament to Taylor's grip on the wing.

He ate alone in silence. Watching. Waiting. He could barely manage a morsel. As the rest of the prisoners finished their meals they began to file out. The staff officers did the rounds and hurried the last few stragglers along. One guard approached his table and leaned in close. His face was pock marked with decades old acne scars.

"Stay behind. Taylor wants to talk." It was an order. Not a suggestion. Jake nodded his understanding as the guard turned on his heel and marched off. He stood as the final few prisoners were leaving. He took his tray to the stacking area where Slick and Arno were doing the same. They left with the last of the guards.

The doors slammed shut. The echo reverberated around the now-empty hall. Jake turned slowly to face Taylor who had not moved from his table at the centre of the room. His neck tingled. His senses on high alert for any sign this would be anything but a friendly chat. He paced slowly; the room silent but for his soft footsteps. Taylor's piercing blue eyes followed him. Unblinking. Hypnotic. Fear-inducing. All in equal measure. They never once left Jake.

Jake spoke first. "I hear you want to talk."

Taylor gestured at the table. "Please, take a seat." He spoke with a cultured, soft accent. Difficult to place but with the clipped tones of an expensive education. Jake pulled the chair back. The metal legs screeched against the concrete floor. He sat and placed his palms on the table. Non-threatening. Taylor sat immobile. Face impassive. He gave nothing away.

Jake took the initiative to open the conversation.

"Before we begin, I want to make it clear for the record. I did not know they were your men. I was just looking out for a friend. I thought they were going to kill him."

Taylor maintained his silence. His eyes skewered through Jake. After an eternity he spoke.

"Commendable. Friendship is a valuable commodity in a place like this. As is loyalty. But there must be a price to pay as I am sure you can appreciate."

"What do you want?" he replied. The weight of the conversation had the potential to define the rest of his life in prison. One false word would spell disaster.

Taylor continued. "Do you know why Zaph was targeted?"

"I don't know the details. Only that he works for you, and it was justified. He said he stepped out of line."

"Correct. It was justified. I must maintain order and sometimes that means violence. In here intimidation is the primary mechanism to manipulate human behaviour." He laughed. "Much the same on the outside to be honest. Fearful men can be controlled. I learnt this in the army."

His face turned hard like stone. "Are you afraid Jake?"

His guts flipped. His heart thumped so loud he was sure Taylor could hear.

He knows. He can see.

The question hung in the air between them.

Don't let him control you.

"No," he lied. "You deserve respect of course. But as I said before, I did not know I was interfering in your business. For that I can only apologise."

Taylor stayed silent as Jakes heartbeat drummed.

Mercifully he filled the void. "You have some fighting skills it would appear. You took out two men. Quite impressive."

"I have had a little self-defence training. That's all. I don't like to be taken advantage of."

Taylor considered this. "You follow Krav. Correct?

Jake nodded impressed. "How can you tell?"

"It's what we were taught in the SAS. More brutal than the schoolboy version you are taught in civilian life, but I recognised the patterns."

He waved his hand as if swatting away an annoying fly.

"Onto the crux of the matter. As you know by now I run the prison. The guards are on my payroll aside from a couple of tediously moral characters. I pay them to ensure my ventures run smoothly. There are challengers to my position from time to time. For the most part they are crushed immediately but I have a problem ahead. There are several Albanians in this prison, mostly low-ranking mafia soldiers. Easy to keep in line. The problem is a senior member of their gang will be joining us in a few days. I have had run-ins in the past with this individual and his men. His imminent arrival is making them restless. Cocky even. They are pushing at the edges of my organisation to see if it will crack. I want a strong message sent quickly. Swift and brutal. I am in charge here. And that leads me to you. You have some exceptional skills which could prove useful. I do not want him killed or even permanently disabled. I want him out of the picture in the infirmary for a week or two to recover. This is your task and the slate is wiped clean. He will not see you coming since you are not connected to my crew. My men will ensure the rest of the Albanians fall in line."

Taylor chuckled to himself. "Your reputation precedes you. I know you took out two guys to land yourself in prison. And you killed one no less. Next you take out two of my men." He waved his hand dismissively." I will hold no grudges if you do as I ask."

He fixed Jake with a chilling stare. His cold blue fixed on Jake. "What do you say?"

No no no. Please not this.

He swallowed nervously. His mouth dry. This was a dire situation that required careful negotiation. He returned Taylor's stare.

"I understand your position. But you also need to understand mine. You know why I am here. Yes, I killed a man in self-defence. But I am no hardened criminal, able to dish out beatings on order. I just want to do my time, fight my case and get home to my family as quickly as possible. Doing this is not going to further my goal and the last thing I need is to make enemies of Albanian gangsters. Respectfully, I must decline. I can't do this for you."

I am going to die in here.

Taylor's stare hardened. "Yet you are happy to make an enemy of me?" He did not wait for an answer. "Disappointing I have to say. You want to go it alone? Let us see where that gets you. You may be in here longer than you think." He paused, placing the tips of his fingers under his chin. "I am going to do you a favour though. You have two days to think it over. Between now and then you are safe. An armistice between us let's call it. After two days you are either in, or you are on your own and fair game. Arno and Slick will be off the leash. As will the two men you destroyed in the showers. You can take your chances with them as well as every other prison wannabe tough guy who wants a pop at you. You will be a marked man. Think it over Jake. But if you come to the wrong decision, I suggest you watch your back carefully because no one will watch it for you."

Taylor stood and extended his hand. Jake took it, sensing the power and strength of the man through that handshake. Without another word Taylor turned and walked off. Jake sat alone shaking and staring at the table in the silence of the empty room.

CHAPTER 17

The next few days were pure mental torture. He saw threats everywhere he looked. Stolen glances from Taylor's crew left him jumpy and afraid. He could sense their desire to unload on him. Yet Taylor's promise stood. For now.

The long hours alone in his cell were the worst. He tossed and turned through the night processing his options. In the morning as he shaved, he did not like what he saw. Was there a hardened edge to his gaze? Colder?

What are you going to do?

Cow to Taylor and do what he asked? Then his remaining time inside would likely be relatively easy. He would enjoy special treatment from the guards and the protection of the gang. But at what cost?

He would be a marked man by the Albanians. Potentially something that would follow him far beyond these walls. Dark thoughts permeated his mind, torturing him as he lay awake at night. Defending himself or a friend in trouble was one thing. He could look himself in the eye and square his conscience that he had done the right thing. But he was no gang enforcer. How could he intentionally go and maim someone. Not anymore. He had left that behind decades ago. Ever since that poor boy.

You can't do it.

He must remain true to himself if he were to retain the inner essence of who Jake Charles was. Else he would never put this dark time behind him.

I'm never returning to that version of me.

In the end the decision was easy. But as time drew on and the task of delivering the news came ever closer, fear and anxiety began to consume him. He would be a marked target. But if that was the price he had to pay, so be it.

He ate breakfast with Zaph the next morning, the one man he could trust.

"He won't be pleased. That much I can say," said Zaph picking at his food.

"What's his story anyway?" Jake replied. "Tell me about him." He leaned forward as Zaph continued.

"Oh, he has quite the story. What ye might call a colourful life. He was a soldier before. Passed selection into the special forces. A captain in the SAS. Ye can imagine the sort of action he has seen. Tours of Iraq, Afghanistan, Sudan. He has fought in every shithole warzone ye can imagine. It all came to a crashing end when he put his commanding officer in hospital for six months. No one knows the reason except Taylor himself. That earned him two years in military prison, which is pretty much the hardest time ye can do. When he was discharged, he started working nightclub doors in London. He brought in other ex-soldiers. The hardest cases ye can imagine working for him. A literal army of killers running the club doors. No one else could compete. He muscled all the other gangsters out of town. Quite a few went AWOL presumed dead. Those left turned tail and ran. Controlling the doors meant controlling the drugs for the whole of North London and The West End. All built from nothing in five years. Eventually the police caught up with him of course. One of his guys was going down for coke dealing. Looking at fifteen years and decided he could not do it. He wore a wire and ratted Taylor out. That was the end of that. He got fifteen years for racketeering, drug dealing, attempted murder, the lot. Yer man who ratted him walked. Taylor rises to the top of every environment he finds himself in. It was like that in the army, on the outside and is the same here. The man is a force. A true alpha. People are afraid of him and for good reason. I have seen him act and it is not something I will soon forget. He is sheer brutal controlled power. Not a man to be crossed for sure. I can only imagine what he has planned for the rat should he ever catch up with him."

Jake listened intently. Fascinated. "Not a guy you want to deliver bad news to then. But I cannot do what he asks." He stared at the floor. "I want to get this over with. Today."

Zaph rubbed his spiky hair nervously. His eyes gave him away. Pure anguish at the position he had landed his friend in. "Look. I get the impression he likes and respects ye. He needs to retain face mind. If ye turn him down, he looks weak. Just watch your back."

***

Jake paced his cell nervously as the call for lunch approached. He was about to deliver bad news to a man who had the power to order him badly hurt or even killed. Yet what choice did he have? Either stand firm to his convictions or commit unspeakable acts that would destroy his soul forever.

You have no choice.

When sick of pacing he exercised vigorously to the point of nausea. When done he collapsed on the bunk.

What are they doing right now?

The girls would be at school. Hopefully distracted from the current situation. No doubt reality would come crashing back when they arrived home to yet another evening without their father.

You must do this for them.

He needed to be able to look them in the eye and say he had remained true to his principles. His thoughts turned to Claire who would be at work. For her the fear would never be far away.

Like him she would readily conjure in her mind the horrors of life inside.

The lunchtime buzzer reverberated through the prison wrenching him back to the present. He joined the throng of prisoners trudging off for lunch. He sat and picked at his food alone. No appetite. Just a fear induced raging thirst he was unable to quench.

After lunch he filed into the exercise yard. Taylor and his crew occupied their usual spot on the benches. They eyeballed Jake as he entered the yard.

Now or never.

He took a deep breath and summoned all his confidence.

He approached.

Before he got within fifteen yards, Slick and Arno stood defending either side of Taylor.

"Easy guys." Jake extended his palms in deference. "I just want to talk."

Taylor stood slowly. "So talk."

"Can we walk alone? I don't like feeling surrounded." He nodded at Taylor's henchmen.

Taylor nodded his agreement, and they began a circular route of the yard. Other groups were doing likewise.

"What's it gonna be?" Taylor asked. "Had time to think it through?"

Jake took a deep breath. "I have. I cannot do what you ask. Please hear me out."

Taylor said nothing. Jake could feel those piercing eyes drilling into him as he walked. He looked straight ahead and continued. "I have nothing but respect for you. I know about your reputation. I know you are not a man to be crossed. But I am just an average guy who finds himself in prison because of an incident I had no control over. I am no gangster and cannot be one of your enforcers. I need to be able to look my girls in the face when I get out of here. I understand there are risks that come with this decision. So be it. I leave the rest to fate."

Taylor stopped and turned to face Jake; his hard face carved like granite. "You've got some balls I'll give you that. For that alone you deserve respect."

He nodded back to his men who were watching them from the other side of the yard. "You know what those guys want? They want those brave balls on a platter."

Jake said nothing as they faced off, neither wishing to back down.

He was the first to sense something wrong.

With their attention so focussed on each other they barely noticed the two men. He heard the footsteps approaching. He registered a flash of silver from his peripheral vision. Two men were closing from the side. Both were carrying crude knives fashioned from sharpened steel. The closest lunged at Taylor with his blade. Jake reacted out of pure instinct. He lashed out with his foot and caught the man on the wrist. The blade dropped to the tarmac. He stepped to the side and smashed a backfist into the attacker's face who crumpled to the ground. Jake's reaction spurred Taylor who turned as the other man lunged at him. The blade struck a glancing blow opening a deep gash. Dark red blood seeped through his shirt. Taylor latched onto the man's knife arm and twisted it back with a sickening snap. He silenced the man's scream with a hammer blow to the throat. He dropped to the ground, coughing gouts of blood. Jake figured he was dead or dying.

The whole yard had noticed the commotion including the tower guards.

"Everyone down. Now." A warning shot rang out. As

one, the prisoners hit the ground laying on their front, hands-on heads. The guards approached and began cuffing all the prisoners. Taylor glared silently at the two attackers. He turned his gaze to Jake and nodded his wordless thanks.

CHAPTER 18

Jake was placed in isolation and questioned after the incident. He assumed the same for Taylor. CCTV caught the crucial moment when the attackers pulled weapons. It was a clear case of self-defence, and no further charges were brought. Two days later Jake was released back into the general population.

Taylor and Jake sat alone in the yard. He had been summoned once more by Slick and Arno. But this time they had been polite. Deferent even. Something had changed.

"I owe you a debt of gratitude." Taylor was bare-chested and glistened from sweat as the sun beat down fiercely upon them.

Be careful. He may be a useful ally but he is still dangerous.

Jake met his gaze across the table. He kept his face neutral. Impassive. "Who are they?" he enquired.

"They were associates of the Albanian crew. It seems their boss got word to them. They were to eliminate me before he arrived then the rest of my crew would fall into line. I got sloppy.

He looked away before his face betrayed something. Shame?

"You saved my life. You won't be touched in here. You have my word. Thank you."

Taylor stood and extended his hand. Was there a certain warmth in that hard face Jake had not seen before. They shook hands. Perhaps some connection between them? Something that might pass as friendship?

"If there is anything I can do, call on me anytime. I won't be in here forever."

"It was nothing. I just reacted when I saw the blade."

They circled the yard together. "You should have joined the forces. You have sharp instincts."

Jake laughed. "Not sure about that," he replied. I don't like violence."

Anymore.

Taylor cocked an eyebrow. "I don't believe you! It's in your bones. Look me in the eye and convince me. No sharp thrill when you took my men out? No rush of adrenaline when you dropped the Albanian? You know exactly what I'm talking about."

Maybe he's right. Am I a thug just like him?

The accusation stung. The hot flush of shame crept up the back of his neck at being discovered. "I take classes so I can defend myself and my family from bad peop…" he stopped himself mid-sentence.

"Bad people like me?" The question hung in the air.

Jake thought this one over for a moment. "You made your choices about what you do for a living. That does not make you bad. Who am I to criticise what you do or how you do it?

Taylor turned away and they carried on circling the yard. "You don't deserve to be in here for what you did. Do you know who he was? The man you killed?"

"Some thug who attacked me after an argument," he shrugged.

Taylor sighed and stopped. He turned to Jake. "I'm afraid it's not quite that simple. I did some digging. The man you killed is called Yuri Vasin. He is the youngest of three brothers who head a Russian crime family. They operate in North London mainly. I have come across them in my professional life. Serious people. You should watch your back when you get out."

Jake considered this. "There was a man at my court hearing. He looked out of place. Like he was there watching me. My family. Will they hurt them?"

Taylor placed an arm on his shoulder. Firm grip. Reassuring. "Don't worry. That's not quite their style. Your family should be safe. But as I said watch your back when you leave. For now, focus on getting out. Who is leading your defence?"

"I'm with a public defender. I can't afford a lawyer. Not without selling the house. She seems competent though."

A smile cracked Taylor's face. "Time to repay my debt. Let me add some big guns to your defence. I have access to the best legal defence money can buy. It's the least I can do."

They carried on circling the yard in the heat. "This is between you and me only. I put away a lot of cash before I got lifted. I have more than I will ever need to live a life of luxury when I get out. Six months then it is sailing the world on my yacht."

Are you lying down with the devil? Want to be in his pocket forever?

He hesitated. But desperation to get back to his family got the better of him.

"That is a generous offer. Thank you. I will take you up on that before you change your mind," he replied graciously.

"Consider it done," he replied.

"What about the Albanians?" Jake asked.

"When they get out of the infirmary they will be transferred. The governor has also arranged for their leader to be moved elsewhere. He doesn't want the trouble. This attack has cemented my position nicely. Worked out well. No one will dare challenge me now."

He clapped Jake on the back. "None of this is your concern. Focus on your defence and get home to your wife and kids." Taylor extended his hand, and the two men shook.

"Thank you Jake. One day I hope I can repay you properly."

***

Jake tossed and turned in bed that night unable to sleep. He lay on his bunk staring at the chink of moonlight as it crept slowly across the ceiling.

Are you sure about this?

He was anything but.

The stress of the past week had affected him badly. Humans are not designed to live in a state of constant dread. High alert. Ready for imminent attack. 24x7 fight or flight. His heart had been racing for days. His appetite depressed. Unable to concentrate.

Now that had gone.

But new doubts were creeping.

Is Taylor a man to get involved with?

Are my family in danger?

He compartmentalised the thoughts in his mind for now. They were for another day. His hearing was approaching fast, and the offer of legal assistance had given him a significant boost. Was there finally light at the end of a very dark tunnel?

***

Jake woke early the next morning from a deep restful sleep. He rose and headed to the sink to wash his face. He examined himself in the mirror. His eyes and cheeks had hollowed some. His jaw more pronounced. A combination of stress and punishing exercise had leaned out his body.

Today he was to meet his lawyer to discuss the hearing. Taylor's solicitor would also be in attendance. Jake went through his usual morning routine pushing himself hard.

After breakfast he was led through to one of the prison's private interview rooms by a guard. He took a seat and thanked the officer for the steaming mug of tea he left with him.

This is new.

Barked orders and threats of reprimand had been replaced by waiter service.

Earned through actions and character? Or Taylor's orders.

Not that he cared which. It was just pleasant to be treated like a human again.

The door buzzed open, and Millbank entered accompanied by a portly distinguished-looking gentleman. He wore a tailored three-piece suit complete with watch chain and bow tie. It was finely cut but failed to hide the struggle at the midriff. Horn rimmed spectacles perched atop a bulbous nose and a bushy moustache. His greying hair was swept back. This man was born to play the role of the barrister.

"Mr Charles. How are you? Simon Carrington QC. Pleased to make your acquaintance. Please call me Simon." He extended his hand and a warm smile.

Jake returned the pleasantries and the group took their places around the table.

"You are looking well Jake. How are you coping?" Millbank enquired.

"Up and down. A few er... challenges navigating the system let's say." He allowed himself a wry smile. "I imagine Mr Carrington has informed you of the events leading to his involvement in the case?"

Carrington interjected. "We are familiar with your assistance to Mr Taylor and most grateful. As I am sure you can appreciate adding a QC to your defence is going to have a significant impact on your case. With your permission I will take complete control and act in your defence. Mr Taylor has confirmed all fees are to be covered. Rest assured you are now in the best legal hands available."

Jake nodded his agreement. "Sounds great. How do we proceed?"

Carrington produced a single sheet of paper and laid it in front of Jake. "Please sign this document. This will pass formal control of your case to me. I will instruct my investigator to work on the case, as will I. From now on, this case has my full attention."

Jake looked at Millbank raising an eyebrow "What do you think?"

"I'm a competent public defender Jake," she replied smiling. "But I cannot offer the resources that Mr Carrington can bring to your case." She placed a manicured finger on the document. "Sign it. This is the easiest legal decision you will ever have to make."

Jake took the paper and scrawled his signature at the bottom. He handed it to Carrington. "Where do we begin?"

Carrington laid bare the details of the evidence. "There is a single witness to the incident itself. He claims you initiated the attack. On the other hand, there are multiple witnesses from the bar who state you were not the aggressor in the run up to the incident. There are a number of avenues to pursue here. Preliminary investigations of said witness reveal a criminal record for robbery, violence, and drug offences. My investigator is digging as we speak." He paused to mop his brow of sweat with a blue silk pocket handkerchief before continuing. "You on the other hand are an upstanding citizen without so much as a parking ticket for the last twenty years, barring some minor youthful indiscretions of course." He leaned in winking conspiratorially. "I won't sugar coat the situation Jake. The law can be a fickle mistress. Never underestimate the stupidity of your fellow man or women," he bowed theatrically to Millbank, "to make irrational decisions. I have seen both judges and juries do so. But I am an expert in nudging them in the right direction." He winked and tapped his nose. "I like to think this will all be over in a trice, but of course I can't make any guarantees." Carrington pushed his notes away. "How does that all sound to you, my boy?" He flopped back heavily in his chair and polished his glasses.

It sounds like you don't have a clue when I am getting out of here.

Jake cleared his throat. "Okay I guess. What do you need from me?"

Carrington clapped him on the shoulder. "It's going to be fine Jake. Your preliminary hearing is in three days. I want you to look after yourself. Stay out of trouble and keep your head down."

"No worries there," Jake replied. "I've had plenty of that but for the most part it seems to be over now."

Carrington hefted his ample bulk out of the chair with a sigh. He extended his hand. "Good to meet. You are in good hands. Relax. I'll be in tomorrow for a full debrief once I have the report on the witness."

Jake stood taking Carrington's hand. "Thank you. I can't tell you how much I appreciate your help."

Carrington laughed a hearty chuckle rumbling deep from within his bulk. "I suggest you thank your guardian angel. He's the one paying my considerable fee."

"Thanks also to you Sarah," he said turning to her. "Will you be involved going forward?"

"I'll be meeting with Mr Carrington to give background information. Also to consult with his investigators. I'll be involved yes. See you soon Jake."

Carrington rapped sharply on the door with his knuckles. "We're done in here."

Jake watched as he sauntered off down the corridor accompanied by Millbank. They made an odd pairing. Millbank striking and fresh. Carrington bulky and distinguished.

His life was in their hands now. And yet he felt no closer to his freedom.

***

He spent the afternoon in the prison library researching the trial process. There were slim pickings, but action and activity made him feel better. Later, he ate dinner with Zaph and relayed the meeting with the lawyers. At Taylor's request, he did not disclose Carrington's involvement. He wanted that kept quiet and Jake had of course agreed.

"Moving forward my man." Zaph punched him on the arm affectionately. "Well pleased for you. Couldn't happen to a nicer fella."

As he was leaving the dining hall, Taylor caught his eye and beckoned him over. He was sitting alone.

"Take a seat," he said nodding to the chair. "How did it go today?"

Taylor's men from the shower fight were on the table behind watching. A vein throbbed blue in the wrestler's temple as he eyed Jake maliciously. Jake sat and faced Taylor. Hands on the table. Non-threatening.

"Carrington is excellent. Inspires confidence. He can't say for sure when I will be out though."

Taylor peeled an apple slowly with a plastic knife. "He is the absolute best. You are in good hands." He manoeuvred the knife expertly from hand to hand. Like a magician manipulating cards. Jake wondered how fast he could end his life with that blunt tool.

"What about those two?" Jake nodded behind.

A smile crossed Taylor's face. "You are untouchable. Everyone on my team has been warned. In any case you have earned their grudging respect." He laughed heartily. "Boy were they miffed at being taken out so easily though. You are a warrior Jake. Make no mistake. Two things earn men's respect in here. Those who fight, and those who keep their mouth shut. You excelled on both counts."

***

He lay in bed after lights out. He pulled the dog-eared picture of his family from under his pillow. Treasure. Claire and the girls posed on the beach; the crystal blue of the ocean sparkling behind them. Happier times before the nightmare had descended. With the photo on the pillow next to him he drifted to a dreamless and peaceful sleep.

CHAPTER 19

"Here's to you darling and your continued success."

The three girls raised their glasses in toast. Claire smiled graciously and mouthed 'thank you', to her best friend Carrie.

"Seriously, the performance was amazing. You should be very proud," Angela chipped in. "And thanks for getting us tickets."

Claire bathed in the warm compliments, enjoying the glow of success and the faint burn of the ice-cold champagne as she swirled it in her mouth. It had been an amazing day. One of her childhood dreams achieved. To play at the Royal Albert Hall in London.

They were all dressed for the show in cocktail dresses. Claire's was black. Simple. Elegant. Her long her was immaculately plaited and wound around into a bun. Angela wore red matching her lipstick. Carrie had gone for a sequined silver dress and matching heels that flashed in the light as she moved. They caught the eye of every man in the bar.

"Thank you. Both of you. You are very sweet and it's my absolute pleasure. You know I would never let you miss my big moment. I've been working towards this since music class. Remember that rubbish we composed for old Mr Sanders?"

"Oh god yes," replied Carrie wrinkling her face. "That old weirdo. He stank of BO and always stood too close."

Angela shuddered. "He always made me feel strange that

one. Swear he would perv at my boobs. Even at fourteen"

Carrie poked Angela. "You did tease the randy old fucker though. What a harlot. Unbutton the top of your blouse. Bat your eyelashes at him. I swear he would actually lick his lips while looking at you."

The three girls broke into uncontrolled laughter at the memory.

"Well, I was rubbish at music wasn't I?" Angela giggled. "Had to get my fun somehow. And anyhow we all looked crap next to little miss perfect here, didn't we?" She tipped her head sideways towards Claire. "It was the only way I could get a decent grade out of him."

They collapsed into laughter again as Claire's attention was drawn to a group of men sat in the corner of the pub. They were loud, raucous, cackling. They carried the faint whiff of danger around them. One of them caught her eye and she found herself staring. He was about the same age as her she guessed. Handsome and chiseled. Strong body in a slim fitting tee shirt. There was something about his demeanour. Something different to his companions. He was smiling and laughing but it was not real. His eyes told a different story. Sad and haunted. Like he was ready to burst into tears.

"Claire, you there?" Angela clicked her fingers in front of her face. She turned back to her own friends and shivered, blinking her eyes. "It might be your big day darling but it's still your round."

"Of course," she smiled. "Another bottle I think." Claire pulled her bag over her shoulder and headed to the bar.

***

The bar was busy with the Saturday evening crowd. Two deep at the bar with punters wating to be served. The bar staff were efficient and attentive moving through the customers quickly. She caught the barman's eye and ordered champagne, handing over a ten-pound note. A large chunk of the payment for her performance. Violinists did not generally get rich she had quickly realised.

"Easy come easy go," she muttered to herself. She grasped the bottle and turned sideways to slide out between the customers behind her. She moved fast. As she turned her head, she was dimly aware of an obstacle in her path but it was too late. She was committed and moving with speed and purpose. She crashed into the man behind her. The bottle slammed into his body and shattered on the floor. Her forehead thumped into his chin hard. She saw stars and felt dizzy. He legs felt light. Like they were going to give way. She wavered, swaying as her head swam from the impact. She raised a hand to her head where she had banged into him. The faintest hint of blood smeared her finger.

He caught her hand in his, steadying her. Her head throbbed. She looked up and they stood like that for a moment in silence. It was the man earlier with the sad eyes. He stared back intensely. The sad look was not there anymore. Something else was in those eyes. They were blue and bright and shining. She smiled and laughed as they stood staring.

"I... I think I owe you a drink," he finally blurted. "I'm Jake. Jake Charles."

"Claire." She replied smiling. "Nice to meet you Jake Charles."

***

He bought himself a beer and another bottle for Claire then found a quiet corner of the pub with a table.

Claire grabbed the bottle. "Back in one sec. Just going to explain to my friends."

Claire delivered the bottle to her friends. She filled her

own glass to the brim then took a hefty slug.

"I've just run into someone. Literally. A guy. We are having a drink together. I'll see you a bit later." She filled her glass again.

"No way. Where is he," asked Angela. "Is he hot?"

"Let's have a gander," Carrie chipped in craning her neck to see past Claire.

"Stop it you two," she replied banging Carrie on the shoulder." It's just one drink. I'll be back soon. You guys finish this and then let's go for dinner."

She returned to the table under the watchful gaze of her friends. He sat with his back to the window facing out into the pub. He stood and pulled a chair out for her. She took it with thanks and sat down to assess him.

She found him intriguing, a curious mix of contradictions. His bright clear eyes and easy smile exuded confidence but his leg bounced, and his fingers drummed on the table nervously. He had a gentle air about him, yet he looked tough. His knuckles were scuffed, and bleeding and he had bruising around his cheekbone.

"Was that me?" she asked touching his cheek tenderly. His skin was warm. His day-old stubble rough against the smooth skin.

His brow furrowed in confusion. He raised his hand and touched hers. Their eyes met. She felt her heart jolt in her chest and her stomach tighten. He looked away lost in thought for a moment.

"No. No it wasn't you. I was at the football today. I had some trouble after the game. Some fans from the opposing team cornered and attacked me."

She raised her hand to her mouth and gasped. "Oh my god. That's awful. Are you ok?" She took his hand in hers and brushed her fingers lightly against his grazed knuckles.

He flinched ever so slightly, then smiled again. "Yes. I'm fine. Honestly. It's okay."

She let his hand drop to the table and their gaze met again. "From the state of your hands, it looks like you did some damage of your own?" She raised an eyebrow, staring at him intently.

He looked away. Could not hold her gaze. Did the shine in his eyes darken? As if some cloud had crossed overhead shading him from the light. They sat in silence a beat.

"I would rather not talk about it," he finally said quietly. He looked up again and their eyes met. He smiled but it was not quite the same. The sadness in his eyes was back.

Right then she felt a jolt of longing to be with him so powerful she could barely contain it. Her heart was thumping wildly. Her skin felt warm and tingly. Like nothing she had ever experienced before. Was this love?

The urge to take him in her arms was overwhelming. To pull him to her and rock him gently, his head on her breast. There was vulnerability in him. Strength too but something else. Something gentle and kind and a little sad. She pictured him beneath her as she sat naked astride him. Leaning forward. Her hands on his muscular chest. Her hair cascading over his face as she kissed him tenderly and rode him gently. Slowly. She felt a familiar quiver in her stomach as it tightened. She shifted in her seat desperately trying to scratch the itch. Struggling to control her desire for him

She blinked and tried to shake the feeling away. To bring it back to the here and now. "Are you a bad boy Jake Charles? Troublemaker? Would I need to worry about you?"

He thought for a moment staring at the table before meeting her gaze. They locked eyes. "People change. I have changed. There is an old me and a new me. I find myself at a pivotal point in my life. Coincidentally on the same day we run into each other. Actually ran into each other as it turns out." he laughed. "Would you like to help shape the new me?"

Her heart continued to race. She found she was smiling. Laughing nervously. She looked away briefly, unable to hold onto the intensity of the moment.

The question hung in the air between them. She met his eyes again. The sad vulnerable boy was gone. Banished like it had never been. The confident man was back in control.

"That's a big responsibility for a girl to take on," she said finally composing herself. She tucked a lock of her hair behind her ear and tugged on it gently. Just to have something to do with her hands. Now she was the vulnerable and awkward one. He stared with such intensity she felt he could see past every careful construct she put on for the world to see. He could see the library catalogue of fears she had nurtured since childhood. Her fear of dark alleys, that she still had to check the wardrobe before she went to bed, her fear of dying old and lonely. And he could also see her sexual desire for him, her animal lust. He could see her shame at displaying this for him. He could see right into her inner being, her everything. Would he like what he saw?

"So what happens next?" She broke the tension the only way she knew how with another question.

"Can we get out of here and go somewhere else?" he asked.

She toyed gently with her hair as she looked into his soft blue eyes. To make him wait or give into the worst (or best) of her animal instinct. Her desire for him was overwhelming. She felt light and airy. Floating even. It would be so easy to take his hand and lead him outside. To walk together through the streets. To find a hotel and explore each other until dawn.

After a long silence she finally shook her head gently. "That's not going to happen. I hardly know you."

"Then let's get to know each other. How about dinner? Tomorrow?" He looked at her expectantly. Something in that face. She saw such a mix of emotion there. He was a contradiction. An enigma. He shared her desire and longing for animal passion for sure. But there was something else. Something fundamental. Like he needed something more from her. She shivered head to toe as a feeling passed through her. Warm and exciting. Like this moment was destined to change her life. She made her decision.

She pulled a pen from her purse and wrote her number on a beermat. Pushed it across the table towards him. "Don't lose it. And don't make me wait around for a call. We are not fourteen. I won't play those kinds of games." She raised an eyebrow daring him.

He smiled, wide and genuine. He nodded and his shoulders dropped as he relaxed in his seat. She realised he had been wound up tight. Nervous despite his attempt to show confidence.

She leaned across the table and placed her hand on the back of his head pulling him towards her slowly. He closed his eyes, and she did too. His hair felt silky to the touch. She leaned forward and kissed him tenderly on the lips. They were soft and he tasted faintly of mint. She inhaled his scent. An underlying smell of aftershave. Something citrussy. But his real scent was there too cutting through it. Not unpleasant like stale sweat but something cleaner. Fresh and manly. Like he had just been working out. The sounds from the bar faded away. She lost herself in the moment until it was just the two of them and this kiss. She touched her tongue briefly to his lower lip. Then bit it gently. She felt the stab of fire in her belly spreading out and engulfing her whole body. Like she could almost orgasm at the slightest stimulation. It took epic force of her will to pull away. But she did.

She stood up from the table and brushed her clothes down. She took his hand and shook it formally. "See you very soon Jake Charles?" She raised an eyebrow. He smiled and nodded silently. She turned and walked away allowing herself a brief look over her shoulder. He sat there staring, smiling. She turned away and felt a wash of something delicious flow through her body. Like ice cream on a hot day. She laughed to herself in pure excitement and joy as she returned to join her friends.

CHAPTER 19

He stood naked and alone in his cell staring at the locked door.

Today is the day.

His fingers and toes tingled. Spidery fingers danced up and down his spine.

Anticipation or fear? He couldn't tell the difference

He dressed. Charcoal grey suit. Crisp white shirt. Black brogues. Carrington had sent his things in the previous day.

He examined himself in the mirror, impressed with what he saw. No alcohol and an abundance of free time to work out had carved out taut lean muscle. The suit gloved his toned body.

He was ready.

A knock at the door startled him back to the moment. The guard peered through the observation slot and the door creaked open.

"Time to go."

Deep breath.

He followed the guard out the door and along the gangplank. Head high.

The sharp odour of testosterone hung heavy in the air. Mostly he never noticed. It was always just there.

Not today. Today, he took it all in. To remember the smell and feelings of this place.

Am I coming back?

He felt sure he was.

The guard escorted him through the corridors to a desk for the sign out process. Then through a side door and out into the wide world. As it swung open the light streamed in from a beautiful early June day. A police van waited.

He would see them today. Claire and the girls. His heart fluttered as he pictured them, imagined holding them, smelling them.

As they sped off his thoughts turned to the man who had died at his hands.

How should I feel?

He had taken this man's life. A mother who had lost her son. Or a family without a father or husband. Yet it could be him bleeding out in that alleyway. His children weeping at the grave of a dead father.

You did the right thing.

Would the criminal justice system agree?

The van droned on through the morning traffic as cold fingers rippled up and down his spine. Like he was off to sit an exam for which he had not studied.

***

Carrington was waiting outside the courthouse as they drew to a halt. He sauntered over, jovial as ever. One of the policemen opened the door and Jake climbed out. A handful of reporters jostled to snap photos.

Carrington clapped him on the shoulder. "Let's get inside. Away from the press." He led him up the courtroom steps.

"Are my family here?" he asked.

"They are indeed. Claire is here. The girls too. They are waiting in the courtroom for you. They can't wait to see you. You have a beautiful family."

He smiled. So desperate to see them. To hug them. To return home after a month of hell.

Carrington stopped and turned to him. Stubby sausage fingers gripped him with a surprisingly firm grip. Carrington beamed as he looked him in the eye. "We are first on the dock today Jake. Straight in. There have been some developments with the witness. No time to brief you fully. Just leave everything to me and answer any questions that are put to you. Time to have some fun my boy." He winked and beamed.

Jake did not share his optimism.

The two policemen escorted them on a meandering route through the lower corridors until they arrived at a set of wooden steps.

Carrington stopped and turned to him. "This leads directly into the dock. You will remain escorted by these two gentlemen. I will take a different entrance. Let's get this done. Good luck my boy." He strolled off with his usual bouncy gait. A man without a care in the world.

"Up we go Mr Charles." The first policemen headed up the stairs. Jake followed close behind. His heart thumped in his dry throat. His armpits were soaked and clammy.

As he ascended into the dock, he surveyed the courtroom. Wood-panelled walls lined the room lending it a distinguished air of history and grandeur. The prosecution lawyers occupied a table to the right of the court decked in their fine gowns and horsehair wigs. Carrington was seated on a table to his left next to Millbank. She gave a brief smile and a reassuring nod.

He turned to the public area behind.

His beautiful girls were there. So grown up and ladylike in

their finest dresses. He longed to reach out and pull them in for a tight hug. Claire smiled through pained eyes and mouthed 'I love you.'

He was there also.

He stood out. An air of self-importance and confidence marked him as different to the journalists and others following the case. Perhaps there was even a resemblance to Yuri Vasin. Older. More distinguished certainly. But the same disarming manner was there. He reeked of control and power. Jake felt the unease creep into his every pore. The man stared. Unblinking. Unflinching. Despite the police presence Jake felt naked and vulnerable.

He turned away unable to hold the man's stare. He took a deep breath and fought to regain his composure.

Focus on the task at hand.

The court clerk stood and cleared his throat. "All rise for the honourable Judge Meredith Spencer."

The court rose at one. Jake followed suit. A distinguished-looking lady entered. He guessed mid-fifties. Her greying hair was immaculately styled. Eyes bright and sharp. Keenly observing everything. They settled on him. His life was in her hands.

She took her seat. The court followed suit.

The clerk stood and addressed the court. "We are here today to hear preliminary evidence and arguments against Jake Charles charged by the crown with manslaughter. Mr Charles, How do you plead?"

He stood again and took a deep breath. Loud and clear for all to hear. "Not guilty."

"Very well." Spenser addressed Carrington "Does the defence have anything to say at this time?"

Carrington hauled himself to his feet. "Your honour. Defence requests a pretrial motion for dismissal. Evidence has come to into our possession which demonstrates my client's innocence. With the courts permission may the defence be permitted to show the court?"

The prosecution lawyer stood. "Objection your honour. The prosecution has not been made aware of any such evidence."

Carrington smiled warmly and turned to the judge. "This evidence came into our possession only late yesterday evening your honour. It completely discredits the prosecution's witness statement. A statement - I might add - that has seen my client, an innocent man sat in prison for the past fortnight away from his loving family." He turned and gestured to Claire and the girls.

Beads of sweat rolled from the prosecution lawyer's brow. He removed his glasses and mustered all his indignity. "Really your honour, I must prot…"

Judge Spencer silently raised a hand cutting him off. "I would like to see where this evidence takes us."

He started as if to object. She glared. A vein in his temple throbbed blue. He slumped in his seat.

Judge Spencer addressed Carrington directly. "Please proceed."

Carrington handed a flash drive to the court clerk. She plugged it into a computer on her desk. After a few moments a grainy image appeared on the large screen mounted on the wall behind the clerk.

Judge Spencer sat forward in her chair watching intently.

Silence descended in the court.

Carrington rose and addressed the court. He painted on his most solemn face, but the wry smile was difficult to hide. The screen showed a black and white image of an entrance to an alleyway lit by a streetlamp

"We are looking at CCTV footage taken from a security camera from a private house facing the entrance to the alleyway. My investigators noticed the camera during their search of the scene and spoke to the owners. They were able to retrieve the footage." He turned to the judge directly. "Something I might add the local constabulary failed to do."

The prosecution lawyer sank lower in his chair, like a chastised child after a telling off.

A dark figure appeared on the screen walking briskly along the road. As he approached the alleyway his face lit up white from the streetlamp glare.

Carrington provided the narration. "I don't believe there need be any dispute this man is my client walking alone into the alleyway."

Jake turned into the alleyway and disappeared.

Silence once again descended in the court.

A car pulled up and a man jumped out carrying a small club. He turned to look around. Again, the face glowed white in the streetlamp.

Jake's knuckles turned white as he gripped the handrail in the dock. Judge spencer glared hard at the prosecution lawyer.

Carrington pulled a single sheet from his briefcase and began to read.

"Following the altercation in the bar, my accomplice Yuri and I were walking home. We were passing through an alleyway when we were attacked by the defendant. He had a knife and stabbed Yuri in the neck. Then he turned on me. I managed to fight him off and he ran away."

He turned to the prosecution lawyer. "Would you care to

ask your lead... My apologies, your only witness to revise his statement?"

The prosecution lawyer hauled himself to his feet. His Adam's apple bobbed as he swallowed repeatedly. His thinning pate shone as beads dripped down his face. He mopped his brow with a handkerchief.

"Your honour. I can only apologise for this embarrassing situation. Clearly the witness has attempted to dupe the police and the prosecution. Of course, we withdraw the witness."

Carrington pounced on his wounded prey. "Attempted and succeeded to dupe it would appear," he chuckled. "Your honour. The defence requests an immediate motion for dismissal. I believe my client has suffered enough at the hands of this witness."

Judge Spencer sat forward and turned toward the prosecution lawyer. "May I assume you wish to withdraw the charges directed at Mr Charles?" she thundered.

"We do Your Honour," he added sheepishly.

"I might also suggest your witness is arrested and charged with obstruction of justice as a matter of urgency."

She turned back to Jake. "Mr Charles. I can only apologise for the dreadful disruption to your life and the shameful incompetence of the police and prosecution. The crack of the gavel reverberated around the court. This case is dismissed. You are free to go.

He closed his eyes. He felt light. Floating almost. Like he could fly away from this place as the words sank in.

Free to go.

He turned to his family. Tears slipped down Claire's face. Violet and Chase sobbed uncontrollably through happy smiles.

Their ordeal was finally over. Daddy was coming home.

CHAPTER 20

Jake's emotional dam finally overflowed. In prison he had buried his feelings deep. Kept them locked away from the watchful eyes of guards and prisoners. He could hold it no longer and the tears came, blurring his vision.

"It's over Jake. We did it." Carrington turned to him extending his hand.

"You did it. How can I ever thank you for your help?" He took his hand and shook it warmly.

"Go to your family."

Jake left the dock passing through a gate into the public gallery. He picked his girls up in turn. He buried his face in their hair, revelling in the warm and familiar but long absent scent.

Claire stood before him radiant in beauty and strength. He put Chase down and pulled her close. "I couldn't have done it without you."

"It's over baby. Let's go home." She smiled and laughed as they hugged tight. Her tears were cold and wet against his cheek. The girls joined in, wrapping their arms around their parents. Finally, they were a family again.

He closed his eyes, savouring the moment.

I am a free man.

He bathed in the loving bosom of his family, finally at peace.

He opened his eyes. There he was once more. Staring. Silent.

There was no uproar. No shouted threats. Just controlled menace. He stared with the eyes of the devil himself, chilling Jake to his core. His moment of joy punctured, and he deflated like a popped balloon. His stomach felt heavy, leaden. Like someone had filled his belly with ice, as cold realisation dawned that a new chapter of misery and fear may soon bear down upon his family.

He put it behind him as they left the courtroom together. Jake and his family were led by Carrington who brushed the jostling crowd aside. Raynes breezed past with a uniformed officer. She stopped on her heel and turned to him.

"Congratulation Mr Charles," she forced through clenched teeth. "I trust there are no hard feelings. You realise I was just doing my job?" She extended her hand. He hesitated then took it. Her fingers were long and bony. Her grip strong. Crushing even. Without another word she strode off with the uniformed officer tagging along in her wake.

Carrington turned to him, eyebrows raised.

Jake shook his head and blew out in exasperation. "Give me two minutes will you. I need a moment." He found the gents and closed the door behind him shutting away the rest of the world. He closed his eyes and took deep breaths.

"I am a free man." He said the words out loud in the silence of the toilets. He filled the basin and doused his face with ice cold water.

His moment alone was interrupted as the door opened behind him. DS Thompson entered and joined hm at the sinks. Jake stared back icily in the mirror as Thompson ran the faucet and washed his hands.

"Hello Mr Charles. I'm glad it went your way today."

Jake turned to him and smiled thinly. "Nothing personal but you will appreciate I have just about had enough of the police." He dried his hands and turned to face him. "Perhaps you should have believed me in the first place."

Thompson pressed a card into Jake's hand and looked him directly in the eye. "If you need anything from the police, please call me immediately. My mobile number is on there. Call it. Day or night if you feel threatened."

Jake took a step back.

Threatened.

The word jolted him like a shock of electricity from the mains as he thought of the man watching him in court.

Thompson continued. His face impassive. "You know who I am speaking of. The Vasins might not take kindly to what happened. Please just be careful. As I said, call me anytime."

He left leaving Jake alone and shaken. He needed to get away from this courtroom. Away from the police. Away from the Vasins. It was time to get back to normal life. He placed the card in his wallet and headed back to re-join his family.

"Jake old boy," Carrington said smiling jubilantly. He clapped him on the shoulder. "Let's go."

Carrington headed for the courthouse doors with Jake and his family following. Claire clung onto Jake like a limpet, unwilling to be parted from him for a second. As if he could be whisked away from her again.

They left the court room for the last time, oblivious to the dark eyes watching intently from the balcony overlooking the foyer. They exited through the main doors and down the stone steps of the courthouse. Reporters jostled for position shouting questions. Carrington directed the Charles family into a waiting car and turned to address the reporters.

"My client has asked me to make a brief statement. He is sorry a man's life was lost in this terrible incident. He wishes to extend his condolences to the family of the deceased. Now he wishes to return home with his family. That's all folks." He held up his hand to silence the barrage of questions and strode down the steps to the wating car. He hauled his bulk into the front seat.

"Onwards please driver. Let's get these good people away. You can drop me at the station." They sped off leaving a trail of reporters frantically snapping pictures at the departing car.

Claire tapped Carrington on the shoulder. "Are they going to print photos of us in the papers? Surely, they can't do that?"

He turned in his seat to face her. "This story has national interest. Self-defence homicide cases always do. It will probably make the papers. And yes, they can print a picture of you and Jake I'm afraid."

"What about the children?" Claire nodded towards the girls.

"Well, that's the good news. They can't print any pictures of the children, so nothing to worry about there. And these stories fade quickly into obscurity. In a few days your pictures will be wrapping up some drunk's chips."

"What's the plan now?" asked Jake. Can we go home?"

Carrington glanced at the children. Chase was reading a book. Violet doodling on a pad. Were they listening?

"I think it would be er…. Better to get away for a while." He raised his eyebrows solemnly and stared directly at Jake and Claire in turn. He extracted a manilla folder from his briefcase.

Mr Taylor owns a rental investment property in Scotland. A bolthole if you like. He has instructed me to make it available for as long as you need it. I strongly recommend you take some time to get away away from...." He paused. "From all the furore surrounding the case. Let the heat die down for now."

The brief moment of joy dropped from Claire's face as she processed what he wasn't saying. She stole a glance at the children. They remained oblivious.

She looked at Jake. Her lips were thin and drawn back. The lines around her eyes more pronounced than he remembered. "We need to get away Jake." Her voice was shaking as she stole a glance back at the children. "We have had... visitors while you were away."

Jake shot a look at her as he processed what she meant He glanced behind at the girls. They were both looking out the window unconcerned. He nodded imperceptibly.

"Who is this Taylor person?" she asked. "Can he be trusted?"

"I will fill you in on all the details later," he replied. "It's not important now but I think he can be trusted. Let's go home. We should pack and leave immediately."

Carrington looked at them both sadly.

He pities us.

Carrington's features softened. "You don't deserve any of this. Taylor's place is perfect for what you need. Remote wilderness. Long country walks around the lake. I've been there myself. Get away and enjoy yourselves."

He nodded hurriedly. "Let's do it."

The car pulled up outside the train station. With some

effort Carrington extricated himself from the car and positioned himself by Jake's open window. "I know this has been tough for you all. Put it behind you now and get on with the rest of your lives. When you arrive at the cottage find Mr Macintosh. He is the groundsman who looks after the place for Mr Taylor. He lives in a cabin in the nearby woods. He will show you the ropes. Make sure you have everything you need. He's a bit of a strange old stick. Typical gruff Scotsman. But he will help should you need anything." He rapped his knuckles smartly on the car door. Goodbye and fare thee well. It has been nice to make your acquaintance." He bowed theatrically then turned smartly on his heel and departed.

Claire stared absent minded out of the window as the taxi pulled away. "Are we sure about this?" she whispered. "Taking gifts from convicts. I don't know Jake"

She turned to him. Imploring him for answers he could not give.

He caught her eye and shook his head almost imperceptibly. He raised a finger and mouthed the words. "Not now."

She turned away again.

Every mile took them further from the hustle and bustle of the city centre and the courthouse. They passed through the open fields of surrounding villages bathed in the sunshine of a beautiful early summer's day. It was a good day to regain his freedom, yet he still felt trapped.

The girls argued playfully. Blissfully unaware while Claire and Jake made mental plans for their trip. As they arrived at their home village on the outskirts of Cambridge, they passed his favourite and familiar places. The village centre with his local pub where he spent many happy evenings playing chess. The girls' school and the park where he took Scruffy running each day.

He looked with longing as the realisation dawned that he had to leave it all behind again. For a while anyway.

They pulled into their road. The house loomed large ahead of him. He felt the sting of tears in the back of his eyes. He was home. He checked the road. No parked cars with men sitting staring.

How long till they come? Today? Tomorrow? Never?

He crouched down and pulled Chase and Violet in close. "Listen carefully girls. We have exciting news." He forced his mouth into a perfect copy of a smile. "We are going on a road trip to an amazing place called Scotland. We are leaving today so we must be quick."

Chase and Violet stole excited glances at each other.

"You must go and pack straight away. As soon as we are ready, we are off."

The girls whooped and cheered. They ran to the door arguing over which toys and makeup were essential.

Claire was facing away. Hands folded across her chest. Shoulders slumped forward. He approached her from behind. Wrapped his arms around her stomach. He inhaled deeply. She smelt of citrus shampoo and rose perfume.

Take charge of this.

"Now is not the time for discussion. We need to get away now. Let's go inside and get packed. We can talk on the journey when the girls are sleeping. Pack light. Essentials only and outdoor gear. Anything else we buy on the way. Go now."

She turned and wrapped her arms around him. There

were no tears, no arguments. Just acceptance. She pulled away in silence.

Claws scrabbled at the front door accompanied by excited barking. Claire pushed it open and Scruffy came tearing out tail wagging furiously. He crouched to meet her. She launched herself at him. Paws on his shoulders; she smothered his face with long wet licks. He laughed and snuggled into the soft fur around her neck. A loving moment of two long lost companions reunited.

They packed fast. Military efficiency with minimal communication. No list was consulted. Decisions made on the fly.

Torch. Matches. Walking boots. Jackets. One case for each of them.

In under two hours they were in the car and on their way. Fearful eyes scoured the road ahead for unfamiliar cars and people. Both gripped with fear of a last-minute encounter. Jake's knuckles were white with tension on the steering wheel. His left knee shook back and forth. Claire's mouth and brow thin and drawn. Like someone pulling her face tight from behind.

The girls stared out of the window listening to their music. Happily engrossed in their own worlds of isolation as they began the long drive North. Every mile away from home represented a mile further from the Vasins. Every car in the rear-view mirror represented a potential threat

Thirty minutes in and Jake's shoulders relaxed back in his seat. One finger guided the steering wheel. His foot tapped in time with the music. He stole a look at Claire. She looked five years younger. The eyes softened. Lips full. The tight, drawn expression gone. She placed a hand on his. They locked fingers tight and drove on in silence.

CHAPTER 21

The top-ranking members of the Vasin family regarded each other in the dim light. The atmosphere was dark and brooding, as was the mood of the three men. They sat convened around a large circular oak table. A half empty bottle of Vodka sat on the table. Each of them cradled a crystal glass topped with the fiery liquid.

Vlad Vasin was the eldest brother and head of the family. He wore a charcoal suit and black shirt. Black hair greying at the temples was swept back to his collar. His skin smooth and tanned. Dark hooded eyes fixed on his brothers as he spoke quietly in his native Russian.

They paid attention.

"Do we know where he is yet? This Mudak. He must pay for what he did."

Sergei Vasin was the first to respond. Sergei towered half a head over his older brother. His scalp was battle-scarred and hair cropped close. His bushy beard hid a crop of nicotine-stained teeth of which several were missing.

"We know where he lives moy brat but we must take care. Our source has given us polite warning. He is civilian and high profile. They not want headlines of messy revenge. This bring heat and damage business. They warn against retribution. We must not appear to have hand in this matter.

Vlad stood and stared his brother down. "Since when do we take instruction from the police? We pay them do we not?

They work for us. What do you think we should do?"

Sergei continued. "We have watched house for last couple days. There is no sign. They have gone to ground. We know not where."

Vlad considered this tapping the table quietly with his finger. "What about the lawyer? He must know where they are. I saw them leave together after the court case."

"I don't know about him," Sergei replied. "I had not yet considered that option. Is wise to bring him into it?"

Vlad sat again laying his palms on the table. "I am disappointed in you Sergei. The lawyer will know where they have gone. Find him and extract what he knows."

Sergei lowered his head. The rebuke stung. "We know not where he lives. I would have to make enquiries."

Vlad took a phone from his pocket and dialled. It answered instantly.

"The lawyer. I want his address." It was an instruction. Not a request.

"What do you care? Just do what you are told. That's what we pay you for." He scribbled an address on a notepad and hung up without another word. He slid the note across the table to Sergei. "Go talk to him. Find out where they are."

"And then... What do you want us to do?"

Vlad slammed his palms on the table as he stood roaring. "I want that bastard skinned. He killed our baby brother. What the fuck you think I want?" Spittle flecked from his mouth. His breathing heavy, laboured. Anger and hatred twisted his features into something grotesque. Like a gargoyle in the half light.

He resumed his measured tone. "What would papa say if he were still alive?" He crossed his chest. "You think he would allow this insult against the family?"

The ice rattled in Sergei's glass betraying his fear. He laid it on the table. He had never witnessed his brother lose control of his emotions. He gestured to their younger brother Dimitri. "We all agree he pay. I want him too. But we have to be careful. We must find way to do this clean."

Vlad took his seat again and sipped his drink. Control regained.

"We have people we can use for this kind of work," Dimitry added. "We can bring an outside agent in."

Vlad snapped his head round. He wagged a finger slowly in front of Dimitry's face. "He must know who. And why. This man took our brother's life. No outsiders. This stays in the family. I want to look in his eyes. To make him suffer as we suffer. That is my final word."

Sergei nodded his agreement. "Vlad is right. I make this man pay myself. We are agreed that we do ourselves. Then can be sure it is done properly. But it brings risk of police attention."

Vlad picked up the vodka and topped up their glasses. "That is my concern. I have leverage. They can be persuaded to look the other way."

Sergei stared his brother in the eye. "Tomorrow we talk to lawyer. Then track this Mudak down." The three men clinked glasses and downed the iced vodka.

"Two of us will be plenty," Vlad replied. "For Jake Charles though. I want a team of four."

He turned to his younger brother. "Get Nicolai ready to move. We will be in touch when we have location. No mistakes."

"Consider it done brother," Dimitri replied. "One small problem. He will be with his family. What about wife and kids? What do we do with them?"

Silence hung heavy in the air. Vlad poured them each another vodka. "We want him to suffer do we not? He has taken our family. Let us repay the favour."

***

Simon Carrington paused from tending his flowers and wiped the sweat from his eyes. He rose slowly from kneeling prone on a cushion and stretched the ache from his bones. The sun beat down scorching him pink like his roses. He turned to gaze across the wide expanse of gardens and the hills beyond.

The Surrey estate had belonged to a prominent Tory MP descended from aristocracy and old money. A plane crash claimed him and his wife in 1947 and the fortune passed to their two teenage sons. It took them less than a decade of women and substance abuse to burn through a family fortune built over generations. Carrington's father snapped up a bargain in the ensuing fire sale and set about renovating the property which had fallen into disrepair. On his own parent's death Carrington inherited the luxurious family home in which he had grown up happily.

Now he lived alone but for the housekeeper Monty who dealt with the day-to-day management of the property and grounds during Carrington's frequent absence. Monty had been with the family for decades and the two men had grown close friends. Carrington often questioned the practicality of maintaining such an enormous house, but he could not bring himself to sell. He did not need the money. His parents left him the property debt-free along with numerous other assets. With the sizeable fees he now commanded, Carrington had amassed enough wealth to see him through several lifetimes.

His swallowed repeatedly to slake the raging thirst in his mouth. His head throbbed at the temple from the heat and exertion.

He downed tools and ambled across the lawn past the pool

shimmering blue and silver in the sunlight. With Monty away for the weekend all was quiet but for the gentle song of the many birds who frequented the gardens. He crossed the patio and entered the kitchen through wall to wall sliding doors to make tea. He sighed contentedly as he surveyed his estate through the kitchen window. Fortune has smiled on Carrington.

The aroma of roasting spiced meat filled the kitchen. Carrington knelt to open the oven and check on dinner. He was entertaining tonight. A Lord and Lady no less and was preparing Moroccan spiced lamb served with rice and flatbreads. Carrington had spent time travelling through Africa and Asia in his youth and had absorbed some rudimentary culinary skills of their people. He made tea and drew a large glass of ice-cold water from the dispenser on the fridge. Time to rest. He returned to the patio and settled on the rattan to enjoy the sunshine.

The sound of the doorbell roused Carrington from his sleep. He rubbed his eyes and hauled himself to his feet. His brow furrowed. He was expecting no visitors. No deliveries. His neighbours were not prone to dropping in unannounced. Who could be bothering him?

He opened the door. The cosh smashed into his nose before he registered it.

The world went dark.

***

Sergei Vasin turned to check the driveway behind him. All was clear.

He stepped over Carrington's body and beckoned Vlad who was watching from the side gate. Both men wore blue surgical gloves.

"Bring him and close the door." Vlad nodded at the crumpled body of Carrington.

Sergei effortlessly hoisted the dead weight onto his

shoulder. The hallway opened onto a broad wooden staircase leading to a mezzanine landing.

The décor was simple and elegant. The house spacious. Tasteful artwork adorned the walls. Double doors opened onto a large open-plan kitchen and dining area. All polished oak flooring and gleaming stainless-steel appliances. Modern. Clean. An enormous oak dining table dominated the space overlooking the patio through wall-to-wall glass doors.

Vlad whistled. "Our friend here is doing nicely for himself. Secure him." He pointed to one of the ornate wooden chairs surrounding the dining table. His quiet and pleasant voice did not betray his cold nature.

Sergei dropped Carrington into the chair. He extracted cable ties from his suit pocket and tied him securely. Arms bound at the wrist and elbows. Legs at knees and ankles. He slid a hood over the prisoner's head.

"Such a nice day. Let's head outside." He dragged the chair behind him to the poolside. "Now we wait."

CHAPTER 22

The agonising throbbing spread from his face deep into his skull.

He opened his eyes to darkness. Panic set in.

He tried to lift his arm but could not move. A rag was stuffed in his mouth. He cried out muffled grunting noises.

What has happened to me?

He tried to piece events together but through pain and disorientation his memories floated away like sycamore seeds on the wind.

His heart thumped heavy in his chest. He sucked in sharp uncontrolled gasps through the gag. He forced himself to take deep breaths to regain composure. He listened intently craning his head from side to side.

"Good afternoon Simon. How are you bearing up?" The voice pierced the silence, Cultured. Crisp. A soft Russian accent.

Carrington tried to respond. He could manage nothing but a muffled unintelligible grunt.

"Let me help you with that Simon. We have much to discuss." The hood slid over his face as it was lifted. Light streamed in. The throbbing in his skull intensified. He shut his eyes. He blinked slowly allowing his vision to become accustomed. Someone was behind him. The rag was pulled from his mouth. He stared in horror. He was bound to a chair facing the large glass doors. The gardens and pool were reflected in the glass, as were the two men behind him.

"Do you know who I am Simon? Why we are here?"

His hands shook uncontrollably. Fear wracked his body.

"I have no idea. What do you want?" His words came in ragged gasps.

"You can call me Vlad. This is my brother Sergei. You should try and relax.

Do as we say and there is no reason for you to come to harm. We are here for a reason. For some information. Give us what we want and we will leave. It's that simple."

Carrington gulped oxygen. He nodded his agreement.

"We have been observing you for some time. You represent a client who is of interest to my family. This person has no ties to you aside from your professional relationship. There is no reason for you to protect him. You have discharged your responsibilities to him now. This person is of course Jake Charles. We would very much like to speak with him but he has disappeared. Where is he?"

Vlad stepped from behind Carrington into his line of view. He recognized him instantly from public gallery at court. Dark unfeeling eyes searched his face. As if Jake Charles location were written upon it.

"He went on holiday. To get away after the trial."

"That's good. An excellent start," Vlad replied. "Where did he go?"

"That I do not know. He told me he was taking off for a couple of weeks. I have no idea where they were heading."

Vlad shook his head slowly. "Simon, Simon. We were getting along fine. You need to know this is a time-sensitive issue for me. I need details before we can leave. Please can I urge you to cooperate?"

Vlad examined his fingernails idly. He returned his gaze to Carrington. He laughed and nodded to his accomplice. "Such a dreadful cliché I know, but Sergei here really is the bad cop in this scenario. If I do not get what I need he will question you. I would encourage you to avoid that."

Sergei slowly drew closer and smiled revealing a crop of nicotine-stained teeth peeking out through his bushy beard. Several were missing. He too stared with eyes devoid of empathy.

"I am less keen for you to cooperate than my brother here. I enjoy this aspect of my work." He drew a large bowie knife from a sheath under his left armpit. The blade was at least eight inches long and serrated down one side. It glinted in the sunlight as he brandished it slowly in front of Carrington's face inches from his eyes.

He turned away imagining...

"Please," he cried. "I don't know where he is. You have to believe me."

Sergei leant in close. He stank of meat and sweat. "I do not believe you my friend. But I will. Everyone talks in the end."

Vlad approached again. "Shall we talk by the pool? Such a lovely day and your gardens are magnificent." They lifted him under the armpits. One either side dragging him backwards. They placed him close to the edge of the pool facing away.

"Have you heard of waterboarding Simon?" Vlad walked slowly back and forward in front of him. Watching closely. Measuring fear.

"Please. I have told you all I know."

Vlad smiled menacingly. "Did you know it was used as an interrogation technique by the Spanish inquisition? It leaves no lasting physical injury when done properly. It was also a favourite in Cambodia under Pol Pot's leadership. Nasty people.

Of course, more recently MI6 and CIA collaborated to kidnap and torture their enemies. They do not call it that. They invented new terms to sanitise and normalise it. Extraordinary rendition Enhanced interrogation. Legal terms invented to permit kidnap and torture. But it is torture, plain and simple and is very unpleasant. I should know. We both do." He gestured to his brother. "If you do not give me what I want, you will too. The result is always the same. Confession is inevitable at the hands of a skilled interrogator." He paused and bent to Carrington, bringing his face in close. "The hardest part is ensuring that you do not kill the subject. The CIA took precautions. Doctors on standby. Defibrillators in case the heart stopped. We must rely on the good judgement of Sergei here." He laughed. "It shames me to admit I did not last long."

He nodded towards his brother. "Sergei is much tougher. They had to go at him for nearly two hours before he finally gave in. But give in he did. Everyone does. Can you imagine two whole hours of being kept on the point of death by drowning? Excruciating. Sergei has intimate knowledge of the technique. He can make things most disagreeable for you." He drew closer still. The smile had gone. His expression devoid of pity or emotion. "I can tell when people have information I want. For the last time, is there anything you want to tell me?"

Carrington's pulse raced. His terrified mind scrambled to unravel his options.

This could all end if he told them.

If you talk, you kill them all.

He looked at the sun-filled sky on this beautiful day.

He knew for sure it was to be his last.

He steeled himself. "I've told you all I know." His voice was steady. Calm. "Jake and his family went away after the trial. He did not tell me where they were going. I am glad he did not. I know you are here to kill me. And when you find Jake, you will kill him too. So fuck you. Do what you need to do. But you won't get anything as I have nothing to give."

Vlad nodded slowly. He looked upon his victim with newfound respect.

"So be it. You are a brave man. You show courage which is rare in this world. Unfortunately it will not help you." He tipped the chair back so Carrington lay prone, legs in the air, head next to the swimming pool. The water lapped at the edge. He squinted from the sun directly overhead.

Sergei returned from the house. He carried a towel and a large jug. "Slowly Sergei. We must give our friend time to acclimatise."

Carrington's mind raced. He knew he could not hold out.

Feed them lies.

Vlad looked upon him devoid of pity. "Last chance."

He was shaking now. Unable to move and completely helpless. Total paralysis. Sergei placed the towel across his face. He could see nothing and already it stifled his breathing. He sucked in hard. Desperate to draw in as much oxygen as possible.

Cold water smothered his face and filled his nostrils. Cascaded down his throat. He held his breath as long as he could. And then he could hold it no longer.

He inhaled sucking water back. A violent burning sensation seared his lungs. He screamed, muffled through the rag as the world faded to nothing.

***

He was wrenched back into consciousness. He vomited violently expelling water from his stomach and lungs. Eyes streaming. Unable to focus. Excruciating pain burned in his lungs. He gulped in a breath. Then another.

He was sitting upright. The towel was gone from his face.

Water and snot gushed from his nose and mouth.

"Please, please, no more," he begged his tormentors.

Vlad approached from behind and brought his face in close. "Would you believe me if I told you that was just fifteen seconds? It does not sound long, but it feels like a lifetime."

"I've told you everything I know. You must believe me. Please no more. If I knew I would have told you by now."

Vlad moved in front of him. Carrington stared into his eyes. Unflinching. Cold. Dark.

"Unfortunately, I do not believe you. Not yet anyway. Must we continue?"

Carrington shook his head. "I don't have anything to give you." He began to sob uncontrollably.

"Again Sergei."

The chair was tipped again and the wet towel covered his face. Water flowed into his nose and mouth filling his lungs and bloated stomach. Pain and fear wracked his body. He spasmed violently against the restraints. His bowels opened. The water in his lungs burned like lava. The darkness consumed him.

***

The light formed a pinprick in the black expanse. It grew closer. Brighter. Warmer. Death's warm embrace?

The image in front of him swam in and out of focus. A shapeless figure looked on in concern. The mouth moved but said nothing.

Silence birthed noise. Ringing bells chiming in his head. The base drum boom in his skull. The violent retching of a wounded or dying animal. The ring of a slap he did not feel.

He vomited again, coughing, gasping for precious oxygen. The stench of faeces filled the air.

"Wake up Simon. Wake up."

Another stinging slap and he was there.

"Nearly lost you there. You are tough but you cannot take much more."

"Please stop. I know where they are." His voice had taken on a metallic timbre. Like a lifelong smoker. "I'll tell you. I'll tell you." he rasped.

Vlad said nothing. He moved in close. Watching. Listening.

"Dorset. They are heading for Dorset. There is a hotel there. The Maypole. That's all I know."

Vlad placed his palms together and bowed. "Those who believe themselves tough always break so quickly. And then I meet someone like you Simon. You have courage. But I must be sure." He turned to Sergei. He pulled the bowie from its sheath and held the tip at Carrington's eyeball.

Sergei's spoke with a guttural, base tone. Thick with the accent of his native Russia. Devoid of the clipped and cultured tone of his brother. "You tell us truth? If not we come back. Will not be nice for you. There are worse tortures than a man can endure. Native American Indians would flay a man's entire hide. One piece and still he live for hours?" He brandished the knife glinting in the sun.

Vlad watched. Scrutinised his face. Like reading a book.

"I believe you are telling us the truth. Thank you Simon. It truly has been a pleasure to meet you." He nodded to Sergei and stepped away.

Sergei withdrew the blade smiling. He raised it high above his head and paused. Then with both hands he buried the blade to the hilt in Carrington's chest

He gazed in shock at the blade handle sprouting from his

chest. His mouth opened and closed like a fish floundering on the riverbank. His lungs squeezed tight. As if some giant was wringing his lungs like a wet towel. The colour drained from the world around him. His eyes rolled back into his head as the world turned black and the welcoming arms of death enveloped him.

***

Sergei withdrew the blade and wiped it clean on Carrington's shirt. He placed it back in the sheath beneath his left armpit. He stood in front of the corpse, muttered a few words of prayer and closed the eyes of his victim.

"Brave man," he said to Vlad who was moving toward the kitchen.

"Have a look around and see what you can find. Be quick. We leave for Dorset."

Sergei followed Vlad inside and began rifling through the kitchen drawers. They yielded nothing.

"I'll check upstairs. He will have a study or an office." Vlad ascended the stairs two at a time. They led to a landing dominated by a crystal chandelier. To the right a hallway led to eight doors. Vlad checked each in turn. Mostly bedrooms for guests or spare bathrooms. He found the main bedroom. Spacious and tastefully decorated overlooking the pool and gardens. The view somewhat tainted by the corpse tied to a chair.

The seventh door revealed what he was looking for. Vlad knew people. He knew where they would keep their secrets. A polished walnut desk sat beneath the window overlooking the gardens.

Laptop. Phone. Writing pad. He fired up the laptop. Password protected. Waste of time. Move on.

There was a drawer on the underside of the desk. Locked.

He felt around searching for a key. Nothing.

He extracted his knife. He worked the tip between the drawer and the housing. The desk was old. Sturdy. He twisted with both hands. The old wood splintered around the lock. He slid the drawer open.

He extracted a slim leather-bound journal. Tasteful. Exquisite. Like everything in the house. Vlad sat and leafed through and read the entries for the past few days. Nothing jumped out at him. He went back to the draw. There was a plastic wallet containing a sheaf of papers. He began to flick through. At first he missed it and went past but some lizard instinct nagged at the back of his brain. He returned to the document. It was a bill for cleaning services for a holiday cottage dated three days ago. He looked closer. At the top of the document was an indentation. He could barely make it out when he held the document to the light. Someone had written something when resting on this page. Maybe a post it note had once been attached. He rummaged in the draw and found a pencil. Gently he began to shade over the indentation with the side of the pencil. Gradually the text was revealed.

Jake Charles –8th June.

"Simon. Simon. So brave and so sly. You did lie to me." He sat back in the chair and smiled.

CHAPTER 23

They followed deserted roads that snaked through the rolling hills of the Scottish Highlands. They drove past shimmering lochs and bluffs covered in heather blooming purple in the summer sunshine. They passed through tiny villages where barely a person was to be seen. Eventually the villages gave way to wilderness. They drove on through valleys surrounded on both sides by towering pine forest. It was hard to believe they were still in the United Kingdom.

"Twenty minutes girls. Nearly there." Chase and Violet gazed open-mouthed in amazement at the stunning scenery.

"So cool," Violet gasped. "Is this what it will be like where we are going? It's so different from home."

"I think so," Claire replied. She opened the pack that Carrington had given them and read from the brochure. "*An isolated and remote cabin nestling in the valley overlooking the loch. Forty-five minutes from the nearest town. We suggest you bring what provisions you need with you. You can enjoy the surrounding countryside, take long walks through the pine forest, and swim in the loch (for the brave and hardy).* It sounds like we are on our own. Just the five of us. This will be like no holiday we have been on before. So let's enjoy it."

Claire placed her hand on Jake's and took a deep breath. Back together as a family. Just them and the wilderness. It felt so refreshing. The stress of the past few weeks was in the rear-view mirror. The girls were relaxed and happy.

Prison. Lawyers. The Vasins. It already felt like a lifetime ago.

They drove on through the forest. The road hugged the water's edge eventually breaking away to the left taking them up a steep hill. They emerged through the treeline as the forest gave way to a clearing.

There it was.

The cottage sat on a hillside overlooking the loch. Jake pulled the car onto the driveway next to an old crumbling stone garage set away from the cottage.

"Here we are. What do you think girls? Shall we go and explore?"

They jumped out of the car chattering excitedly. "Can we look inside?" Chase panted. "I want to see my room."

"Come on let's go." Jake opened the boot and Scruffy jumped out licking each of them excitedly.

He unlocked the front door and the girls pushed past scrabbling up the stairs, squabbling about who was getting the bigger room. Jake took Claire's hand and stepped inside.

The house smelled old. Musty. Exactly like a house that had been unlived in and locked up for the winter. He had to stoop to avoid the gnarled wooden beams that traversed the cottage. The skeleton that had supported the house for a hundred years.

A heavy wooden door adorned with wrought iron led through to the kitchen diner. Cosy and functional rather than modern. A fireplace sat in one corner stacked with a wood supply in a large wicker basket. A heavy oak dining table sat in front of patio doors that opened onto an expansive deck.

Jake unlocked the doors and pushed them open. The freshness of summer flowed in as the old musty air flowed out. Like the cottage was breathing a sigh of relief to be lived in once more.

Jake stepped out onto the deck. It was cut around a circular firepit with boulders cemented around the edge. He pulled the covers off a garden swing chair and sat gazing out at the loch and mountains beyond.

Past the deck the lawn sloped gently away to the edge of the water. A boat was tied to a rickety wooden jetty that jutted into the loch. Golden sunlight danced across the surface. Birds swept low across the shimmering water. Off in the distance in the centre of the loch a wooden platform bobbed on tractor tyres and served as a resting place for passing birds.

Claire joined him and they sat hand in hand listening. The gentle lap of water against the jetty. The wind whistling through the trees. The staccato call of the cormorants as they rested in the sun.

It was a glorious location and Jake fell in love at once.

The burden of the previous weeks melted away. Like he was shedding the skin from one life ready to embark on a new and exciting future. Ready to emerge and grow into his new self. A life of freedom and love to be spent with those closest to him.

They sat in silence absorbing the tranquillity of their new home. Minds freed from worry. All the while blissfully unaware of the pure evil stalking and closing in.

***

She stared at the skeletal hand lying limp in her own. It looked so fragile. Like the skin was made of tissue paper wrapped around spindly veins that pulsed blue. It was cold to the touch. Life clung to the old lady. Her blood limped through her arteries wafted by a weakening heart. Her chest rose and fell slowly as her lungs fought the losing battle against gravity and managed to suck in yet another rattling breath.

She lay on her back, wafer thin eyelids closed and fluttering. The skin of her face and neck was ghostly white and loose. Thin grey hair fanned out on the pillow. Her mouth hung open. Lips drawn back against yellowed teeth. Like looking at a living cadaver. She had been given days to live by the doctor. It was hard to believe she would make it through the next minute.

Raynes kissed her mother on the forehead. She left the room without looking back as silent tears slipped down her cheeks.

***

Thompson sat towards the back of the café facing the door leafing through a file. He closed it and stood as she approached. He smiled thinly. His lips pulled back tight in grim sympathy.

"How is she doing?"

She shook her head slowly. "Any time now."

"I'm sorry." He sat back down.

She sat and ordered coffee. Strong and black no sugar.

"What you working on?" She nodded to the slim manilla file on the table in front of them.

He coughed and glanced at the file furtively. He picked it up and slid it into his battered leather case. "I'm moving on Raynes. I've put in for a transfer request. Crawford has rubber stamped it."

Curious she thought, her interest piqued as he slid the file away. She noticed he could not meet her eye. Her coffee arrived. She thanked the waitress and took a long hot gulp that burned bitter as she swallowed.

"Where are you going?"

"I'm joining a unit in London," he lied. "It's time for a change. This Charles case has left me burnt out. What about you?"

She stirred absently at her coffee. "I'm taking some time

off. Crawford is pissed at the fuck up. No doubt the same reason you have chosen to bail out." She stared at Thompson with disdain, unable to hide her distaste. "It's mum's final days and I want to be with her. After she ...." She tailed off and took a deep breath. "After she is gone, I will get back to work I guess. No doubt Crawford will find a replacement to reform this crack team we have forged." She laughed and gestured between the two of them. It came out hollow. They both knew it was a lie.

Thompson looked her directly in the eye. "What about Jake Charles, and his family?"

She recoiled, as if the very name was poison to her. As if it made her physically sick. In reality it did. Jake Charles was responsible for the worst strike against her career in a decade. She swallowed. Her voice wavered "What about him? He is free to go."

"The Vasins. Aren't you worried they will target him? He killed one of their own. They are not the type to forgive and forget."

Raynes shrugged. "I'm a detective. Not personal protection for the public. Someone else's problem."

Thompson nodded and looked at her thoughtfully. "Someone else's problem. I suppose you are right."

She stood and drained the last of her coffee. "I guess this is goodbye then?" She offered her hand. He stood and took it, and they shook wordlessly. She strode off.

"I am sorry about your mother." He spoke to her retreating back. She waved a dismissive thanks and left without turning round.

He sat for a while staring blankly at the wall as he thought long and hard how to deal with the thorny issue of Jake Charles and his family. His phone rang. He recognised the number, knew who was calling. He flipped up the green icon and put the handset to his ear. He sat in silence without acknowledging the caller, listening intently. His face impassive, betraying no emotion. "Agreed," he said finally. Let's move ahead with the operation."

CHAPTER 24

The convoy proceeded North. Vlad and Sergei tipped the spear with Dimitri and Nicolai following. A full moon illuminated the empty blacktop snaking off in front of them.

The two men sat in silence brooding over recent events. And what was yet to come.

The killing of the lawyer had whetted Sergei's palette. A thrilling encounter. He took a certain sadistic pride in his work. Enjoyed it even. That moment as you stare into a man's eyes. Bright. Shining in fear. He could almost cry as he watched them fade to dull grey marbles. He shifted in his seat as he felt himself get hard.

For Vlad it was all business. Purposeful. Necessary. A required transaction to achieve a desired outcome. Zero emotion. Just cold calculation working towards his goals.

He thought often about the lawyer since they had left. Not everyone was so courageous when the end came. He could recall the face of every life he had taken. Snapshots in his mind that sometimes haunted his dreams.

His first. A rival gang member as a young man in Russia. A fearsome-looking brute of a man. Built like a side of beef with hands like shovels. He broke early and cried for mama as Vlad beat him to death. From that day he had learned the power that fear and violence gave him over his fellow man. A power that could command an extraordinary influence over others and bend them to his will.

Appearances could be deceptive. One look at the pampered lawyer would lead to the assumption he would fold and disclose all at the first hint of pain. Yet he held out to the end. Courage and conviction in the face of certain death. For this he earned Vlad's respect.

And then of course there was Vasily Gruut. Ten years before. A death he could never forget…

Vlad was a rising star in the criminal underworld of Moscow when spotted and recruited as an assassin for the KGB. In those days a fine line existed between the criminal fraternity and the intelligence authorities. A revolving door the KGB exploited in nurturing talent.

Smart. Sharp. Hungry. They trained him well. He supplemented his income from crime by committing murder in service of Mother Russia. Cold and emotionless. He was the perfect weapon. His keen instinct for violence was exploited. Encouraged even.

Over time he built an empire. And of course, a black book of enemies.

Rival gang members and acquaintances of those he killed. All held a grudge. None were more dangerous than Vasily Gruut, a rival who controlled Moscow's heroin and people trafficking trade. Vlad was careful to pack that world away. Compartmentalize it. He would never allow it to intrude on his family life.

He married Alena just shy of his thirtieth birthday. The very definition of love at first sight. He saw her across the nightclub bar. His breath stolen from his lungs. He knew there and then he had to be with her. Raven hair framed a face of exquisite Slavic beauty.

Alena was fierce and proud. Intensely loving and protective of their twin six-year-old girls Taya and Tatiana. They had inherited their mother's fire and beauty.

He wanted them to experience a normal life. Devoid of the mayhem and destruction that he traded in. He took great care to ensure his work did not follow him home.

It was a postcard winter's day. Cold. Crisp. Silent but for his footsteps crunching in the freshly fallen snow. Smoke curled from the chimney fading into the endless blue. He clutched chocolate from Switzerland and fluffy teddys for the children. He smiled anticipating their joyous faces and excited squeals at his return.

Alena's keys were still in the lock. Not so unusual. She could sometimes be forgetful.

He turned the key and opened the door onto an ugly, hellish new world where things would never be the same. The door swung inwards. He saw them. Time stood still marking this moment. There was only before and after.

The three of them sat on chairs in the hallway, posed in a grotesque scene. Eyes dead. Throats slashed in a hideous red smile. Blood pooled on the ground around them and splattered the walls and stairway.

He sunk to his knees. The sound he made barely human. Closer to the howl of a dying animal. Despair and rage, emotions coursed through his body, as pure and cold as the snow outside.

How long did he lie there? He could not say. It could have been minutes or hours. He knew the killers had left; else he too would be dead. What was left to live for anyway? He contemplated ending it all. So easy. The knife used to slay his family lay on the floor in front of him. Left behind as a gruesome calling card. Taunting him. Daring him. It could all be over in seconds.

But some tiny flicker of fire inside stopped him.

Don't make it so easy for them.

He would be named slayer of his wife and children in a ghastly murder/suicide. There would be no justice for his family and the killers would go free. Revenge ignited inside.

They will pay.

Instincts and training took control. Grief would come later.

He had to call it in. Let the authorities take over and collect evidence. Not that there was any doubt.

The knife left behind was a clear warning. *Stay away.* This was the work of the Gruut crime family.

Vasily must die.

He would not be easy to get to. A cautious man who took precautions to protect himself. He rarely travelled. When he did he was heavily guarded with bodyguards close by.

Vlad's face was known to them all and they would be on the lookout.

Any frontal attack was suicide. He would be cut to pieces before he got within twenty metres. He would need to find another way.

Every man has a weakness. Find the chink in the armour where he is vulnerable.

Vlad watched and waited. Time passed.

He learned every nuance of Vasily's behaviour. Studied his every move. This was now his life's work. He cultivated informants on his payroll who provided him with information.

Then he was ready to strike.

Vasily was a cautious man but lazy in one respect. He committed the fatal error of any high-profile target.

Repetition.

He liked to party. His vice was girls and he liked them

young. Vlad watched for more than two years as the pattern emerged. Roughly once a month he would bring the girls to the penthouse suite of Moscow Towers Hotel. Vlad knew this because he employed the concierge on a handsome retainer. Like so many others in his pocket across the city who whispered secrets into his ear

The hotel would present a difficult target. But not impossible.

From his sources, he knew that Vasily's two bodyguards would be stationed outside the door. Ready to react at the first sign of trouble. The front door was not an option.

Killing this man was not enough. He required seclusion. Privacy. Time. He must gain entry and extract Vasily undetected.

The years had passed. Vasily would have forgotten by now. Vlad was just another obstacle that required crushing and had no doubt crawled off to some hole to lick his wounds.

Plans were laid meticulously. No room for error. Any slight deviation would trigger failure. If caught he would be executed on the spot.

Vlad arrived at the hotel just before 3 am driving in through the main gates. Green spotlights lit up the foliage with an ethereal glow. As expected, there was little activity.

The hotel comprised of a horseshoe-shaped building of twelve floors wrapped around a large pool and bar area. The pool glowed blue from underwater lights. Mirror calm in the half moonlight.

He followed the road which snaked around the perimeter of the grounds. He pulled up at the top of the ramp and presented a security pass. This had been procured earlier that day in exchange for a bottle of Jack Daniels. Western luxuries still opened doors in Moscow. The gates buzzed open. He descended into the underground car park and pulled into a spot next to the service elevator.

He pulled his baseball cap low and grabbed his kit bag. He used the service elevator. No chance of running into late night revellers. Floor 11. He followed the corridor to one of the two rooms he had booked weeks before with a fake identity.

The concierge had called to confirm arrival at 11 pm. Vasily, a girl and two bodyguards. They would not leave until after 10 am the next morning. Same as last month and the month before and the month before that. Routine.

Vlad sat on his balcony overlooking the hotel complex. Watching. Waiting. He had a direct line of vision across the pool to Vasily's suit one floor up. He would strike at 4 am when the lights would be long switched off. Vasily and the girl would be asleep, the guards lethargic. He had sat and observed this routine many times.

3:07 am. The room darkened. Crucially the balcony door was left open. A habit he had observed of Vasily in the summer months.

3:50 am. Ready to go. Ten minutes in and out.

He exited his room and followed the corridor around to his other room, directly beneath Vasily's. All was quiet. Straight through to the balcony doors. They slid open silently. He climbed to the suite above. A black figure in the shadows. Unseen.

His heart hammered in his chest. Seconds from extraction. He withdrew a tranquiliser gun from his rucksack. He slid open the balcony door and entered the room. Light footsteps. Silent.

His eyes slowly adjusted to the gloom. He stopped and waited to feel the room and sense the occupants. Two shadowy shapes on the bed. Breathing steady and slow in heavy sleep. He levelled the gun in front of him and crossed the room.

Vasily stirred and sat up. Some part of his lizard brain

sensing danger. Vlad squeezed the trigger. A soft click followed by a thud as it pierced Vasily's chest. He collapsed back onto the bed with a sigh. Vlad pulled back the covers and squeezed a second shot into the girl's buttocks. She never stirred.

He forced himself to stop and listen. All was silent. No whispers from the guards. No movement outside. They had heard nothing. Else he would be dead by now.

He hoisted Vasily onto his shoulder. A big man, heavyset and overweight. Vlad was strong and focussed. He carried Vasily across the suite and onto the balcony drawing the door closed behind him. The breeze brew cool across the sweat dripping from his brow. He withdrew a length of rope from his rucksack and secured it around Vasily's waist. He heaved the dead weight over the edge of the balcony and lowered him to his own below, swinging him in and over the glass balustrade, landing with a thud. Vlad swung over the edge and landed silently next to the unconscious Vasily. He wrapped the body in a sheet and dropped him into the laundry cart the concierge had arranged.

He stopped to catch his breath. His hands and feet tingled as the surge of adrenaline subsided. Anticipation of what was to come became his focus. He parked it for now. Not the time.

His kit bag joined Vasily in the cart. He exited the room and took the service elevator back to the basement. Unhurried. Face down away from the security cameras. Stay alert.

He opened the side door to the van and heaved Vasily in, sliding the door closed quietly. He gunned the engine the car and pulled away. Slow. Controlled. Nothing to arouse suspicion.

The time was 3:58 am. Less than nine minutes to execute the extraction. He opened the window. The cool air bathed his sweating body. He drove on heading for his next destination and the grim destiny of Vasily Gruut.

CHAPTER 25

An image assembled and dissolved again into darkness. A face? Some far-flung corner of his mind recalled the likeness.

A voice from the silence? Like a muffled trombone. He picked up snatched phrases of recognition buried in the sea of noise.

He drifted back into the void.

**

The world rushed back. Cold. Uncompromising. He came too with a shouted gasp. Freezing water cascaded down his face and chest. He looked around desperate to make sense of his surroundings. Where was the cosy bed and the warm company of last night?

A dark and shadowy figure stood in front of him. As his eyes adjusted to the light the man came into focus and spoke. The voice was soft and cultured. A faint sneer curled the corner of his mouth. The eyes did not smile though.

"Hello, Vasily."

He tried to move his arm. Nothing happened. Bound hand and foot. He was completely immobile, naked, and shivering.

"Vlad. My oldest friend. Been a long time. How's the family?" He chuckled softly, blinked the water from his eyes and took in his surroundings. Fluorescent strip lighting hung low from the ceiling. Most were smashed but a few were functional, bathing the space in a dim glow. The slow drip drip of water from broken pipes the only sound but for his own ragged breaths.

Vlad paced slowly toward his prisoner, his boots scuffing the bare concrete floor. "It has been a long time. We have not spoken since..." He trailed off. "Since before my family died. You murdered them. Our business is our business. From time to time, we have differences of opinion. But do we not resolve that between ourselves like gentlemen? Why Vasily?"

Vasily shrugged. "To make a statement." He stared at Vlad with cold hatred. "And yet here we are. You know my entire army will be out looking for me. Dozens of soldiers. Do you have any idea what they will do to you?"

Vlad raised an eyebrow considering the question. "Nothing good I imagine. But what can you take from a man from whom you have taken everything already?"

"There is always more to take," he growled. "You of all people should know that." "What is your plan? Kill me and then what? A lifetime of running. Hunted. Pursued to the end of the earth? Set me free and we can forget this happened. Maybe we can work together? Imagine how strong we could be. We would rule all of Moscow." His eyes shone bright in the dim light.

Vlad paced slowly back and forth in silence, considering the offer.

"I have not brought you here to bargain."

"Everyone has their price my friend." Vasily's confidence was growing. He clenched his jaw and smiled. "Name your terms and let us be done with this foolishness."

Vlad turned away. "You are mistaken. There is nothing you can give me now but your suffering.

The shine in Vasily's eyes dulled. The confident smile melted away as the cold sweat of fear washed over him. "What are you planning to do with me?" His voice wavered.

Vlad came in close. His face directly in front of Vasily. Eyes dead as night and filled with menace. "I have had many years to determine a suitable punishment. So many choices." He turned on his heel and began pacing again. "I have studied the art of pain for many years. Been fascinated ever since I was a small boy. The facility, the desire even of humankind to inflict the grossest acts on his fellow man. Throughout history it has endured, across all cultures through to the present day."

Vasily began to struggle against his bindings. His voice trembled now. "Please. Don't be stupid. Whatever you do to me will be visited upon you tenfold."

Vlad ignored him. "So many options. Crucifixion. As old as crime and punishment itself. Burning is quite agonizing as I understand. To begin with at least. But once the nerves are burned away, the pain disappears." He scratched his cheek and laughed. "And that would not do! I always liked the creativity of the native American Indians. They would stake a man to the ground next to an ant's nest, and then sit watch while their victim was slowly devoured. It would take hours. Helpless and shrieking from that first bite as the realisation dawned on the horrors of their eventual fate. I think on those poor souls praying for death while their torturers sat and smoked their pipes, watching as the bones were picked clean. I would have enjoyed that, but sadly no such ants in Moscow."

Vasily's breathing quickened. The hopelessness of the situation closed in around him as he realised he would die in this room. "Please. Stop this. I'll do anything."

Vlad ignored him and continued. "Have you noticed yet what you are tied to?"

Vasily swivelled his head trying to see behind. He could see nothing. He looked down. He was naked and spread-eagled. Like the Vitruvian Man. Arms out to the side. His legs parted beneath him.

Vlad did not wait for an answer. "It is a wagon wheel. Very old in fact. Not easy to come by."

"What are you going to do with me?" he replied. He flexed at his bindings, but it was no use. The ties cut into the skin of his wrists as he struggled.

"You left the knife to warn me against retribution. To scare me off. It was a message. You are untouchable with your army to protect you." Vlad turned away and kneeled next to a gym bag on the floor behind him. "Everyone is vulnerable though to a determined pursuer willing to take risks."

He reached in and produced a wooden club. Ancient. Gnarled. The handle bound in black leather. It was about a foot long and expanded into a bulbous knot as big as a melon at the business end. He weighed it in his hand.

"I have selected something special for you. You broke me Vasily. Now I must break you."

Vasily began to sob and shake his head. "I'm sorry. I'm sorry. Please forgive me. I'll give you anything you want."

Vlad shook his head and wagged his finger slowly. "It's too late. Come now Vasily. Take your punishment like a man."

He tested the club in the palm of his hand. The dull smack echoed round the warehouse. The knot was sanded smooth and oiled, shining in the gloom. "I made this especially for you. It has given me great pleasure. I harvested it from an oak in the forest near my dacha. Alena's favourite place in the whole world. We used to sit beneath that oak in the summer. Reading. Listening to music. Just being. They are all buried beneath it now."

Vlad approached and lightly touched the skin of his victim's arm. Caressed it gently. "Where shall we begin?"

Vasily was snivelling now. Shaking with fright. Urine ran down his leg and dripped onto the dusty floor. Vlad paused for anticipation, drawing strength from fear.

He smashed the club down on Vasily's left forearm with a sickening crack. He screamed, piercing and continuous till his breath was no more. He turned to look in shock at his arm, bent grotesquely between the wrist and elbow joint. Shards of blooded, white bone stabbed through the skin.

The scream dwindled to frightened snivelling. He pleaded for mercy as the horror of what was happening to him dawned.

Vlad paced slowly. Allowing time for grim reality to drive home. "Shall we continue? Seven more to go."

"Please. Stop. I beg y...." he whimpered.

He was cut short as Vlad moved swiftly. He raised the club again and dropped it down on the right forearm. A second crack followed by the anguished howls of a wounded beast.

He closed his eyes in a desperate effort to shut out the real world. He vomited. Snot and tears cascaded down his face and chin.

Vlad slapped Vasily around the face. "Stay with me."

He worked methodically around the body. He smashed the upper arm bones, followed by the shins, and finally the femurs. Vasily's shrieks of pain and pleas for mercy spurred with each sickening splinter of bone. When he passed out, Vlad threw another bucket of water on him to rouse him from unconsciousness. To ensure he remained lucid for the entire sickening experience. Between each limb, Vlad paused to savour the snivelling wretch's suffering.

Vasily hung limp and unconscious from the wheel. A grotesque imitation of a human body. Vlad emptied another bucket of water in his face. "I want you to experience the finale."

He started with the right arm. He snipped the tie and threaded the arm through the spokes of the wheel. The grating crunch of bone on bone and the muffled whimpering of Vasily accompanied his work. He tied him once more at the wrist to resecure him in position. Then he moved onto the other limbs, completing the same grim procedure until he was completely entwined in the wheel. He doused him once more for good measure.

"Wake up Vasily. We are done here."

Vasily opened his eyes. His mouth hung open, flecked with spit and vomit. Excruciating agony emanated from every sinew and muscle that strained against his bonds. Every miniscule movement inflicted insufferable pain that would persist until death mercifully took him. He moved his head and stared aghast, wailing at the jellified limbs woven through the spokes of the wheel.

Vlad stepped back and surveyed his work with satisfaction. "You will hang here till you die. Think on what you have taken from me. I have one last gift for you though."

He reached into the bag and extracted a pouch of clear fluid with a flexible tube terminating in a syringe. He hung it from the wheel above Vasily. Just a little something to ensure you enjoy the experience fully."

He pierced the vein of Vasily's left arm and taped the syringe in place. He opened the stopper. Vasily took a deep breath and groaned. His pupils expanded and his breathing shallowed.

"I procured this from an acquaintance who works on a neonatal unit. It is used on premature babies or those suffering from alcohol or opiate overdose. A slow release of caffeine and sodium benzoate will help keep you hydrated and prevent you from dying from lack of fluid or blood loss. It will also stimulate your nervous system to prevent you from a deep sleep. I understand this should keep you alive for at least two days. Goodbye Vasily."

He took one last look at the twisted and broken body, imprinting the image in his mind. He gathered his things and left without looking back.

***

It was almost a week later when the grim discovery was made. An anonymous phone call from overseas had tipped the police to the whereabouts of the body who discovered it, decomposing and stinking. The pathologist estimated that the victim had survived for three days before finally succumbing to his injuries.

***

He cried out and woke with a start, clammy with sweat. He sucked in lungfuls of air and clawed at his chest which thumped like a drum. Sergei stole a glance at his brother. "You okay moy brat?"

He wiped a sleeve across his soaked forehead and sat up breathing heavy. "I'm fine. Just my usual nightmare about him. About them...." He turned away to hide the shine in his eyes

"Long time ago now brother. You should let it go."

Vlad gazed out the window. The motorway had long given way to rolling hills and wilderness. The dark of night banished by the dawn glow rising from the hills. "Where are we?"

"We are in Scotland," Sergei replied yawning. "I must rest. You take over."

Sergei glanced in the rear-view mirror. Dimitry was close behind. Their eyes met. He signalled and both cars pulled off the tarmac onto a gravel incline. The four men got out and checked the area. There was no-one to be seen. Sergie opened the map and laid it flat on the bonnet. He beckoned for Dimitri and Nikolai to approach.

"We are here." A cracked fingernail marked the spot on the map. "They stay here." He stabbed a second finger and traced the route between the two points. "Three hours. Dimitri, take over.

Me and Nikolai must rest. When arrive we stay well back. Away from house. Observe target. Clear?"

A silent nod and the group took their places. Vlad gunned the engine and took off in a cloud of dust with Nikolai close behind.

His nightmare was now long banished. Every fibre buzzed with anticipation. He flexed his fingers and closed them tight on the steering wheel. There had been many kills since that night long ago in a Moscow warehouse. But this felt special. Laying pursuit. Stalking his prey to a wilderness hideaway to snuff out a life and exact revenge. He bit down on his lip and savoured the coppery taste of blood as he closed on his target.

CHAPTER 26

Jake found the woodstore next to the garage. It was well stocked with seasoned pine. He stripped to the waist and got to work with an axe he found hanging from the wall. Twenty minutes later he heaved a basket of wood inside and built a roaring fire in the hearth, bathing the cottage in a warm golden glow. He sat with Claire, hand in hand sipping wine in silence in as he pondered his life decisions.

Perhaps it's time for a change? He turned the thought over. Examined it. Probed it gently. He yearned to shed the skin of his old life and start anew. Maybe this wilderness hideaway offered something they just couldn't get from Cambridge. *Could we live like this forever?*

They cooked, ate and laughed as a family. A second bottle of wine appeared. After dinner they snuggled together on the sofa by the fire to enjoy a movie from the selection on offer in the cottage. Scruffy settled in his lap. He stroked her fur gently.

Later they carried the exhausted girls upstairs and put them to bed.

Claire and Jake crept downstairs and made love by the roaring fire, delighting in the warmth and closeness of each other. Something had drifted from their relationship in recent years. Floated away like breath on the wind. That night in the highlands they rediscovered each other. Then in bed they made love again and slept entwined.

***

The dawn light streaming purple through the skylight woke Jake early. He pulled on shorts and tiptoed downstairs. Embers still smouldered in the fireplace bathing the house in cosy warmth. As he opened the heavy door, the cool morning air wrapped its chill embrace around him.

The early morning sunshine peaked between the hills igniting the mist-covered loch in hues of gold and purple. Jake sucked in a lungful of cool mountain air. His breath condensed in clouds as he exhaled.

He took a seat on the patio and examined the folder Carrington had given him. The pack contained instructions to contact Mackintosh at the gamekeeper's cabin, along with an aerial map of the property. He took his bearings. The cabin was beyond the orchard, adjacent to the back garden in a heavily wooded area. He followed the path through the garden and into the orchard before it emerged into a thicket of dense brush. To his right the loch flashed silver and blue in the early morning sunshine. To his left a tall pine forest. The path ahead snaked through the brush emerging into a valley and up into the mountains beyond.

The map indicated a track off to the left into the pines, but Jake had not seen any track as he passed. He doubled back and looked once more. This time more carefully. It was almost imperceptible, but he found it. The brush had grown over the path, so it was almost impossible to see unless you knew it was there. But the ground was slightly compressed and there was no growth where feet had fallen.

He followed the path wading through the waist-high scrub pushing the thick foliage aside. This was not a path well-trodden. By now he had lost sight of the cottage. The track passed through the dense brush and emerged into the pines that rose forming a canopy arching over the footpath. Like some tunnel into a fairy-tale kingdom. Sunlight struggled to penetrate leaving a gloomy yet tranquil aura. The aroma of pine wafted gently on the breeze. He stopped to listen to the morning birdsong and the hammer of a woodpecker in the distance.

After a hundred meters or so the track began to widen. It snaked round to the left and emerged into a clearing occupied by an isolated log cabin. The forest enclosed the clearing but for one open section affording a view across to the loch in the distance.

The cabin itself was constructed of native pine. The only inkling of modern materials was the glass in the windows. Everything else appeared to be sourced from the forest. Half log steps rose from the path to a deck area outside the front door of the cabin. A fire was smouldering in a cleared area of brush; the faint smell of burning embers lingering on the breeze. A pot of water bubbled clouds of steam. Yet no man could be seen. Like the Mary Celeste.

Jake began up the steps to the door but was halted by a voice from behind.

"Can I help ye, laddie?"

He spun around startled but could not see who had spoken. The voice came from the shadows in the trees. He squinted, peering into the forest to identify the owner, but could see nothing in the gloom. Slowly, a man emerged from the trees.

"I'm sorry. I didn't mean to intrude. I am Jake Charles. I'm looking for a Mr Mackintosh. I was told to find him at this cabin."

"Aye, and who might have told ye that?" the man asked stepping forward.

Jake could not place the man's age. He seemed somewhat stooped and appeared to limp slightly affording him an elderly appearance. Perhaps in his sixties. He had steel grey close-cropped hair. A matching moustache covered his entire upper lip drooping down either side of his mouth. His face was deep lined and weather-beaten with a rather gaunt hollowed appearance. Piercing grey eyes sparkled bright.

"Mr Carrington arranged for me and my family to stay at the cottage. He said I should find Mr Mackintosh who would help us with anything we needed while we were here."

"Carrington. A fine gentleman. Well, ye've found him. I'm Mackintosh. Pleased to make yer acquaintance."

Jake extended his hand and Mackintosh clasped it in a vice-like grip. He pumped Jake's hand vigorously.

"Nice to meet you too," Jake replied. Up close he noticed the faint but not unpleasant aroma of smoke, sweat, and the forest. Mackintosh was clearly a man who lived close to nature.

"Are ye settled in the cottage?" Mackintosh enquired.

"Yes thanks. We arrived last night. It's quite beautiful here. I think we will go for a walk today."

"Aye, a beautiful morning to be sure. But pack for bad weather. It can turn fast around here and catch ye out. Don't be fooled by the sunshine," Mackintosh warned.

The stillness of the forest was interrupted by a faint, almost imperceptible noise in the distance. Somewhat alien in the tranquillity. It sounded like a motorbike, but he could not be certain. Mackintosh's head snapped in the direction of the noise. He stared intently. As if he could somehow see the source through the dense trees and foliage.

"Is everything okay?" Jake enquired tentatively.

Mackintosh said nothing for a moment. Lost in thought. "Aye, no bother," he said finally returning his gaze to Jake. "You'll no find me here that often. If ye need anything, ye can leave a note."

"Thank you," he replied. "I'm sure we will be fine."

Mackintosh stood in silence. Clearly nothing more to say.

A man of few words, Jake mused.

"Well thanks once again Mr Mackintosh. Be seeing you maybe." Jake turned away from the cabin and followed the track back through the brush. As he rounded the first bend, he stole a glance back up towards the cabin. Mackintosh remained like a statue where Jake had left him. Staring intently.

Strange fellow, Jake reflected heading through the brush.

He turned to look again. Mackintosh was no longer in sight.

Jake continued back down the path through the brush, emerging into the orchard. He returned to the cottage to begin preparations for their day out.

He found a key on the set Carrington had provided and tried the garage door. He pushed against complaining rusty hinges and stepped inside. No one had been inside for some time. Cobwebs glinted in the sunlight streaming through the grubby windows. He wafted them aside and opened a window to ease the damp musty smell.

Although long neglected, the garage was well stocked. The left-hand wall revealed a variety of equipment for outdoor living. A foot long bowie knife in a leather sheath. Petrol-driven chainsaw. Spades, shovels, and other assorted tools. To the right a locked cabinet was bolted securely to the bare brick wall. He tried the smallest key and sprang the lock open raising his eyebrows as he surveyed the contents. There was a hunting rifle and shotgun with boxes of ammunition for both.

What really caught his eye though was a sleek crossbow and a quiver filled with arrows. It was made of oiled oak and polished steel. He picked it up and weighed it heavy in his hands. Years ago, he had fired a bow and arrow on a stag party day out but had never had the chance to fire a crossbow. He figured why not. He slung the strap across his back and collected the quiver. He grabbed the hunting knife and strapped it to his belt for good measure.

"What are you up to?" Startled, he jumped and spun around. Claire stood in the doorway; her dressing gown wrapped tight against the cool morning air.

"Shit. You made me jump. Don't do that. I'm armed" He laughed and turned to show her the crossbow on his back. "Check this place out. Filled with guns and ammo."

"I don't want the children near any guns Jake," she replied sternly. She stepped forward and examined the crossbow. "Is this safe?" she asked frowning.

He pulled her in close for a cuddle. "Perfectly safe. Don't worry. I know what I am doing. I figured we might spot a rabbit or two. See if we can catch some dinner."

She turned on him with a raised eyebrow. "Are you sure about that? You know they don't even like to think about where bacon comes from."

She smiled and ruffed his hair. "Let's go and wake them for breakfast."

Jake locked the cabinet and closed the garage door behind them. He took Claire's hand as they wandered slowly back to the house. He stopped and pulled her into an embrace as they stared to the hills beyond the loch. "Could you live somewhere like this?"

For a moment she said nothing. Just tightened her grip around his waist and buried her face into his neck inhaling deeply. She thought back to the blackness that had consumed her recently. The fear that clawed at her stomach and chest like an alien trying to burst free. The anger and hatred she had felt outside the school gates.

It had all gone. Floated away like smoke in a breeze. The colour and vibrance of the world were back once more. She could feel again. Live again. Love again.

"I don't know. Maybe. It's crossed my mind once or twice.

Could you?"

The question hung unanswered as they stood and held each other. Like they were the only two people in the whole world.

"See in the distance?" He broke the long silence pointing to the mountaintop that rose from the edge of the loch. "That's the highest point for miles. After breakfast let's pack a picnic and go hiking. The girls will love it."

"I love you Jake Charles." She pulled him closer, and they kissed passionately.

The sound of giggling and footsteps drumming on the stairs broke the moment as the girls flew through the front door like a whirlwind. Chase led the way throwing herself at Claire. "This place is awesome. So many places to play hide and seek. Can we go exploring?"

"That's the plan," replied Jake. "After breakfast we are heading up there." He pointed to the peak in the distance.

"Oh dad," groaned Violet hands-on-hips. "It's miles away. Can't we play in the orchard instead?" Chase stood next to her sister nodding her agreement.

"Maybe later sweetie," he said pinching her playfully on the cheek. "Fresh air. Exercise. Back to nature. It's just what we all need. Scruffy's going to love it too."

They guided the girls back through the door. "How about bacon and eggs for breakfast," Claire said. "Then you can help me make some sandwiches."

Jake and Claire busied themselves in the kitchen with breakfast which the four of them devoured in ten minutes flat. While the girls went to wash and dress, Jake prepared the picnic. He found a dusty bottle of red in the wine rack and threw that in for good measure.

Once the bags were packed, he headed out into the

sunshine to study the map and plan a route. The others were still getting ready so he figured he would test the crossbow. He examined it closely. It looked straightforward with a lever and ratchet for applying tension. He drew it back until the mechanism clicked into place. He loaded a bolt and weighed the weapon in his hand. It was lighter than he expected yet sturdy. He aimed at a tree twenty yards away, lining the sites up on a discoloured piece of bark. He squeezed the trigger gently, testing the pressure required. It did not take much. The trigger gave and the bolt flew from the crossbow with a rush and a loud thud as it embedded in the trunk. He smiled and approached the tree. His shot was accurate. The metal tip of the bolt had bitten deep into the tree, a thumb length left of the spot he aimed for. He worked it free gently, taking care not to damage or bend the bolt. The tree was a dense hardwood oak and it had driven in at least a couple of inches.

Claire and the girls appeared from the house, also packed and ready to go.

"All good?" he said. "Let's go exploring?" It was shaping up to be a glorious day. The early morning cool had now given way to the warmth of the sun, which rose high above the mountains and had burnt away the morning mist that had covered the loch at dawn.

Jake kneeled and spread the map on the ground. "Gather around girls. Today I'll teach you some useful skills. Starting with map reading and navigation. See the hill over there?" He pointed into the distance. "That's where we are heading. And here it is here," he said drawing their attention to the map. "We are here. You can see the cottage marked on the map. We will take this path which runs alongside the loch and winds up the hill all the way to the top. Do you think you can follow the map and get us there?"

The girls looked at their parents with disdain, hands-on-hips. "Of course daddy," Chase said. "We might be kids, but we are not idiots. Although it does seem a bit pointless when we could just use your phone."

Jake laughed. "Always the phone! No phones today girls, only for photos. You guys are in charge. Lead the way please intrepid explorers."

Violet and Chase folded the map and the family set off down the path towards the loch's edge. Jake and Claire followed hand in hand with Scruffy barking excitedly and bounding around alongside them. Their journey was underway.

The path led down from the gardens through a wooded area. Goosebumps raised on Jakes neck as they descended into the trees. Out of the sunshine it was dark, cool and fresh. Birds sang their chorus and Scruffy snuffled excitedly in the undergrowth, investigating the sounds of woodland creatures.

Soon the woods began to thin, and the path exited onto the loch's edge. The change was startling as they emerged into the warmth and light of the sun blazing over the towering hills on the other side. A few solitary walkers dotted the mountain ridge like marching ants. The sun glittered off the shimmering lake like a thousand stars. Flocks of birds swept low across the surface and on the far side Jake could make out a stag at the water's edge drinking.

The girls skipped on ahead lost in the moment, chattering excitedly.

As they strolled hand in hand, he thought back on their earlier conversation. It dawned he could happily leave the town life behind and live in such a place. The forced confinement of prison had exposed a yearning in him to seek out and enjoy the open expanse of nature. A profound feeling of calm enveloped him like a cloud.

They continued on a leisurely pace skirting the edge of the loch. They were close to the far end now. The path ahead began to rise from the water's edge, snaking up the hillside to the summit. He stopped to look back to where they had started. The cottage was little more than a speck in the distance overlooking the water.

"It's going to get tougher now girls," he said. "Time to start climbing!"

They pressed on up the hill. The path followed a ridge with the ground falling away on either side. The ground was grassy and dotted with grazing sheep which scattered as they approached. In places the going was tricky as the path turned rocky and steep. This required a scrambling approach which the girls attacked, squealing with joy. They continued climbing for another hour, soon closing in on the top of the hill.

"Come on kids," he urged them on. "Nearly there now. Another fifteen minutes and we are at the top. Then it's lunchtime."

The promise of food and rest delivered the energy boost required for the final push. They pressed on finally cresting the top. They emerged onto a tabletop plateau at the summit of the mountain. The top of the world. The highest point in any direction as far as the eye could see. Jake raised his arms and turned slowly savouring the panoramic views.

"Here we are. Isn't it amazing?"

For once the kids seemed genuinely dumbstruck. They stood in silence turning slowly. Looking in awe at the incredible view in every direction. Claire distributed bottles of water and they sat to enjoy lunch in the tranquil setting. A cool breeze and the haunting call of a bird of prey were the only sounds. Jake watched him hover. The master of his kingdom at the top of the world.

After they had finished eating, Jake stood and took his bearings. Away in the distance to the North, dark storm clouds were forming over the hills. They were some way off so gave Jake little cause for concern for the moment.

"Listen up guys," he called them together. "It's taken us two hours to get here so it's about the same to get home." He pointed back to the cottage in the distance. "That's home. We can complete a circular route if we continue along this ridge towards that smaller hill. It descends through the valley and passes some interesting features according to the map. Home in plenty of time to relax, make dinner and crash out for an evening movie. Sound good?"

"Definitely," said Violet nodding. Chase was busy doing twirls, oblivious to the conversation.

They packed up and stuck off. The path was rockier than before. Hard going down the shale covered hillside. It soon levelled out, easing on the legs. They briefly lost sight of the cottage as the path dipped between two hills. Eventually the path emerged through the valley, opening onto a glorious pasture covered with wildflowers blooming in the summer sunshine. The cottage while still a speck in the distance was visible once again.

Something caught Jake's attention as he looked down towards the cottage. Was something moving on the road? He stopped and rummaged in the rucksack, drawing out the binoculars he had packed earlier. He focussed on the cottage. Now sharply in view thanks to the powerful magnification. He swept back up the road until he found what he was looking for.

Two cars were heading up the road towards the cottage. The first chilling tendrils of alarm began to form in his stomach.

"Strange," he said out loud to himself. Claire stopped.

"What is it darling?" she replied. Her voice wobbled. A tone higher.

"There are two cars heading up the road towards the cottage. There is nowhere else to go on that road."

"Maybe the lawyer got his dates mixed up," she pleaded.

"Perhaps someone else was booked to stay at the cottage this week." He could tell she did not believe it.

"They are stopping," he replied He watched closely already knowing what this meant.

The driver's door of the lead car opened. A man got out. Jake trained the binoculars on him. His insides turned to ice. There was no mistaking him. The man from the courtroom.

"Get down and take cover. All of you. Get the dog on the lead."

He crouched one knee to the ground. He watched as the passenger door opened and a second man got out. Shaven-head and heavily bearded. Two more men oozing menace exited the second car.

"It's trouble. We need to move. Now."

Claire understood. No more questions. She busied herself getting the girls ready. "Come on girls. Let's play a game of hide and seek."

They also knew. Something was very wrong. But they had the good sense to do what they were told. They crouched behind some bushes out of view. Claire fumbled for Scruffy's lead and caught her by the collar. She barked excitedly. The sound pierced the peaceful quiet of the wilderness and echoed off the nearby mountains.

"Shit. Quiet Scruffy," Jake whispered.

The driver's head snapped around. He seemed to look straight back at Jake through the binoculars. There was no mistaking the sound. It had given them away in a flash. They could not be seen, but they had been discovered for sure. The man raised an arm, waving leisurely in their direction. As one would to an old friend. The passenger also now looking in their direction drew his finger across his throat. The ball of dread in Jake's gut grew and throbbed.

The awful realisation dawned on him that he and his family were alone in the wilderness. The weather was closing in and they were in mortal danger.

CHAPTER 27

The cottage loomed in the distance. Vlad pulled the car to the side of the dirt track and Dimitri stopped close behind skidding on the shale. They were still at least a mile away, but Vlad ever cautious did not want his enemy alerted to his presence until he decided the time was right. He stepped out of the car. Watched. Waited.

The cottage was directly ahead overlooking the loch to the right. Further in the distance a grassy pasture rose into a valley between two mountains. The other three men exited their cars awaiting Vlad's instructions.

"We wait here and observe. I want to know they are alone. No surprises."

The quiet was shattered by the bark of a dog echoing around the mountain. Vlad's head snapped in the direction of the sound. It was difficult to say for sure, but his eyes were drawn to the valley. Did he detect some movement? It was a long way off. The back of his neck prickled with the familiar feeling that he was being watched. He smiled and waved, staring directly where he had sensed the movement. This was a psychological game now. Four hunters on the chase. Their prey up in those hills somewhere. Frightened. Desperate.

Vlad shivered in anticipation. He itched to be on the move.

"Let's go," he said, getting back into the car. "Park up by the cottage and get prepared. They are up there somewhere and there is nowhere to run."

***

Jake watched them get back in their cars and speed off towards the cottage. They were coming for them.

Panic began to flare. Fear for his family's safety overwhelmed him. His breath came in ragged gasps as he looked wide eyed in desperation at his wife and children. Their own terror stared back.

"Dad, what's wrong? You're scaring me," Violet cried.

Hold it together. Isolate you fear.

He closed his eyes. Took four deep breaths. Then opened them again. He forced a pained smile.

"Nothing for you to be afraid of sweetie. Everything is going to be okay."

He didn't believe it. Not for one second.

They had to run and hide. No other choice. He glanced behind, back up the mountain. The first wispy tendrils from the slate grey clouds were curling over the summit like demon's fingers. Edging closer.

They were trapped.

But perhaps the weather could work to their advantage? Provide some cover. His attackers would have guns, but he was also armed. They would not be expecting that. Some small element of surprise. Was it enough?

He checked the phone. No signal. He began to formulate a plan.

They would approach from the path next to the loch or up through the valley. Four men. They would almost certainly split into two groups and cover both options.

Claire's hands were shaking. He was the same. He took them in his and looked directly into her eyes. He spoke quietly so the children would not hear. His voice wobbled. Lips drawn back tight. Panicked eyes betrayed his terror.

"We must work together so listen carefully. There are four of them. We need to run and hide. Head back to the peak. The storm will give you cover. Put on the waterproof jackets and move as fast as the girls can manage." He fumbled in his pocket and withdrew the card Thompson had given him. "There is a signal at the summit. I checked earlier. Call Thompson and get help immediately. There was a third pathway heading away from the summit. Take that and follow it. I will hold them up till the police arrive. I love you. Be strong."

He pulled her into an embrace. Would it be their last?

She nodded fighting back tears. She pressed her forehead to his.

He turned to the children. They seemed smaller. Frailer. Like they were trying to shrink away from a frightening world.

"Girls. It's time for a game of hide and seek. Get your coats on. Do what mum says. No arguments now." He hugged them both. "I love you. Time to go. Don't be afraid."

"Is someone here to hurt us daddy?" cried Chase. He bent to cradle her face in his hands and looked directly into her eyes. "No sweetie. You will be fine. They just want to talk to daddy. I want you to go with mummy."

She nodded weakly. Claire took their hands and marched them off up the valley with Scruffy.

Will I ever see you again?

He watched them leave as he prepared for what amounted to his certain death. There was no way he could stop four men. His only chance was to slow them down and give his family time to make their escape. He checked his kit. The knife hung heavy from his belt. He primed the crossbow and loaded a bolt. He had a dozen.

He chose his spot carefully. If they came through the valley, they would be forced to follow the path below him. He crouched behind a rocky outcrop that afforded a clear line of vision down the track. He could also see the path that traversed the loch. He lay in wait. Primed. Fear, adrenaline, and raw anger fuelled him. He was not going down without a fight.

***

One final look back at her husband and they took off. Her children's survival depended on her now. Jake was on his own. There was nothing she could do to help him other than get to the top and call for help. Thick, dark clouds rolled over the crest of the mountain. An ominous deep rumble echoed around the valley like the gods waking from a long sleep.

Heading up into the storm went against every fibre of her being, but they had no other option. The children's faces were ashen. Their wide eyes fearful, seeking solace that she could not give. But thankfully they complied without complaint and kept pace with her.

She estimated they would reach the summit in thirty minutes. She checked the phone constantly willing it to give her some signal. As soon as the call was made, they would head down the other side. As far away as possible and pray that Jake could survive long enough.

"I'm tired mummy. Can we stop?" begged Chase as they marched on.

"No darling. We must keep going. I need you to stay strong a little longer. You can rest when we get to the top." They pressed on, heads down against the spatter of rain that had now begun. Sweat poured from Claire, both from the effort as well as the cold fear consuming her. The sunshine had gone now. Obscured by the dark clouds that had gathered. She glanced back down towards the cottage. The sunny, welcoming valley now transformed into a darker, more chilling place.

Will we die up here today?

She buried the thought. The mothering instinct to protect her children outweighed all other emotions and feelings. They closed on the peak. Ten minutes to go.

Flashes of lightning lit up the clouds from within like tinted cotton wool. Shades of pink, white and slate grey. The clap of thunder rent the air around them. Chase and Violet darted in and clung to her, trembling like frightened rabbits.

She pulled the phone from her pocket. She cried out in blessed relief at the three bars of signal.

She crouched and handed the backpack to Violet. "Take cover under those rocks and rest while mummy makes a phone call. Help yourself to a chocolate bar from the bag and have a drink of water."

With shaking hands, she keyed in DS Thompson's number and hit the dial button. It rang straight away. Relief washed over her that it had not gone straight to voicemail.

"Come on. Come on. Answer," she urged the phone. Five rings. She felt panic rising. He was not going to answer. She hung up crying out in frustration and tried again.

"Answer you fucker," she screamed. As if she could by way of some supernatural force will the man at the other end to pick up.

Three more rings. "Hello. Who is this?"

Tears of blessed relief slipped down her cheeks mixing with the rain.

"Thompson. It's Claire Charles. Jake's wife. Listen carefully, we don't have much time."

"What's wro..." he started.

"Just fucking listen," she interrupted.

He fell silent.

"We are being chased. By associates of the man that died. Four of them. We are in the Scottish Highlands staying at a cottage." She gave him the address and quickly outlined the rest of their plan. "Please. You must send help at once. There is a mountain to the Northeast of the loch. The highest point for miles. I am taking the children down the path on the Northern side as far away as we can. Jake is lying in wait on the Southern flank to try and slow them down."

"OK, I have all that," Thompson replied. "Stay calm. You are doing fine. Stick with the plan and get the children as far away as you can. I am mobilising an armed response team to your location. We will be there as quickly as possible. Get going now."

Claire sobbed with relief to hear that help was on its way. "Please hurry."

"I'm hanging up now. I want you to stay focussed. Get yourself and the children out of there."

She packed the phone away and turned to her children with renewed hope. "Come on girls, time to move, help is on the way."

CHAPTER 28

The four men kitted up in silence. Combat pants. Boots. Lightweight fleece and jacket. Each checked and holstered their Glock 17 9mm pistols. Each carried a knife sheathed under their armpit.

"We should have rifles," Sergei noted.

"But you are such a terrible shot moy brat," joked Vlad. He clasped the back of his brother's head and pulled him in close eye to eye. "A rifle is so impersonal. We are not out here hunting stag. This man killed our baby brother." His eyes were wide. Shining with excitement. "We will not gun him down from half a mile away. I want him to feel it. I want to feel it as the blade slips in his gut. Watch the life drain from his eyes" He stabbed a finger into Sergei's belly. "I can taste his fear already." He pointed to the mountain. "Up there, running scared with his family. Savour his terror." He turned away from his brother focussing his attention on his preparations.

When he was done, Vlad pulled the map from the car. "We are here," he pointed to the building marked on the map. "They are on foot with children so will not have been planning to go far. They were somewhere in this valley region. My guess is they will run for that mountain. He marked on the map and then pointed up the valley to the real thing. "That is four kilometres away with two approaches. He indicated both routes on the map. "A storm is approaching," he said nodding to the darkening sky. "They must make escape directly into the storm or return to the cottage. Sergei and I will take the path by the loch. Dimitri and

Nikolai take the valley. We meet at the top. The first team to spot them fire two shots."

The three men nodded their agreement. With their plans set the four took off in pursuit.

***

Jake waited and watched. With his family on their way to relative safety he considered his options. He only had one that stood any chance. Hide. Strike. Run.

From his vantage point between two rocky outcrops, he had good cover and field of vision. The darkening skies would aid his concealment. Could he take one of them out and make a break for it? He scanned the path by the loch. No movement. Claire must come through and reach Thompson. He was their only hope now. He laid low, tuned to the sound of his environment. The rustling of leaves in the wind. The call of the birds. The low rumble of thunder in the distance.

The clouds pooled overhead bringing with them the soft pitter-patter of rain. The gentle breeze of earlier replaced by a consistent wind whistling down the valley. He crouched and trained his crossbow on the path, primed and ready to fire at centre mass. The midpoint of the chest.

Level the odds. Do not overthink it. Take the closest target. Run.

He repeated the mantra over and over.

He closed his eyes, breathing deeply. Desperately trying to control the surge of adrenaline, the thumping of his heart, the clammy sweat dripping down his back. He opened them again. He was ready.

***

Vlad moved fast along the path. He broke into a jog, silently scanning all he passed. Sergei tucked in close behind. They moved as one. Two men operating as a single unit.

Training kicked in. Muscle memory from campaigns fought in far-flung corners of the world. Just another mission. A target to hunt, capture, kill.

Vlad's gun was securely holstered under his left armpit. He was an expert marksman, able to draw and fire in less than a second so carrying the gun was counterproductive. He could move faster when not holding it.

They know we are coming.

He had not forgotten the feeling of being watched from afar.

He moved swiftly along the path remaining alert for movement in the bushes around him. The objective was the mountain summit. Twenty minutes at their current pace. He remained watchful for exits his target may have taken to lie low and hide. To the right lay the loch. A body of water half a mile wide. No chance of escape without a boat. To the left harsh scrub and thickets. Difficult if not impossible to conceal four people and a dog. The children would hobble them. Slow them down. He savoured the predatory buzz like electricity in his veins. He quickened his pace.

The path began to incline away from the loch. The hill had a steep face on its Eastern flank plunging directly into the loch. No way to pass. Vlad started up the rise, his legs burning with lactic acid.

His eyes scanned the terrain. Laser focussed. Every change in the environment processed and assessed. He turned to check on his brother. Sergei was close behind tucked in on Vlad's shoulder. Beads of sweat formed on his forehead. He was breathing heavily. Vlad eased the pace minutely to compensate. Fifteen minutes to the top. He pressed on without pause through clenched teeth.

He checked ahead for possible ambush points. Always cautious. Where the path ran close to an overhanging rock, he took a wide berth indicating to Sergei to do the same. Ten minutes now. They were close.

***

Dimitri watched as his older brothers took off. He was tall, muscular. He moved languidly, like a cat. Blessed with the strength and ferocity of Sergei and the street cunning of Vlad. Yet none of the impetuousness that had shaped Yuri's downfall.

He looked to Nicolai. "Ready?"

He nodded and they were off. Nicolai was not related by blood yet had killed on behalf of the Vasins on numerous occasions. The most loyal of soldiers and a trusted man to bring on such a mission. Dimitri towered over Nicolai whose curly mop of black hair framed a smiling olive-skinned face. Almost cherubic. Despite his Russian roots he appeared more like a Greek islander. His soft features and slight frame concealed a ferocity that many a man had underestimated at his peril.

They skirted past the cottage and through the back garden. No sign of activity. The back gate opened onto a path which meandered on a gentle incline through the orchard before threading through an area of dense brush. They waded through the thicket and into the valley beyond.

The early summer blossom bloomed pink and red in the afternoon sunshine in stark contrast to the clouds closing in on them. They would soon be engulfed in the storm. Dimitri moved at pace. Light on his feet and graceful for such a tall man. He scanned his surroundings continuously for noise and movement. Nikolai was close on his shoulder, in his peripheral vision.

Dimitri tried to think like his prey, assessing the likely actions of a man pursued by four armed attackers. Hiding was a possibility. More likely they would take advantage of the head start and make a run for it and call for help. With the nearest police hours away, this was of no concern. This would all be over long before they could mobilise.

***

He stiffened as he saw it. Clear movement by the loch. Two men moving fast along the path.

They have split up. Two heading the other way.

There was nothing he could do about the pair by the water. His heart throbbed painful in his ears.

Where are the others?

He did not have to wait long. He spotted them crossing the valley below a few minutes later. They moved fast, precisely. The first man, tall and heavyset had a gun in his hand. The second smaller man at first glance seemed unarmed, but Jake was sure he would have a weapon. They were five hundred metres away and closing fast. The valley converged onto the stony path that led to Jake's vantage point and continued up the hill behind him.

Timing is everything. Shoot too early and miss. Too late and they will be upon you.

The rain drove in heavy now running down Jake's face and obscuring his view. He blinked the water from his eyes. Lightning flashed, illuminating the landscape and the two approaching men before surrendering to the gloom. A clap of thunder, deep and booming rolled through the valley and echoed from the hills. Closing. Two hundred meters. Jake's heart thumped in his throat. Adrenaline coursed through him sharpening his vision and focus.

The crossbow rested on the rocks in front of him. Steady aim. Perfect line of fire. He had chosen his site well.

He briefly lost them as they followed the path out of Jake's view. He kept his breathing slow. Calm. Controlled. One hundred meters out. Firing range in twenty seconds. He had his spot marked. Fire when the first man was ten meters away.

Fifty meters out. The taller man came back into view. No sign of the second pursuer.

Where is he?

His chest tightened.

Forget him. Concentrate on the target in front of you.

Jake closed one eye and took aim. Weapon trained dead centre of his chest. His finger tensed on the trigger.

One chance only.

If he missed, he would be pinned down and executed. Failure was not an option.

Ten meters. He relaxed and breathed out slowly as he squeezed the trigger. A soft click and the bolt whistled through the air finding its mark with a soft thud barely audible above the wind.

Direct hit. The pursuer stopped dead in his tracks and dropped his gun. He stared in confusion at the shaft sprouting from his chest. He clawed at the bolt with both hands and sank to his knees. His lips drew back in grimace baring his teeth. A low guttural moan escaped from deep within. This was death, and he knew it.

One down. I have a chance.

Elation. A fleeting moment. Like a jolt of electricity to his spine fired up into his brain. He scanned for the other attacker. He was nowhere to be seen.

"Drop your weapon, do it now." The voice was deep. Thick with a Russian accent.

Jake froze. He glanced slowly to his left. The second man stood on a rocky outcrop above him. He stared down the barrel of the gun trained on him. There was no escape. He had been outflanked and outsmarted.

Is this the end?

A flash of lightning blinded him. In the gloom that followed the man's silhouette seemed to double in size and then he was gone. Jake stared at the empty space. He swiftly reloaded the crossbow and broke cover. He ran to the outcrop where the gunman had stood just seconds before. The rocky ledge fell away to a plateau ten feet below. He lay, neck twisted at a grotesque angle. His eyes were open, staring like the dead eyes of a stuffed animal. His head was mishappen. Smashed on the rocks from the fall. Blood and grey brain matter seeped from his skull and washed down the cliff with the rain.

The rock was slippery. A twist of fate in Jake's favour?

While he was not a man of religion, he thanked the gods silently for the good fortune.

He turned to the man he had shot. He jumped back down onto the path and approached warily; the crossbow trained on the man. He lay sprawled on the ground. He clutched at the bolt and gasped torturously, breathing frothy bubbles of blood.

Jake was on him in a flash, knife in hand. He kicked the gun away and grabbed his collar. Poised. Ready to strike. The dying man stared up at Jake, the last person he would see. His life ebbed away, and his eyes glazed over as the final breath rattled from him.

Jake wasted no time. He collected the gun and searched him. He pocketed a second ammunition clip. The odds were still dire but had shifted slightly. Grim determination fuelled him as he turned up the hill and set off in pursuit of his wife and children.

CHAPTER 29

Needles of rain stung Claire's face, lanced in sideways by the gusting wind. Lightning flashed. Rumbling thunderclaps wrenched the air. Violet and Chase shivered in cold and fear, teeth chattering as they clung tight to their mother. Claire hung up the phone and kneeled, pulling them in tight.

"Girls listen to me carefully. Please do not be frightened by the storm. It won't hurt you. Everything will be okay, but we need to move quickly and play a game of hide and seek. Dad and some other men are going to try and find us. But we must be quiet, do you promise me?"

Her voice wavered as she said it. She didn't believe herself.

They nodded quietly. She looked at each of them. Violet. She could tell. Their eyes met and they shared a look but played along for Chase's benefit. Violet knew better than to ask questions.

"Sorry pal but I can't take you with us," Claire whispered softly into Scruffy's ear. "Stay safe."

She was a friendly and soppy pet. No use as a guard dog and a liability who would give them away with excited barking. It broke her heart, but she had no choice. She looped the lead around a nearby tree.

"Quick march back to the top of the hill. We are nearly there, then it's downhill the other side as fast as we can. Just like the Grand Old Duke of York." She forced a tortured smile and stood up, pulling the girls gently along with her.

They set off as quickly as she dared. The girls were flagging but they had to move. Help was on its way. Was there a chance?

They pressed on into the wind and rain. The girls panted heavily as the climb became steep and the path snaked up between rocky patches and overhangs. They were closing in on the summit. Maybe ten more minutes and they would be there. Then it was a fast descent to relative safety.

Just keep moving until help arrives. She chanted it internally as a mantra.

Almost there. Just a few hundred metres to go. Onwards they trudged in silence. The final approach loomed with the path snaking up behind a rocky outcrop and onto the plateau.

They had done it.

The route for their escape now headed down to their left. She urged the girls in that direction.

"Good afternoon."

The voice was barely audible in the howling wind. She stopped dead in her tracks, her heart thumping in her throat. He sat cross-legged on a rock staring intently. A gun lay in his lap. He was quiet. Controlled. But there was no mistaking the menace.

The girls instinctively ducked behind their mother, seeking protection she could not deliver.

"Privyet" A second man appeared from behind a rocky outcrop also armed with a gun in his hand. He was shorter and stocky with a bushy beard and a shaven head. Like his companion he projected the same terrible air of menace, chilling Claire to the bone.

"What do you want?" she growled at them. Hatred twisted her voice. She would kill these men given half a chance.

"My name is Vlad." He nodded to his companion. "This is my brother Sergei. Your husband took something from my family. We are here to repay the favour. Where is he?"

"He's not here," she replied defiantly.

"I can see that. But you did not answer my question. Where is he? I am assuming that he is back down there somewhere." He nodded back towards the valley. "You have split up because you thought you would have a better chance that way? Well maybe you do. Maybe you do not."

Without warning Sergei fired two shots into the air. She hugged the children tightly as they sobbed quietly. There was no escape. They were trapped.

***

Jake drove on into the howling wind and rain running as fast as he could manage.

He was certain the other two pursuers would be close to the top by now. Would Claire make it away before them? He clung to a wispy thread of hope.

Two loud cracks in a volley rattled round the mountains. Not thunder. The unmistakable recall of gunshots from the summit.

No, it can't be.

He dropped to his knees not daring to think what it might mean. Tears pricked his eyes as visions of his wife and children laying in blood flooded his mind. Slaughtered by a madman.

He buried it. It just could not be.

It's a signal.

Two teams in separate pursuit would have a simple alerting mechanism. When you find the target, fire off two shots. This could only mean one thing. His family were now captive at the summit. They held the high ground and would use his family as bait to flush him out.

In his favour the path Jake was on offered good concealment. He could not be seen from the plateau until he was in striking distance. He was their objective but what was the intention? Logically there were two possibilities. They would either kill him up here on this mountain or kidnap and take him somewhere else. Either way they would slaughter his family. Leave no witnesses.

He made his decision. This had to finish on the mountain today. Fight and survive or die. Half of them were now dead. Could he do it again?

Not far now. Five minutes out. Jake finalised his plans as he ran. What came next was anyone's guess. But Jake was going to play the hand he was dealt, and he would never give up.

***

The children sobbed quietly, hugging themselves tightly to their mother as the gunshots rang through the surrounding hills. They screwed their eyes tight in a futile, childish effort to blank out reality.

"Please don't hurt us," Claire begged Vlad. "For God's sake they are children. What kind of man are you?"

"Your husband murdered our baby brother. That we cannot forgive," Vlad replied. "We are here for him. If he has courage there is no need to harm you."

Claire's mind raced, processing multiple streams of information quickly. The police were on their way. Should she alert her captors to that end? Would it serve or hinder her purpose? If they knew the police were coming, maybe they would run?

Doubtful.

More likely they would realise time was limited. Maybe act in haste and harm them. On reflection she decided to stay quiet.

"What happens now?" she asked. She drew the children in tight to shield them from the driving rain whipping across the exposed plateau. Dark stormy clouds rolled just meters above their heads.

"We wait," Vlad replied softly barely audible above the whistling wind. He stood and beckoned her to him. "Please come. Hands behind your back."

Claire complied approaching with caution. He slipped a cable tie from his pocket and secured her hands tight so she could barely move them.

"You too please," he said to the children. They looked to their mother for guidance. She nodded. Vlad secured them also.

Claire monitored the movements of Vlad and Sergei carefully from her peripheral vision. Watching for any routine or weakness she might exploit. Vlad paced the plateau peering down the path from time to time. Was there an element of anxiety creeping into his demeanour? He was expecting Jake to be captured by now. Sergei had disappeared out of sight.

What are my options?

Running was not a possibility. They would be gunned down in seconds.

Was Jake still out there? She had not heard gunshots so was it possible he was still alive? Perhaps there was a chance, however slim. The longer they could string this out, the better their chances of survival. She needed to try and level the odds.

She scanned her immediate environment. They were seated on a large rocky plateau with plenty of sharp stones strewn on the ground. If she could palm one there might be a possibility to launch an attack. Her priority now was to work free of her bond without being detected. She felt around behind her and found a jagged rock. She began to work at the tie. It was tough going. Thick. strong. But she persevered single-minded and earnest. Given a half chance she would launch a surprise attack. If Jake was still alive, their only hope was that swift and decisive actions might just give them a chance of survival.

***

The Vasins have them. He could feel it.

He ran through his plan in his mind. They would see him approach. There was no avoiding that as the path trekked across a ridge which led to a rock covered shelf about thirty meters short of the main summit plateau. He could get that far in safety. There was no way for a man stationed at the summit to hit him with a handgun at that range. There was nowhere to hide on the ridge. From there he would be able to talk. Maybe he could bargain his life in return for his family's freedom. Beyond that it was difficult to see a way out.

The Vasins held all the cards.

He continued to climb the ridge. The wind tugged gently at his jacket. It was weakening as the rain died away to drizzle. A flash of lightning illuminated the rocks ahead of him throwing shadows. Did he see a man hiding?

As he drew closer, he slowed. Fear permeated his very being like the claws of death on his scalp. Fear of imminent death. Fear for the safety of his family. The ultimate fear they may already be dead.

Focus.

He pushed negative feelings aside and pressed on fast, darting left and right as he ran to keep his movements unpredictable.

The path levelled out as he emerged onto the rocky shelf. He glanced all around furtively, sick with the anticipation of a shot ringing out. But none came.

Then he saw them. Thirty meters ahead on the mountain summit. Claire was seated with the girls. They seemed unharmed. One of the men stood guard over them. The other nowhere to be seen. He took cover behind a rock.

Vlad shouted across the void to Jake. "Where is my brother and his companion?"

Jake shook his head. "I'm sorry. They didn't make it."

Grief and anger flashed across Vlad's face. His head dropped before he returned his gaze to Jake, twisted with hatred. "Too bad. Now you have three deaths to pay for."

"I didn't start any of this," Jake shouted. "You came after me. And for what. Because of your brother. He attacked me. Tried to murder me in an alleyway. All I did was defend myself. What would you have done?"

"None of that is my concern. You killed my brothers. Now you must pay."

***

He's still alive.

Her heart jolted in her chest, and she sucked in a sharp breath when she heard his voice.

This could only mean the other two were dead or disabled. All was not lost. There was still hope. She persevered at the tie, her hatred of these men, and desperate fear for the safety of her children fuelled her with determination and resolve.

Break the bonds. Find a weapon. Strike.

The situation remained dire. But the odds had swung minutely. There was a chance, albeit a slim one.

While Vlad's attention was diverted, she worked frantically at the tie. Still some way to go. She felt around behind her and chanced upon a large rock. Flat. Sharp. And with enough heft to do some damage. She palmed it and wedged it down the back of her jeans.

Something had changed in Vlad's demeanour. The hairs on the back of her neck stood up as she sensed agitation in his voice. He was getting angry and losing control. Raging at the loss of his brother and at Jake for killing him.

"Girls listen to me carefully," she whispered. "I want you to close your eyes. Close them tight and do not open them until I tell you. No matter what you hear. Do you understand me? Not a peep?" They both nodded and screwed their eyes shut.

He paced the plateau like a caged tiger, clenching and unclenching his fists. His icy control was slowly ebbing away. "I have had enough now Jake. I have your wife and children. Drop your weapon. Put your hands in the air and come towards me slowly." He pulled Claire roughly by the hair. She screamed in pain as he yanked her from the ground.

"Do it now please Jake. I don't want to harm her, but you know I will."

He had her gripped firmly. One hand on her hair, the other on her right arm. A tear slipped down her cheek. She shook her head slowly, imploring silently. *'Please don't give up Jake.'* If he complied, all was lost.

Vlad released her arm and slid his hand up the small of his back. He withdrew a hunting knife, brandishing it in front of her face. She shrunk away as the polished steel blade flashed silver. He held the tip close to her eyes. She imagined it slicing through muscle and tendons.

"I'm tired of this Jake. I'll remove her head if you don't give yourself up. Then I will do the same to your children."

***

Jake's breath came in rapid gasps. Panic. He watched helplessly as Vlad brandished the knife in front of Claire.

What can I do?

Expose himself and he would be gunned down in an

instant. Then his wife and children were as good as dead. Stay hidden and he would be forced to witness their torture and murder. He checked the gun. They were thirty feet away. Vlad's body was partially concealed by Claire's. He visualised drawing and shooting. Even an expert marksman would have shunned the plan. Too risky, but he was out of ideas.

As these thoughts flashed through his mind, Vlad brought the knife up to her cheek and drew it slowly across her flesh. Her scream pierced the air as her skin peeled open like an orange. Blood welled in the wound and spilled down her front splashing onto the wet rocks.

He flinched in horror and made his decision. He had to take a chance. He pulled the gun from his belt, cautious not to give his movements away. He kept the gun out of Vlad's line of sight, concealed by the rock he was crouched behind.

"Drop gun. Do it now." Jake felt the cold steel muzzle of a gun pressed against his temple. He had no choice. The gun clattered to the floor. Sergei lifted the crossbow from Jake's neck and tossed it aside. He manoeuvred behind and pushed the barrel into the base of Jake's spine forcing him forward.

"Move. Or lose kidney." Vice like fingers gripped his shoulder, pulling him back against the gun and forcing him into an awkward angle. He was marched across to the plateau. The storm had abated. The rain spattered light spots. The howling wind had dropped to a steady breeze and a chink of sunlight was breaking through the clearing clouds.

"Nicely done moy brat." Vlad nodded his approval.

There was no way out. His weapons were gone. He was at their mercy now.

He sensed movement off to his right, from behind the shelter of a rocky outcrop.

Vlad turned to the figure as she emerged from the

shadows gun in hand. "DCI Raynes," he said. "So nice of you to join us."

CHAPTER 30

He knew before he asked the question. Whispered so she could barely here it. "What are you doing here Raynes?"

She stared at the floor unable to meet his gaze. Finally, she forced herself to raise her head. But she could not meet his eyes. Hers were haunted. "I'm sorry Jake."

Vlad came forward and stood directly in front of her. "You will tidy up as per our arrangement. No trace back to the family."

"How could you?"

She looked away again, back to the floor. As if wishing for it to open and swallow her. Her voice was quiet. Broken. "You stumbled into something Jake. It's been going on for longer than you can imagine. Now there is no other way."

She looked up, her gaze briefly falling on Claire and the children. Sadness and guilt crossed her face.

She took a deep breath steeling herself. "Do what you have to do quickly and leave," she said to Vlad. She turned away unable to watch what was about to take place.

Hatred fuelled Claire, anger coursing through her veins like fire. She wanted to kill these bastards so badly she could taste it. She was close now. The tie was weakening as she worked it against the edge of the rock behind her. Suddenly it gave and her hands were free. No one had noticed. She kept them tucked behind her. The stone that she had stashed earlier was still there, tucked down her jeans. She felt its heft and weigh. Visualised herself swinging it into his face.

Sergei spun Jake round to face him and cocked the gun. The barrel centred on his forehead. He turned to look at Claire and his children for the last time. "I love you," he mouthed at his wife before turning his hatred on Sergei. Determined to stare his killer in the eye.

"Not yet. First you watch."

Sergei manoeuvred behind Jake and grabbed his hair roughly. He forced him to his knees in front of his family. Vlad paced slowly looking from Claire, to Violet, to Chase. Like he was making a selection.

"No. No. Don't do it." He pleaded in despair.

Vlad grabbed Chase. His youngest baby. He pulled her roughly to her feet. From his kneeling position he was almost eye to eye. She kept them screwed tight. Vlad brought the knife to her neck.

She raised her head and opened her eyes, staring straight into the tortured past of her would be killer. The knife grazed her soft skin as he looked down upon her face. He paused. His face changed. Softened.

"Tatyana". He barely whispered it, gazing down as a loving father. Back in his dacha in Russia all those years ago. The knife slipped from his fingers and clattered to the ground as a tear slipped down his cheek.

And then several things happened at once.

Claire leapt up snarling. She swiped Vlad viciously across the temple with the rock. He staggered back. The skin had separated to his skull. Blood welled in the wound and dripped down his neck.

He stood dazed. Eyes glazed and staring at his brother when the top right portion of his head exploded in a mist of pink and white. The sound of a gunshot rippled through the mountains. Sergei's corpse dropped to the stony ground.

"No," Vlad screamed. Despair and anger contorted his features as he stared at his brother's twitching body.

Jake scrambled to gain purchase on the rocky ground and launched himself at Vlad. He was stunned and slow to react but managed to raise his gun and squeeze off a shot catching Jake in the shoulder. It failed to stop him. Momentum carried him through, and he smashed his forearm into the bridge of Vlad's nose. Cartilage, bone, and blood pulped into a spongy mess. They fell to the ground together, tumbled over the edge of the mountain and landed hard on the rocky path ten feet below. Stunned. Immobile. Vlad's gun disappeared over the edge.

Raynes looked on in stunned confusion at the turn of events. With her attention diverted, Claire took her chance and launched at her like a wild animal, smashing the rock into the side of her head. Her eyes rolled white into the back of her head and gravity took over dropping her to the ground like a rock. She lay motionless and blood soaked. Probably dead Claire figured.

***

He pulled himself to his knees desperately trying to draw air into his winded body. The odds were levelled and the fight was on. Mano a mano. Both unarmed. Jake went for him. He slammed his palm into Vlad's broken nose, temporarily blinding him. Training kicked in and Vlad reacted quickly lashing out with his knee into Jake's groin at full force. He doubled over, retching into the mud. Vlad came back aiming a kick to his face, but Jake rolled away and it only caught a glancing blow. He kept coming. Jake scrambled back on his elbows as Vlad lashed out again. Jake kicked out and connected the heel of his boot with Vlad's standing knee. Momentum carried Vlad forward while his knee stopped dead in mid-air. With his foot planted he had no chance. His knee bent back with a sickening crack, and he collapsed on top of Jake screaming.

Jake still had the knife attached to his belt. Sergei had failed to spot it earlier beneath his jacket. He pulled it from the sheath and rolled on top of Vlad. With one forearm constricting Vlad's throat, he went for the ribs. He managed a weak block and they both struggled for control. Jake pivoted from the waist and smashed his forehead down onto Vlad's broken nose. A wicked blow. His entire upper body torqued from the waist. Gravity did the rest. He pulled the knife back and struck again for Vlad's ribs. With his strength waning, Vlad made a feeble attempt to block. The blade pierced his midriff an inch. His lips drew back in a grimace. Jake dropped his weight driving the knife deeper. Vlad gasped. Eyes wide open and staring. The fight was drained from him. He was mortally injured and knew it. Jake pulled the knife from his side and lifted it above his head ready to strike the killing blow. Their eyes met. Vlad's shallow breathing was coming in ragged gasps.

"Finish it," he whispered.

Jake plunged the blade into the centre of Vlad's chest. He grasped the hilt with both hands and twisted violently, forcing a final tortured groan from Vlad's broken body. Blood spilled from the corner of his mouth and his eyes glazed over. Jake collapsed and rolled away from the dead body. He lay on his back exhausted.

It was over.

CHAPTER 31

Claire drew the girls tight into her arms, her motherly instinct to protect and shield them from the violent scene splayed out around them. They looked up at her with wide fearful eyes, both trembling uncontrollably. She found a knife next to Sergei's corpse and cut them free from their bonds. She grasped their hands and ran down the path with them, rounding the corner to where Jake lay next to Vlad's lifeless body. The girls threw themselves on their father, burying their heads into him.

Jake sat up, drawing them into his embrace. He wiped the blood from their faces. "Are you hurt? Please tell me he didn't hurt you."

"We are okay dad," replied Violet. They refused to look over at the dead body, turning their backs on the bloody sight. Jake stood unsteadily with the girls clinging to him. He pulled Claire in and hugged her deeply. He took her chin in his hands and examined her face. The wound on her cheek was deep and bleeding badly but it was a clean cut and would heal with medical attention.

"You beat them Jake." He spun around startled. Raynes stood above on the plateau. She looked down upon them, gun hanging limply by her side from a shaking hand. Blood cascaded down her face from the deep cut to her temple. "I'm sorry but I had no choice." Her features sagged like a sad clown; no strength left to force a smile as the cold reality of what she had done bit.

"You fucking bitch," Claire spat at her. "How could you? You would have let us die up here. Let those animals slaughter innocent children. What kind of woman are you?"

"The worst kind," she replied softly gazing off into the distance. "The very worst."

"Put the gun down Raynes," Jake said heading back up the path. He approached slowly. "It's over."

"Stay back. Don't come any closer." Raynes lifted the gun, waving it erratically with shaking hands.

Jake stopped short of her, hands out in front. "Please put the gun down. Whatever you have done to this point, don't make it worse for yourself."

She fixed her eyes on him. "How can it be worse. But you are right in one respect. It is all over." She lifted the gun and placed the barrel under her chin.

"No Raynes," he shouted. "Don't do it."

She wavered and stared at him through bloodshot eyes. Her finger tightened white on the trigger. The hammer drew back, and the barrel inched around as she wrestled with her conscience. Something seemed to click inside, and she relaxed the tension on the trigger. She dropped the gun. It clattered to the stony ground and Jake kicked it away. Her head dropped to her chin, and she fell to her knees crying out a deep mournful groan, like an animal crying for a dead cub.

Jake was first to register the sound. He turned to find the source. Barely perceptible and far off in the distance but building. The faint whip of helicopter blades echoed from the far side of the loch and all around the valley. Jake scanned the horizon, searching for the source of the sound, impossible to isolate the direction of approach

Then he saw them. Two choppers were approaching fast, skimming low across the loch. The pitch of the engines rose a tone as they hugged the mountainside, rising to the summit. The lead chopper circled, drawing in closer. Claire and Jake covered the children's ears against the whipping blades and roaring exhaust. A marksman had a rifle trained on Raynes.

DS Thompson hailed her through a loudspeaker. "Let's see those hands Raynes. On your head please." She complied and lifted her hands lacing her fingers round the back of her head. She struck a lonely figure kneeling on the stony ground, tears mingling with the blood from her wound and dripping down her cheek.

The downforce from the blades whipped up debris from the mountain as the choppers descended and landed at the far edge of the plateau. They touched down sinking onto their wheels. Jake and Claire turned away, sheltering the children as best they could from the noise and wind. The roaring engines quietened as the pilots cut the power and the slowing whip whip of the blades diminished as they lost their momentum.

Thompson jumped out flanked by a uniformed officer and a SWAT unit of four dressed in black and carrying automatic weapons. One kept his gun trained on Raynes while the others fanned out to secure the area.

Thompson ducked low beneath the slowing blades and collected her gun from the ground. He stopped in front of Jake. "Jesus. What happened here?"

Paramedics climbed from the second chopper. Jake beckoned them over. "See to my wife first. The children are shaken but okay."

He turned to Thompson. "They are all dead. Two more down in the valley as well as these two." He nodded to Sergei's headless corpse and then to the body of Vlad prone on the path below them, the knife embedded in his chest.

One of the paramedics examined Jake's shoulder while another assessed Claire. "The bullet has passed straight through, but you have lost some blood. Let's get you to the hospital." They wrapped foil blankets around the four of them and guided them towards the chopper.

"Scruffy," shouted Claire stopping suddenly. "Our dog is tied up back down the path. We must get her," she implored Thompson.

He placed a hand on her shoulder. "Don't worry. We will conduct a thorough search and retrieve her. You get off to the hospital now. She will be looked after."

She nodded her agreement, and they boarded the chopper taking their seats. The paramedics secured them each in place. One turned his attention to Claire, placing a pad over the wound securing it in place with tape. Another tended to Jake. She removed his shirt and pressed thick pads against the entry and exit wound in his shoulder. He winced against the pressure.

"Something for the pain," she said, rummaging in her bag. She produced a syringe and gave him a shot in the arm. The effect was instantaneous, and the pain drifted away in a hazy cloud of bliss. He leaned back in his seat squeezing Claire's hand tight. The girls sat either side of their mother, snuggled in close. Relief and exhaustion etched on their faces.

The starter motor coughed, and the engines roared to life. Jake pressed his forehead to the window and surveyed the desolate scene as they rose from the mountain top.

Vlad and Sergei were splayed out dead on the ground, pools of blood seeping slowly onto the surrounding rocks. Thompson stood with Raynes on the plateau while the SWAT team descended through the valley.

The chopper hugged the mountainside and sped them away across the shimmering loch. The storm had passed. The cloud parted revealing a blood orange sun hanging low in the sky. The water illuminated fiery hues of red from within as if the lake itself were ablaze.

***

Thompson approached Raynes cautiously. She slumped on her knees sobbing uncontrollably. "Would you like to talk me through what happened here today?" he questioned.

The bluff and fight had long since left her. "It seems you are not who I thought you were," she replied softly.

"My role as your DS has been cover. I operate out of a specialist unit targeted with rooting out corruption, eliminating the bad apples. Police the police if you like. You have been on our radar for some time. Is there anything you would like to tell me?"

Raynes lifted her head defiantly and looked directly at him, eyes red and raw from crying. "I had no choice. You have no idea what they are capable of." Her eyes darted from side to side as she processed the turn of events and the implications of her actions dawned. "I am saying nothing else until I have spoken to a lawyer."

Thompson clenched his jaw tight. "A lawyer indeed. Perhaps you can engage the services of Mr Simon Carrington QC?" He pulled a slim black phone from his jacket pocket and held it up in front of her. The voices of Vlad Vasin and herself were clear and unmistakable.

"The lawyer, I want his address."

"What are you going to do?"

"What do you care what I am going to do? Just do what you are told. That's what we pay you for."

"Okay, okay. Give me one second."

"He lives in a mansion in Surrey. It's 29 Acacia Road, Guildford. Just don't drag me into this mess."

She closed her eyes and sobbed.

"I know why you did it Sam? But he was tortured and killed you know."

She shook her head slowly. "You know about the money,

right? I owed them a lot of money. But they also threatened to kill my mother. Did you know that? To rob me of final few years with her. I had no choice. I never believed they would hurt the lawyer though. You have to believe me."

He looked on with pity and disdain in equal part. "I gave you a chance to come clean. Remember, back in the café?" He produced the phone again and played the recording. His voice came out crisp and clear.

"What about Jake Charles, and his family?"

"What about him? He is free to go." She closed her eyes in shame at hearing her own voice.

"You knew even then didn't you? You knew what he had planned for them. They are an innocent family. We raided the Vasin's headquarters an hour ago," he continued. "They found a three-inch dossier with your name on it. It seems they had quite an insurance policy on you. We know about your problems with drugs and alcohol. I am sorry Raynes but it's no excuse. People have died and there will be consequences." He pulled cuffs from his pocket and secured her wrists. "DCI Samantha Raynes. I'm arresting you for conspiracy to murder. You do not have to say anything, but it may harm your defence if you do not mention when questioned, something which you later rely on in court. Anything you do say may be given in evidence. I suggest you get a good lawyer Raynes. You are going to need one."

He nodded to the uniformed officer who led her to the waiting chopper. She slumped to the ground sobbing as the gravitas of the situation landed. Raynes knew only too well how police officers fared in prison. Tears cascaded down her cheeks as she was pulled to her feet and guided to the chopper to face her fate.

CHAPTER 32

The light streamed into the hospital room. It was another beautiful summer's day, somewhat unusual for this part of Scotland. Jake and the family had been afforded adjoining private rooms in the hospital given the families ordeal while they recovered from thier injuries. Jake's wound was healing nicely, and the doctor had informed him that he could leave that afternoon.

He sat in a chair next to the bed, dressed and ready for discharge. The local papers were filled with the carnage that had occurred in the highlands. Stories of Russian gangsters and vigilante heroes were rare in this part of the world, and it seemed Jake was quite the celebrity. The girls lay snuggled on the bed with Claire taking an afternoon nap.

Jake stiffened at the sound of footsteps approaching in the corridor outside their room. He glanced anxiously at the door, still jumpy when unfamiliar people approached. He relaxed as DS Thompson appeared in the doorway.

He smiled warmly and knocked. "Hi Jake. May I come in?"

Jake returned the smile and folded his paper. "Sure. Please do come in. Take a seat."

"I brought you some grapes. Standard hospital gift I hear." He placed them on the table next to Jake. "I also brought something more unorthodox that I feel the doctors would disapprove of." He gave a conspiratorial wink as he pulled a small bottle of whisky from his pocket and passed it to Jake, who cracked a wide smile and nodded his thanks.

"I've just run into Doctor Ferguson. He tells me he expects a full recovery with no lasting damage."

"Yes, I think I... we...have been extremely lucky all things considered. I'm being discharged today. We are going to stay around for one more day and then it's back home."

Thompson nodded. He took the seat next to Jake. "I am all but finished here with my investigation. Heading back to London imminently myself. My superiors require a full briefing on this case. I wondered if we could have a quick chat before I head off?"

Claire woke at the sound of voices. "DS Thompson, how are you?" She sat up, the movement also waking the children.

"Hi Claire, how is the cut healing?" Thompson asked.

"Oh, I'm just fine thanks. I am told I will be left with a very faint scar. Clean cut since the knife was so sharp. At least it will give me something to talk about at dull parties."

Thompson laughed warmly. "Indeed you will." Could Jake and I have a moment please? I need to talk with him alone."

Claire looked to Jake who nodded his approval. She gathered the girls in her arms. "Well you two monkeys. How about we head to the canteen and get some drinks?"

"They do milkshakes, can I have Strawberry?" shouted Violet.

"Chocolate for me," cried out Chase in reply.

"Sounds good to me. Let's go." She leant across and gave Jake a peck on the forehead. "Anything for you?"

"No, I am good thanks. It seems DS Thompson has brought supplies." He showed her the bottle.

"Very nice. Well enjoy and save one for me." She winked

as she headed out the door. The girls skipped along behind chattering excitedly.

"You have a lovely family Jake," he said smiling warmly. "How are the kids coping?"

"They are doing great thanks. A few nightmares here and there but that is to be expected. It's quite remarkable how well they have fared, to be honest."

"That's great to hear." Thompson grabbed a couple of glasses from the bathroom and poured them both a hefty slug of whisky.

"Cheers." They clinked glasses as Thompson sat down creasing his brow gravely. Clearly the pleasantries were over. Time to talk business.

"Good news first. I have checked with my colleagues in the organised crime unit. They assure me there will be no comebacks on you. The Vasins are finished. All gone. They expect to wrap up the entire syndicate with the evidence they have found. Those few still alive are going to be spending most of their lives behind bars. There is no one left to seek retribution."

Jake felt himself well up in sheer relief at this news, his emotions getting the better of him. This had been gnawing at the back of his mind for days. That the Vasins would never stop, never leave him and his family alone. But now it was all over. They could get on with putting their lives back together.

"What about Raynes?" he inquired.

"Raynes is a sad story," he replied. "She has been battling addiction problems going back to her youth. Drugs, alcohol, you name it. Expensive habits. On top of all that her mother is sick. Dying in a private care home. It seems she has been in debt to the Vasins for years. They started out as her suppliers. When she could not pay, they got their investment back in information.

We have recordings of her and the Vasins. Also a file as thick as a phone directory. She will go away for a long time. She is currently in a mental institution under assessment. Not in a good way from what I hear."

"I can imagine. Very sad" Jake replied thinking about her actions on that mountain.

"We have been tracking her for some time," Thompson continued. "She came by motorbike to assist the Vasins. We had a tracker on her and traced her to a nearby hotel where she had booked in under an alias. We were following behind and waiting for our chance to strike. When your wife called, we scrambled the choppers and fortunately got there just in time." He paused, taking on a serious tone "I'm afraid it's not all good news Jake. There is something I need to tell you, but I wanted to wait a couple of days until you were recovered and feeling better. I'm afraid this might come as a bit of a shock. Carrington is dead. It seems the Vasins sought him out to get to you. When they were done with him, they killed him. I am sorry."

Jake's heart sank as he thought of the jovial barrister. Guilt flooded him at Thompson's words.

"He did not deserve that," he whispered. "It's my fault."

"No it's not," Thompson replied shaking his head firmly. "You must not blame yourself. You had no control over the situation Jake." He looked at the floor sadly. "But I did. I should have foreseen this action by the Vasins. The mistake was mine." He sat in silence for a beat then continued. "I do understand your feelings of guilt. I have seen it many times before on cases I have been involved with where people died. There are counselling services that specialise in how to deal with this kind of trauma and the many ways it can affect you. With your permission, I will put them in touch with you." Thompson paused, allowing Jake to collect his thoughts then continued. "I would suggest you and the family accept help. Most people seem to think they are fine after traumatic events. Then further down the line the demons emerge. I've witnessed hardnosed police officers crumble. The children will need a safe space to express what they are feeling too."

Jake's mind whirled, scrambled by the news about Carrington. "Sure. Thanks," he said quietly. Lost in sadness.

Thompson pressed on. "Before I leave, I need to ask a couple more questions to tie up some loose ends in our investigation. Something does not quite add up."

"Of course. What do you want to know?"

Thompson consulted a notepad. "The cottage is owned by an overseas investment company. It all seems to be above board and legal. The cottage is listed as a holiday rental property. Booked in Carrington's name. I am guessing he did this on your behalf?"

"That sounds right," Jake replied. "He had been there himself and spoke of it highly. It sounded like a perfect place for us to get away for a while."

"Perfectly understandable. You also happen to mention a gamekeeper called Mackintosh who looked after the cottage and the land around it."

"That's right. I met him the next morning after we arrived, "Jake continued. "Strange old fellow, he stayed in a log cabin not far from the cottage. I only met him briefly and we did not have anything to do with him after that."

"Have you seen or spoken to him since?"

"No, I haven't, and I am ashamed to say with everything else, I forgot all about him, have you spoken to him?"

Thompson's face took on a perplexed look. "Well, here's where I can't seem to tie everything together." He paused before continuing. "We have been through the cabin, the one Mackintosh supposedly stayed in. We cannot find any trace of it having been inhabited recently. The management company pays a cleaner from the town to clean both properties once every other week. They also use a local gardener from time to time for the upkeep and maintenance of the land around the cottages. Neither the cleaner nor the gardener has ever seen or heard of this Mackintosh. No one in the town that we have spoken with knows of him. It appears that you are the only person who has ever met this man."

Jake recognised the last statement was phrased more as a question, possibly even an accusation. Thompson left it hanging in the air. He sat in silence watching Jake carefully. Confusion muddled Jake's brain as he stumbled through his next words. "But....he was there, I'm...not lying, why would I lie about this, what would I have to gain?"

"Relax Jake. I have interviewed many people over the years, and I have a nose for truths and lies. My gut instinct says you are telling the truth. It's just a mystery I can't work out right now. Anyway, we will continue to make enquiries to find him."

Jake considered what Thompson had said. He tried to form some sort of logical explanation, but he came up with nothing.

Thompson continued. "The other loose end is Sergei Vasin's death. In your statement, you described how you shot one of the gunmen with a crossbow bolt. You went on to say that another appeared to have slipped on rocks and broken his neck. Vladimir Vasin was killed by the knife wounds he sustained in the fight with you. This is all in line with what we found when forensics combed the area. Sergei Vasin is where it gets murky. You described his head as having exploded." Thompson flicked through his notes. "He was indeed killed by gunshot to the brain. Of that there is no doubt. Yet you say you did not shoot him. Is there anything else you know or have subsequently remembered that can help us shed some light on this?"

Jake considered the new information. "I have no idea. I thought maybe it was one of your snipers who took him out from the chopper."

"No. It was not us. We arrived after Sergei's death. It is a mystery." Thompson paused again, inviting Jake to speak.

"Maybe Raynes had a change of heart, guilt-ridden as she was? She could have killed him. I was not watching her," he suggested.

"No. Her gun was not fired," Thompson replied. "Forensics have confirmed that. Usually we do not like loose ends that cannot be explained. Having said that, in this instance I am not overly concerned. Neither are my superiors in London. One high ranking corrupt officer put away, and a problematic organised crime family confined to history. Case closed as you might say."

"Quite," replied Jake, still trying to process the information

"A curious coincidence though? There is an unidentified and as yet untraceable individual who you met near the scene. And one of the brothers was shot by an unknown assailant. Are you sure there is nothing more you can tell us about Mr Mackintosh? We really would like to speak with him"

He was there. He saved us.

I'm afraid not, "replied Jake. "I don't understand it myself. You have my statement and description. That's all I can give you."

Thompson observed Jake for a beat. "Well, we will continue to make our enquiries to try and track Mr Mackintosh down. But so long as nothing gets into the public domain about this detail of the case, then a couple of loose ends are erm … Quite frankly irrelevant." He let his statement hang in the air, eyebrows raised.

Jake took the hint. "I have no appetite to revisit any of this, especially in public."

"Good, good. Well, I will be heading back to London now.

I have a feeling that due to a sudden vacancy, a promotion for a certain DS may be in the offing." Thompson stood, draining his glass. "Please take my advice and make use of the counselling. You have my card. Please don't hesitate to call if you need anything.

"Of course," he replied. "Please don't take this the wrong way, but I am kind of hoping this is my last interaction with the police for some time." Jake smiled and extended his hand.

Thompson took it and they shook warmly. "Goodbye, Jake and stay safe. I am sorry for the ordeal you and your family have been through, but I am glad this turned out okay for you all things considered." He left Jake nursing his whisky, his mind working to comprehend what he had just been told.

CHAPTER 33

The mid-morning sun warmed Jake's back as he sat holding hands with Claire as they sipped coffee. Cyclists and skaters streaked by in flashes of pink and green neon while children played on the grass. Chase and Violet splashed with Scruffy in the nearby water fountain, shrieking in delight as the plumes of water rose soaking them all. They had packed the car that morning and checked out of their hotel. They decided to enjoy the local park once more before heading home, finally ready to put the dreadful events of the mountaintop behind them.

They sat in silence across the table from each other watching the children play. The day was calm and bright. Jake was lost in thought with mixed emotions. Sadness at the loss of Carrington. Relief that their ordeal was over. Happiness that the girls seemed to be making a swift recovery. Curiosity about Mackintosh

A nudge from Claire jolted him back to the present. "What's on your mind mister?"

"Oh, you know, this and that. Just playing things over in my mind. It's going to take a while to put this behind us."

She stood and planted a soft kiss on his forehead. "Finish your coffee, you have barely touched it. I'm going to take the girls to the swings for a play before we go."

She strolled over to the children, the sun shining on her chestnut hair. Still after all these years, she was as lovely as the day they had met. He turned back to the mountains in the distance, yellow hazed in the sun from the gorse covering the lower slopes. It truly was a beautiful corner of the world. Perhaps one day they could return to bury their demons. But for now, they needed to put this place behind them and return to their prior life. Find some level of normality again.

He sipped at his coffee and turned to watch Claire and the girls. They squealed in delight as she pushed them on the swings. Scruffy jumped up trying to join in the game. His heart swelled with love and appreciation. Pure joy at being alive. As the sun warmed his back it was difficult to believe that only days earlier, they had come so close to tragedy.

He turned back to the table and jolted in surprise. Mackintosh was sitting opposite, staring straight at him with those piercing grey eyes.

"Jesus, Mackintosh," stuttered Jake in confusion. "You made me jump. How did you get here? I thought, I thought..."

"You thought what laddie?" interjected Mackintosh scrutinising Jake.

He recovered his composure. "Well, I'm not sure. Either you were dead or ... Perhaps I was going insane. You were a figment of my imagination. It appears I am the only person to have ever seen you."

A wry smile creased his granite face. "Aye son. I'm real as the next man. But I keep myself to myself. I'm not one to let people know my business and like to keep it that way."

"You know the police are looking for you? They want to question you about what happened. On the mountain a few days ago.

"Oh, I know all about the Russians. Good fortune was with us there. It could have gone either way for a wee bit. And by the way, call me Mac. All those that know me do, but that's not many I can tell you. Too many lost in far-flung places in service to their country." He sighed as he looked off into the mountains. Remembering.

"It was you up on that mountain, wasn't it?" Jake whispered. "The shot that took out the brother on the summit. The shadow behind the man on the pathway. He didn't slip, did he? It was all you." Jake spoke the words as statement of fact rather than a question.

Mac sat quietly, his grey eyes twinkling in the sun. Jake realised he had read this man so wrong on their first meeting. Now, he understood him in an entirely new light. As if seeing him for the first time. His face was not old as Jake had first thought. It was a face shaped and defined by life experiences no normal man could imagine. Not aged in the usual sense. Rather it was chiselled and spoke of a fierce toughness. Exposure to inhospitable climates. The melancholy of fallen comrades. "You know Taylor, don't you? From the forces? He sent you."

Mac's tone softened as he remembered. "Aye, I know Taylor. Probably better than any man alive. Saved my life on more than one occasion....as I have his." He trailed off, seemingly lost in thought.

Jake stared at the table, a lump forming in his throat as he thought of the debt of gratitude he owed this man. He returned his gaze to Mac and saw a certain kindness in that face. "Thank you, Mac. I don't know what to say. Or how I can ever repay you for what you did for me and my family."

"If Taylor says a man he likes, and trusts needs help then that man becomes a friend of mine. It becomes my duty to assist where needed. He would do the same for me. Worked out okay in the end. You should take some credit yourself for the success of this mission."

"Success of this mission," Jake repeated it, enjoying Mac's turn of phrase. "Once a soldier eh?"

The two men sat in silence a beat before Mac suddenly stood up. "I must be off now. But I have something for you." Mac pulled a crumpled postcard from his jeans pocket and slid it across the table towards Jake. The picture on the front showed a marina. Typical of those found dotted throughout the Mediterranean. "I understand the weather is lovely there in early September." Mac winked with a wry smile, then turned and walked away never once looking back.

Jake watched him carefully as he left. He had mistaken him as thin in the arms and torso. Almost skinny. But Jake could see he possessed lean strength and poise. His gait exhibited graceful lightness of foot. Almost predatory and cat-like in his manner.

"Thank you, Mac," he muttered under his breath. He looked at the postcard closely. It was not a place he had heard of. Likely one of the smaller of the Greek Islands. He turned it over. On the back in scrawled black ballpoint, it simply said Bay C, Mooring 22.

"Dad." The girls dragged him back from his thoughts. They flung themselves in his lap and smothered him in kisses. Scruffy jumped up onto the bench and planted long wet licks on his face.

"Did you have fun? Ready to go home?" he said, kissing them each in turn while ruffling Scruffy's fur.

"Was that a man I saw you talking to darling?" Claire asked quizzically.

"Just someone asking for directions and suggesting a good holiday destination," he replied pocketing the postcard. "Probably best I explain later over a drink or two."

She adopted her confused face, wrinkling her brow and nose, looking at Jake sideways. The face she reserved exclusively for him when he was not making sense. She made to continue questioning but thought better of it. She shook her head and turned to the girls. "Come on kids, back to the car. Time to leave."

With one last look up at the mountains, Jake stood taking his wife's hand. He turned to kiss her softly on the lips. "Let's go home."

EPILOGUE

They arrived late in the evening, showered, then headed out for dinner at a waterfront restaurant. Later they returned to the hotel room and made love. Then sipped champagne on the balcony overlooking the moonlight sea, talking into the small hours. The girls were with Claire's parents for the week, giving them time alone to enjoy a peaceful holiday. To relax. To reconnect.

Jake woke early as he usually did. Claire preferred to sleep late. She snoozed on, wrapped in crisp white Egyptian cotton sheets. He made coffee and slid open the balcony doors. The early morning warmth flooded the cool room. The blazing sun hung low on the cobalt Mediterranean Sea igniting a shaft of shimmering orange from within. He finished his coffee, headed back inside, and planted a light kiss on Claire's forehead. She begrudgingly half-opened one eye and smiled.

"I'm off for a little wander to explore," he said. "I won't be too long. Breakfast when I get back." Without speaking she waved him away, blew a kiss and closed her eye again. She rolled over, drew the sheets tight around her and settled back to sleep.

Jake dressed in shorts and a t-shirt and slid his feet into deck shoes. Sunglasses on. He let himself silently out the door. At this hour the hotel was quiet, and the lift arrived quickly. He strolled across the hotel foyer. The young lady behind the reception desk nodded to him.

"Kalimera," She smiled revealing bright white teeth contrasting against her olive skin. Her long raven hair was tied in a ponytail. He smiled and returned the greeting as he passed through the foyer to the pool area. Steps at the far side of the pool headed down to some lower streets which meandered through the town towards the marina. The pool area was empty at this hour. Sprinklers released a fine mist onto resplendent purple, red, and pink flowering bushes, releasing a floral-scented aroma which wafted on the morning breeze. The fine spray cooled his face as he passed. The morning cacophony of cicadas buzzed from all directions.

He reached the steps and descended to the street below. He followed a narrow alleyway in the general direction of the seafront. Brightly coloured wooden doors and window shutters adorned the whitewashed houses, which dazzled in the early morning sun. The alleyway emerged onto a cobbled plaza bordered by restaurants and tavernas with a central fountain gushing water into a shallow pool.

The town was slowly coming to life. Waiting staff in crisp white linen busied themselves setting tables ready to catch the early breakfast crowd. He crossed the plaza into a narrow street that dipped sharply towards the see. The street was closed off at the far end by a boundary stone wall where stone steps descended to the seafront. He followed them and emerged onto the promenade which skirted a brilliant-white sandy beach. Early morning swimmers bathed in the crystal blue waters while sailing boats skipped along the horizon. He paused to inhale the salty aroma of fresh sea air and to savour the moment. Life had taught him to enjoy the present. To live for today.

The promenade hugged the beach in a long arc maybe a kilometre in length which snaked away to his left towards the harbour. He followed the promenade past the beachside restaurants and bars to the marina. Wooden jetties jutted into the water where hundreds of moored boats bobbed in the gentle sea.

He reached into his pocket and pulled out the postcard

that Mac had given him months earlier in Scotland. The picture of the marina matched perfectly to where he was standing right now. He turned the card and re-read the short wording in the top right corner. Bay C, Mooring 22.

He followed the promenade to bay C. He crossed the jetty, passing boats of all different shapes and sizes. Everything from one man rowing boats to the towering white luxury yachts of the obscenely wealthy. Some were locked up. Some a hive of activity where the owners sat on their decks, reading and enjoying early morning coffee in the sunshine.

He figured mooring twenty-two would be near the end. He followed the gangway left, then right through ninety degrees. Twenty-two was indeed the final mooring. He stopped and looked at the boat secured to the wharf. It was a sailing yacht, perhaps forty feet. Brilliant white with blue trim. Varnished wooden decks. Well maintained. Functional rather than flashy. Big enough for the open ocean. A home to live in permanently if you wish.

A figure emerged from below, bare-chested and wearing white swim shorts. He moved gracefully, silently. Taylor looked straight at Jake, a wide grin spreading across his face, his blue eyes twinkling. He raised a hand briefly in greeting. Jake could not help but crack a smile himself as he jumped aboard to greet his friend.

THE END

ACKNOWLEDGEMENT

Writing a book is a solitary and at times lonely endeavour with many long hours of typing away, editing, and re-editing all the while consumed with dreams of success, tinged with lingering self-doubt. But I got there in the end, and it would not have been possible without a significant dash of help and encouragement.

At this stage, I would normally thank my publisher, my editor, my agent, etc. But I don't have any of those people. I do want to thank all those who took the time to read and comment on my fledgling drafts, giving me honest feedback and helping me shape the book to come. Please do forgive me if I have overlooked you and your name does not appear here. Yousif Barr, Phil Vipond, Damo Bell, Adam and Katy Kelly, Timmy Ayres, Mark Mckinstry my brother Stewart, but most of all to Steve Quinn, an amazing human being who sadly is no longer with us. We miss you dearly Steve.

Thanks also to my awesome friend and partner in misbehaviour Steve Austin, who helped creatively with the cover artwork design. He is a supremely talented individual and an all-around top guy. Thanks also to Amir for bringing these ideas to life. To my amazing girls, Scarlett, Olive, and Rose. Thanks for your optimistic (if misguided) encouragement that I will, "sell loads of books and be famous."

And of course, to Natalie, my amazing wife and partner in life. Thanks for all the special years and for your support and encouragement. Love you baby!

ABOUT THE AUTHOR

Fraser Kingsley

Hunted is the debut novel by Fraser Kingsley and was born from a simple kernel of an idea:

What terrifies me the most? What are my deepest-rooted fears?

Fraser lives in the UK with his wife, their three girls and their beloved cockapoo, Honey.

Printed in Great Britain
by Amazon

33382716R00151